DAUGHTER

With a scream she rushed at Mursilis and Hattusilis and, cat-like, drove her nails into their faces.

'Wear these scars!' she shrieked. 'And never forget that you will pay for this!'

Astonished, the two men fended her fury off with their arms.

'Lady! Lady!' they shouted. 'Your husband is alive. His attacker is dead. Why do you treat us so?'

Sobbing, she turned away from them and flung herself on Tutankhamun, covering him with kisses.

'I'm all right,' he whispered hoarsely, in quite considerable pain. 'The dagger . . .' he muttered. And she saw he was clutching the iron dagger in his hand. It was covered in blood.

DAUGHTER OF RA

Moyra Caldecott

ARROW BOOKS

Arrow Books Limited
20 Vauxhall Bridge Road, London SW1V 2SA

An imprint of Random Century Group

London Melbourne Sydney Auckland
Johannesburg and agencies throughout the world

First published in 1990

© Moyra Caldecott 1990

Typeset in Garamond
by JH Graphics Ltd, Reading

Printed and bound in Great Britain by
Courier International Ltd, Tiptree, Essex

ISBN 0 09 959870 1

For Oliver my great love, and for Mary and Pat, Jeannine and Ann, and all my Egyptian friends – with love and gratitude.

CONTENTS

'Hail to you, you owners of souls, who are devoid of wrong, who exist for all eternity! Open to me, for I am a spirit in my own shape, I have power by means of this my magic, and I am recognized as a spirit.'

Spell 72, *The Book of the Great Awakening*

From *The Book Of The Dead* by R. O. Faulkner, British Museum Publications, 1985

1
THE CORONATION

The boy stood barefoot and almost naked in front of the gigantic cedar doors of Amun's temple – a simple kilt of fine white linen his only garment. Behind him were the most important priests and dignitaries of the Two Lands. He knew they were there. He could feel the pressure of their determination that he would be the king they had waited for since his grandfather Neb-maat-Ra, Amenhotep III, Great Bull of the Two Lands, had stepped into the solar boat and gone to join his ancestors in the Land of the Ever Living.

He was frightened. When this door opened he would no longer be Prince Tutankhaten, free to roam the palaces of his father and his grandfather, free to swim in the lakes with his sisters, play with other children, say what he liked. He would be Pharaoh, with all the world dependent on his every whim, his every word. He would wear clothes stiff with gold and jewels and would have to move with dignity. No longer would he chase his friends through the garden and throw stones at the birds. When these great doors opened he would enter a prison from which there was no escape. He would have to endure endless boring ceremonies; mouth again and again the words he had been taught; perform monotonous rituals; listen to the lengthy sacred texts endlessly intoned. He would be expected to know everything, see everything, *be* everything. He would be the sole conveyor of the gods' power to earth.

As the only surviving son of the king among many daughters he knew he would have to take on this role

one day. His mother Kia, for one, had never let him
forget it. But when he had been learning to be a pharaoh
he had looked on the lessons as elaborate games, remote
from reality. Reality was the fun he had with his sisters
and his friends. The hot, closed rooms of the House of
Life where he was trained and instructed in the skills
and knowledge he would need as Pharaoh he had
endured as best he could, only waiting for the hour of
release. His heart skipped a beat. If only he had paid
more attention. But even if he had – no one expected
him to inherit the throne at the age of nine. No one had
prepared him for this.

He knew Ay was close behind him – Master of
Chariots, Companion of the Great King, Vizier in
charge of all things under the King. Ay who had been
powerful in his grandfather's court and because of this
had not disappeared with all the rest who had been close
to his father.

Everything had happened so quickly – his father's
death; Nefertiti, the Great Royal Wife, taking the
throne; the murder of his uncle Djehuti-kheper-Ra
whom he had liked and trusted; and, most frightening
of all, the violent disorder in his father's capital,
Akhetaten, in which so many of his family and friends
had perished. He shuddered to think of what it must
have been like for the beautiful Nefertiti and his
beloved sister Merytaten when the mobs turned on
them and beat them to death. How could such things
happen? General Horemheb said it was because his
father had destroyed the rule of Maat, of Order and
Justice, in the Two Lands by turning against the old
gods who had kept the country in peace since the
ancient days. 'See,' he said, 'what happens when the
common people have no gods to respect and obey; when
they have only themselves to consider.' But his father

had not left the country without gods. There was the
Aten, the greatest god of all, who held the whole earth
in its care.

The young prince had not seen the ugly massacre at
Akhetaten, nor General Horemheb's fierce vengeance
on those who perpetrated it, because he had been safe
with his sisters on his grandfather's estates at Per-hay,
near Waset. But he had witnessed the confusion that
followed and seen a distraught Kia at one moment
preparing for them to flee, and at the next, grooming
him to be King.

Big men with dark faces came and went. His sister
Ankhesenpaaten listened impassively to what they had
to say and dismissed them from her presence.

Then one night his younger sisters, his greatest
friends, Nefernefruaten, Neferneferure and Setepenre,
disappeared like so many other people he had known.
Only Ankhesenpaaten and his mother remained.

He had never been close to Ankhesenpaaten. She was
older than him, and never seemed to evince the joy of
living the other daughters of Nefertiti did. Now it seemed she was to be his Queen, his Great Royal Wife.
Because his mother was not royal, his sister Ankhesenpaaten, daughter of both Akhenaten and Nefertiti, and
indeed carrying extra status by having been married to
the king, her father, would give his claim to the throne
unshakable legitimacy.

General Horemheb stepped forward and placed a
huge and heavy stone-headed mace in his hands. He
knew what he had to do and did it.

He lifted it with all the strength in his thin arms and
struck the door – once, twice, three times. The sound
brought a chill to his heart as the immense panels of
cedar, heavily laden with inscriptions and images in
bronze, gold and silver rolled slowly back. He entered

the sacred precincts – a minute figure overshadowed by
the huge statues of his ancestors, by gigantic columns,
by the tall priests who came forward to meet him, clad
in stiff ceremonial garments, wearing the masks of the
gods – the very gods his father had taught him were evil
and had banished from the Two Lands. He looked at them
uneasily. What was he to believe? Ay and Horemheb, who
now seemed to hold the power in the Two Lands since
Nefertiti's death, assured him that his father had been
insane and the country was in danger because the old gods
had been mocked and driven out. They quoted instance
after instance of how the Two Lands had suffered under
his father. He was told that it was his responsibility to
restore them to their rightful places and to rescue from
destruction the kingdom he had inherited.

The figures before him looked both ridiculous and
menacing. Men with animal masks.

'They are just pretending,' he told himself, and
repeated it several times as they drew nearer. Horus
with the head of a falcon, Lord of the Sky, representing
divine kingship, the sacred son of sacred parents;
Anubis, god of the Tomb, with the head of a jackal to
remind us that through the jackal's gut the dead are
recycled into life; Khnum who fashions life on a potter's
wheel, wearing the head of a ram; Set, the god of
storms, the dangerous god, with the head of an animal
no one can name; Sobek, the crocodile . . . All these and
more gathered round him and led him forward. The boy
was frightened. His father had impressed on him that
there was only one true god and that could not be
represented by anything on this earth.

'Only the globe of the sun and the sun's rays can give
you an idea of his glory,' he had said. 'Only the Aten
that shines on all the world at one moment can even
begin to show you what lies in his heart.'

He had witnessed his father and his father's servants smashing the statues of the other gods and yet no retribution had fallen on them. Or had it?

Tutankhaten frowned, remembering his father's sudden death and what had happened afterwards. For a while Nefertiti had ruled in his father's place. Nefertiti, the beautiful one, whom his mother loathed. Nefertiti, the proud, who watched him sometimes with the cold eyes of a cobra. He could not know, young as he was, that there was a struggle going on for power in the Two Lands, and the faction against his father Akhenaten, was working secretly to overthrow him and place his son on the throne. For a while, his father's friend, some said his brother, Djehuti-kheper-Ra, had looked as though he would rule Khemet. But he had been found dead in an alley. Nefertiti and Merytaten, Akhenaten's wife and eldest surviving daughter, had been murdered by a rioting mob. Nearly everyone he knew was either dead or had gone away. He was thankful for Ay, his father's and his grandfather's confidant, for giving some sense of continuity, some feeling of familiarity and security. He glanced briefly over his shoulder at Ay for guidance, momentarily forgetting what he must do next. Ay nodded him forward.

The priest with the mask of Horus took his hand and led him to a second door, twenty cubits high and fashioned from fine white limestone. Beside it was a colossal statue of one of his ancestors, Aa-kheper-ka-Ra, Djehuti-mes I.

Then a priest garbed as the god Atum, the creator of physical form, took his other hand. The door ground open slowly and the young prince entered the 'hall of purification'. He stepped into a shallow crystal bowl of sacred water and four priests, each at one of the four cardinal points of the world – north, south, east and west – poured purifying water over him from four slender crystal vials. He felt the cool liquid on his skin and he shivered. There was no going back now. No pharaoh had ever ceased to be pharaoh while he lived.

Did he imagine it or did the statues that surrounded him, the carved images on the walls, suddenly seem different? Were their stone eyes *seeing* him? He felt his flesh goose-pimple and lowered his eyes at once to the paved floor. Blindly he followed where he was led.

The next hall was called 'the house of the king' and was where the coronation ceremony itself would take place.

There had been a ceremony at Akhetaten in a coronation hall hastily erected for the purpose. But Ay and General Horemheb had said that that was not enough. All the gods of Khemet must declare him King, not only the Aten. The great temples at Ipet-Esut and Ipet-Resyt had been partially restored for the purpose. Tutankhaten, if he had not been concentrating so hard on the floor at his feet, would have noticed that many of the reliefs of the gods were still chipped and scratched out and some walls were still smoke-blackened, the vivid colours of surface paint peeled and flaked.

His heart was beating uncomfortably fast as he passed between the papyriform columns and the two magnificent golden obelisks. Huge Osiriform statues of Djehuti-mes III and IV towered over him. He entered the chapel of the north, the 'house of flame', and the chapel of the south, the 'great house'. The gods of the north and south crowded round him, encircling him, chanting the ancient, sacred (and largely unintelligible) words of the coronation ceremony.

He was expected to grasp a live cobra and stare into its cold, yellow eyes.

He was sick with fear as he felt its scaly body in his

hand, and then the High Priest seized its tail and whirled it round his head so fast that it made almost a continuous circle. He did not feel another priest put something over his wig, but when the now dead cobra had been removed, he found that he had the royal uraeus on his head, the cobra of gold with eyes of topaz that was to protect him forever. He began to feel stronger – more confident. He felt the transformation from boy to king beginning.

One by one the crowns were placed on his head with ritual gesture and chanted words. He had been told by Ay that the crowns were divinities in themselves and when they were on him he would become the divinity itself and be great in magic. His father had never claimed this for the crowns that he wore.

'They are no more than symbols of office,' he had said. 'It is you who will give them power – not they, you.'

But Tutankhaten could feel the difference in himself as they pressed upon his forehead. He straightened his back and lifted his head. No longer did he gaze nervously at the paved floor, but raised his eyes to stare boldly into the eyes of the masked priests and beyond them at the statues and reliefs around him. He met the eyes of the gods as an equal. He was Divine Pharaoh and no one ever again could tell him what to do.

The beginning of a smile broke through for the first time since the bewildering events of the past few months had disturbed the familiar routines of his life. He might well enjoy being Pharaoh! He would not be alone – the power of all the mighty beings beyond this world were with him. Even General Horemheb, whom he had feared up to now, was subservient to him in his role as Divine King.

His father had been wrong. The crowns were magic.

He could feel their strength pouring into him and he spoke the words of a pharaoh in a voice that surprised even him because of its strength and depth.

Ankhesenpaaten, his Great Royal Wife, his Queen, would be having a simultaneous ceremony in the Temple of Mut, Amun-Ra's consort. She would be surrounded by goddesses as he was surrounded by gods. She would be robed by priestesses clad in the robes of goddesses. The crown of Mut's magic feathers would be placed on her head. Did she feel the changes he felt? But then he remembered that this was all not so strange to her. She had been through something of the kind when she reached puberty. She had been crowned the consort of her father – but not Great Royal Wife for all her royal blood. Never before had she been Great Royal Wife, Divine Queen. How would it be to go to bed with her, he thought. It was a relief to him that she at least would know what to do! His thoughts were just beginning to stray along these lines when he felt a touch on his elbow and knew that he had missed his cue.

Amun-Ra was granting him immortality and his thoughts were straying to an image of his sister-wife naked!

The double crown was on his head, the golden cobra at his brow, Amun, the Hidden Wind, was breathing into his nostrils the breath of eternal life. He drove the image of his sister from his mind with difficulty.

'Eternal Life?' What did it mean? He could not envisage it no matter how many texts about it his tutors made him read.

'It is not everlasting life,' his father had once said in answer to a question. 'Though that too is granted. It is life without time, without place, without extension in any sense. It is now and yet not now. It is here and yet not here. It is everywhere and yet nowhere. It is neither before nor after . . .'

At this point the prince had given up listening. He regretted that now. For it was to be his – and he did not understand what it was.

Later, sitting on the throne that the great Thutmosid kings had sat upon, the god Amenhotep II, and his own grandfather, the greatest of them all, he forgot to ponder such questions and wondered rather how he would be able to carry out all the things that were expected of him as Pharaoh in *this* life.

Priests impersonating the hermaphrodite god of the Great River, the river that gave Khemet life, were twining the lily and the papyrus, the plant symbols of the south and of the north lands, around the legs of his throne, and he spoke the words of invocation:

> *'Master of vegetation, Lord of the fishes and the birds, great water god whose powers transform a dead land to a living, be at our side, now and forever.'*

Without the swelling of the waters, without the floods that deposited the rich black mud, his country would be lost. A pharaoh must surely be more careful about his relationship with Hapi than with any other god. Yet, Tutankhaten thought, a slight frown creasing his smooth young forehead, there had not been famine at the time of Akhenaten and he knew for a fact that Akhenaten had refused to honour the river god, though he had not attacked his sanctuaries with such diligence as he had those of Amun.

Tutankhaten had been gripping the two sceptres in his hands so tightly that his fingers ached. He loosened his hold slightly and one almost slipped from his grasp.

It was the one still embellished with the sign of the
Aten. The inscription read:

> *the face of the king, son of Amun, dazzles like Aten
> when he shines.*

'I'll never give it up,' he whispered to his heart, and
held it firm again. Ay and Horemheb had not declared
the Aten anathema as Akhenaten had Amun. All
ancient gods were to be venerated and the Aten was no
exception. But, young as he was, he suspected that if he
showed an inclination to follow his father's way too
closely he might not live long. He did not understand all
the implications of the changes that had so rapidly
occurred, but he was shrewd enough and alert enough
to know that he was walking on a glass floor, and if he
was clumsy and took one step without the guidance of
these two men, his whole world would collapse under his
feet.

He thought about Ankhesenpaaten again, but this
time remembering the look in her eyes when she was
told by Ay and General Horemheb she was to be Great
Royal Wife. There was nothing of the joy and gratitude
he would have expected – only a look that suggested she
was weighing up the pros and cons coldly and sus-
piciously. She bowed to him as her future husband and
king, but her eyes did not meet his, and he was shocked
by the suppressed anger he sensed in her tense body. He
had never been as close to her as to his other half-sisters,
but he had not suspected that she hated him. Did she
hate him? Or were the Vizier Ay and the stern General
the focus of her rage?

As the priests intoned the ancient words over him and
clothed him in his coronation robes, he tried to remember every detail of that extraordinary confrontation.

Ankhesenpaaten had been seated by the window looking out into the garden when they arrived. She stood up
immediately and faced them. She ignored him from the
start and it was as though he and Ay did not exist. Her
eyes went straight to the General. Nothing was said for
what seemed a long time. The two looked into each
other's eyes and Tutankhaten, who had felt so uncomfortable in that silence, now knew why. Though nothing
could be seen it was as though the two were fighting a
duel. Ay put his hand on his shoulder as though to hold
him back from a battle. What was this palpable hatred
between the young princess and the weathered General?
Tutankhaten was so ignorant of the power struggle that
had destroyed his father that he could not understand
it. To him the General had been the one to punish those
who had used violence against his family. He
remembered that his mother Kia, who had lived in
obscurity away from the court for some time, had been
recalled and reinstated honourably – but only after the
arrangements for his marriage to Ankhesenpaaten had
been completed. He remembered something now he had
overlooked at the time. He barely knew his mother for
he had been brought up at the court – either with his
grandparents at Per-Hay, or in the beautiful City of the
Sun, Akhetaten. But he was present when she was told
who was to be his Great Royal Wife, and he knew now
her reaction had been unfavourable. A daughter of
Nefertiti could never be close to her heart.

They were intoning his titles.

'King of Upper and Lower Egypt; Neb-kheper-Ra,
becoming like Ra every day; Son of the Sun;
Tutankhamun, living image of Amun; Ruler of Abedju,
the sacred city of Osiris; Lord of Diadems: Beloved of
Amun, Son of Amun, born of Mut, Lady of Heaven . . .'

He had been told that his name would be changed

from Tutankhaten to Tutankhamun, but until it was said in the great echoing hall, accompanied by trumpets, he had not grasped it.

At last he stood alone in the most sacred sanctuary of all before the shrine of Amun-Ra himself, standing in golden splendour in his golden solar boat.

At this moment he knew that Ankhesenpaaten, now named Ankhesenamun, would be in the sanctuary of Mut in the southern temple of Ipet-Resut. She would be raising her arms to the goddess as he was to the god. She would be speaking the words from the timeless texts as he was speaking them. She would also be clad in fine linen, weighed down by jewelled necklaces and belts, a crown upon her head. He felt strangely as though they were together in one place, though many leagues separated them. Amun and Mut, great god, the Hidden One, the Breath of Life, and his consort, the Mother, the bearer of all living beings, seemed to stand side by side, and he and his Great Royal Wife were taken into their embrace and made their instruments upon earth.

He looked into the blue lapis lazuli eyes of the golden god and it seemed to him they were no longer jewels but living eyes that could see into his soul. He was seized with terror and longed to flee, but his limbs seemed paralysed and he could not move. He could not even lower his gaze but felt the eyes of the god boring into his until he was nearly fainting from the strain of it. He found tears flowing down his cheeks.

His heart cried out many wild things – but no words passed his lips but the ones he had learned by rote and was expected to say. In his heart he pleaded for forgiveness for what his father had done – and what he had done under his influence. He swore to uphold the worship of Amun-Ra and never let it die. He swore a thousand vows he later wished he had not, but the relentless stare of the god was torture. He wondered if it was too late. Would the god extract vengeance for what had passed? He wished he had not been chosen Pharaoh. Not only would he be the god's instrument on earth, but he would be in the god's power to an extent no other being on earth would be. He would be bound in all the nine parts of his being and there would be no escape – ever. Not even in death.

It seemed to him the god was becoming ugly and distorted as the gold shimmered through his tears. Darkness seemed to be closing in around him and he felt himself falling.

And then he knew no more.

The nine-year-old boy had fallen forward in a faint, his crown dislodged and lying at the god's feet.

The High Priest fetched him out.

No word was ever said about it.

Sacred water and incense revived him, and, dazed and only half conscious, he was put into his golden carrying chair and taken out through the many doors and gates of the dark temple into the blazing sunlight of the city. There the crowds surged forward and fell at his feet. Bewildered and unhappy the child stared out from beneath the double crown at the thousands upon thousands of people screaming and shouting his name. Trumpets blared. Drums rolled. Petals rained down upon him.

He could see the sweat pouring down the necks of the high nobles who, for this momentous occasion, had vied with each other to take the place of slaves and carry the new pharaoh triumphantly to meet his Great Royal Wife.

From the southern sanctuary of Mut, Ankhesenamun was also being carried – but she did not look into the faces of those who crowded round her and screamed her

name. She looked above their heads to the sky. A cloud
had crossed the sun and its long rays could be seen
clearly reaching down towards her.

Quietly she bowed her head and murmured the words
of a prayer to the Aten she had learned at her mother's
knee:

> *'How manifold are thy works. They are mysterious
> in men's sight. Thou sole god, like to whom there is
> none other. Thou didst create the earth after thy heart,
> being alone, even all men, herds and flocks, whatever
> is upon earth, creatures that walk upon feet, which
> soar aloft flying with their wings, the countries of
> Khor and of Kush, and the land of Khemet. Thou
> settest every man in his place, and makest their
> sustenance, each one possessing his food, and his term
> of life counted; tongues made diverse in speech and
> their characters likewise; their complexions
> distinguished, for thou has distinguished country and
> country . . .*
>
> *Thou makest the seasons in order to prosper all that
> thou has made, the winter to cool them, the summer-
> heat that they may taste of thee. Thou has made the
> sky distant to shine in it and to see all that thou hast
> made, being alone and shining in thy various forms as
> the living Aten, appearing gloriously and gleaming,
> being both distant and near . . .'*

2
THE FIRST LOVE

Not yet twelve years old Ankhesenpaaten had borne a child, a daughter, to her father the Pharaoh Akhenaten. The dynasty was running out of princes carrying the royal blood. Nefertiti had produced only girls and while Akhenaten loved them dearly, a son of royal blood would make the future of the dynasty more secure. Also, for Akhenaten it was not just a matter of the physical succession, but, because of his obsessive belief that only he and his close family were capable of carrying the power of the Aten on earth and mediating it to his subjects, he was determined to produce a son carrying the pure blood of the Aten. In marrying his daughter he was not doing anything unprecedented. Sitamon, his sister, was married to her father and given the status of Royal Wife. But it was not until nearly the end of his life that Akhenaten realized that Sitamon had borne a son to her father of purer blood than himself. If it had not been for the determination of his own mother, Great Royal Wife Queen Tiye, a commoner lifted to royal status by the love of his father, he himself might not have come to the throne. The existence of the Prince Djehuti-kheper-Ra, son of Sitamon, had been kept secret and he had led a life of obscurity far from the court until a few years before Akhenaten's death.

Ankhesenpaaten had entered the parental marriage with resignation. She did not cry out when the first coitus took place and she did not cry out when she gave birth. She knew her father was disappointed that her child, who soon died, was a girl and assumed that she would have to bear more children. But he appeared to abandon the attempt to father a son on her and became so absorbed in other matters that she lived untouched and almost unnoticed among the other wives of the House of Women.

Sometimes she was lonely and longed for the care-free days of her childhood. But when she joined her sisters and her former friends she found nothing was the same. She was bored and irritated by their games and realised she had outgrown their childish chatter. Her greatest pleasure became listening to the adult gossip of the court – watching, observing, absorbing all she could – while giving nothing back. If her parents had thought to question her she would have been able to tell them about every intrigue, every disaffection, every minute shift of loyalty, long before anyone else noticed anything.

She watched Djehuti-kheper-Ra, her father's friend and confidant, and could have told Akhenaten long before it came out, that the man was obviously closely related to him, and that he met with the priests of Amun from time to time in secret. She monitored every expression on his face before and after such meetings. She noticed his love for her elder sister Merytaten, and his hopeless desire for Nefertiti – probably before he himself was aware of either.

She moved so unobtrusively about the court, there was hardly a thing hidden from her. She never spoke of anything she knew. Her satisfaction was in knowing it when others were still ignorant.

Her mother once accused her of loving no one, of being cold and feelingless. But this was not true. There was a need to love and be loved. It was just that in the first bewilderment of having to play the role she was expected to play she had built up such defences around herself that she no longer knew how to live without them.

Nefertiti was increasingly busy with complicated and difficult matters. The early days in the Golden City of the Sun when the family were together and together were seen to represent the ideal of living under the Aten, were fast disappearing. Maketaten, one of their daughters, died. The priests of Amun, like wounded and dangerous animals, hit out at every vulnerable point. Akhenaten the dreamer became Akhenaten the oppressor. In order to force his ideas on the Two Lands he was resorting to means that as a youth he would have abhorred. Nefertiti was playing dangerous games, trying to hold the whole together. She had not much time for her third daughter – but when she did take note of her she was worried. She seemed much older than she was. The expression in her eyes sometimes almost frightened her. Merytaten had her love for Djehuti-kheper-Ra. The three youngest girls were still children and unaware of the dark clouds gathering over the sun. But Ankhesenpaaten? Ankhesenpaaten knew everything that was going on – and kept it buried in a brooding heart. She even knew that it was General Horemheb who had poisoned her father.

It was this impression that Ankhesenpaaten gave of being so cold and calculating, so old and worldly-wise, that made Kia dislike and distrust her. Tutankhaten's mother had a much simpler personality than Nefertiti and her daughter. She loved and hated what she saw on the surface of things and never dreamed that what she saw was not necessarily what was really there. When at last she was brought back into the life of her son she fell upon him with almost suffocating affection, treating him as the baby she had been separated from for all those years. Ankhesenpaaten resented this of course and Kia sensed this resentment.

Akhenaten had been fond of Kia and had found her warm and direct nature comforting. It was perhaps for this reason Nefertiti had sent her away. She could see that sometimes her husband would rather be in the undemanding company of Kia, having his scalp or back massaged to the accompaniment of a pleasant little folk song, than in her own company making passionate love or talking excitedly about important matters that affected this world and the next.

When all the ceremonies and festivities of the marriage to Tutankhamun and the coronation were over there came a time when the young King and his Great Royal Wife were alone together.

Tutankhamun looked at Ankhesenamun seated at the table in their chamber. A long day of tedious and exhausting official business was over. The Queen was holding up a polished silver mirror and quietly wiping away the cosmetics from her face with a well oiled pad of soft cotton. Most women in her position would have had servants to do this for her, but Ankhesenamun preferred to do it herself. Her women had removed her jewels and her garments and stored them away, and then silently left. They knew this last rite was always Ankhesenamun's own. It was as though, slowly, carefully, she was removing the layers of a disguise, the layers of another persona. At first she had not let her husband observe this process and see her as she really was, but this night she knew that she could not avoid intimacy any longer. Something in her yearned for it, and something else made her want to run away.

She had known this boy since infancy. She had taught him his first words. Now, still a child with the soft rounded cheeks of a child, she was expected to initiate him into manhood.

As she combed out her hair she could feel his eyes fixed on the breast he could just glimpse under her raised arm. She began to feel the tingling she had felt when she had been listening in to the erotic tales of the women in the House of Women. From them she had learned more about the possibilities of the sexual act than she had ever learned in her brief marriage to her father.

She continued to comb her hair long after it was needed, moving casually and seductively, feeling the young boy's eyes on her all the time. Since her father no male had touched her, and with her father she had felt nothing but a dull sense of duty and a certain revulsion.

Listening to the women had set her off exploring her own body and now she was longing to feel how it would be with another. Tutankhamun was too young to give her full satisfaction – but he was a virgin and had learned no bad ways. She, if she was careful, would be able to teach him to give her pleasure. She had heard enough of the complaints of the women to know a man should not be allowed to get away with only pleasuring himself.

He stood beside the bed when she lay down, awkwardly, not knowing whether he dare make a move towards her or not.

She kept him standing there for some moments feasting his eyes and then she reached out her hand for him.

Eagerly and clumsily he lay down beside her, putting a hand tentatively on her breast – not knowing what to do next. She could see that he was hot and desperate, but fiercely shy. She turned her body against his and gently started to stroke him. She took his hand and taught him how to stroke her and in what places.

That first time was not a complete success, but the barrier had been broken and they both knew it would not be long before their nights together would be the most precious parts of their lives – the only times when, burdened as they were with state duties and responsibilities beyond their years, they could seek out and find a secret pleasure for themselves and a relationship that kept them from despair.

During the first year of his reign Tutankhamun barely spent a month in Akhetaten. The royal entourage was always on the move. Ceremonies had to be performed at all the major centres, in each case to re-establish the gods of that centre and the new king's commitment to them. At Men-nefer the King was named the son of Ptah, the Creator, and Sekhmet, the Destroyer, the male and female deities of that great city. At Khemnu he was named the son of Djehuti and Seshat, the god and goddess of wisdom and of scribes. At Abedju he was identified with Horus, the son of Osiris who ruled the Underworld, and his sister-wife Isis.

At every centre Ankhesenamun was at his side, the importance of the balance of male and female energy constantly emphasised. But whatever ritual significance it might have, Tutankhamun was glad of her presence and at night when the watching eyes and guiding hands of Ay and Horemheb could not reach them, they performed their own and very personal ritual to release tension and make them forget their cares.

Exhausted, Tutankhamun fell asleep quickly, but more often than not Ankhesenamun lay awake for a long time beside him, thinking. The chamber was never very dark for since the violent events at Akhetaten, Tutankhamun had insisted on having at least one lamp burning all night. She stared into its flame and pondered the enigma of gods and humans. If the gods and goddesses were great spirit beings free of the restrictions imposed on humans by encasement in flesh, why were they so dependent on humans? Why must humans appeal to them, sacrifice to them, name their names? Surely they existed whether people recognized them or not? Surely they did their work whether people asked them to or not?

When her father was alive she had often been bored and irritated by his obsession with religion. It seemed to her life was a performance – a continuous enactment of set pieces, and those who were deemed successful were only those who gave the most convincing performances. She was fascinated by masks and as a child spent a great deal of time constructing them. She wondered what had happened to her collection of masks. She smiled wryly remembering the times she had frightened her nurse and her companions by appearing unexpectedly out of the shadows wearing one or other of her masks. Or did the nurse or the companions only shriek with pretended alarm? Was their reaction a performance too?

Part of her pleasure in eavesdropping and in observing all that happened at court came from figuring out what act, what script, what manoeuvre was being used to produce what reaction.

At a very early age the words of hymns and prayers ceased to have meaning for her and became patterns of sound to fill the silence – scripts to be followed and learned by rote, signifying nothing.

Even at the death of her infant daughter she wept because she knew it was expected. One mourned dead people loudly and theatrically. Only once when she was alone with the frail and sickly little body before it was embalmed, and there was no one there to see her act, did she wonder what it might have been like if the little creature had lived and shared love with her. The twinge of sorrow for an opportunity lost was not feigned.

She turned her head and looked at the boy at her side.

His dark lashes lay against a flushed cheek. His full and
rounded lips were slightly parted and she could hear his
breath stirring very softly, very regularly. She felt sorrow that so young and so naive he was plunged into a
corrupt and savage world, the puppet of forces that
cared nothing for him. She put her lips against his
forehead and kept them there, drifting at last towards
sleep, gathering him in her arms.

Day after day lists of names were brought to the young
Pharaoh by Ay and Horemheb and he was either told
that they were names to be trusted and that they must
be appointed to such and such a post, or that they were
names not to be trusted and they must be either banished or destroyed. Most of the names meant nothing to
him. Only Ay and Horemheb knew the faces behind the
names. The boy put his royal seal where he was told and
made no demur. Later, men were brought before him as
he sat upon the throne and again, on the instructions of
Ay and Horemheb, he either appointed, rewarded or
condemned them. Petitions were read out, but it was
not his decisions that were implemented.

Ankhesenamun was very well aware of the power of
the Vizier and the General and the helplessness of the
boy on the throne. She watched all that happened with
growing bitterness, but even if it had been in her nature
to interfere she could not. Both his grandfather and his
father had broken with tradition and brought their
Great Royal Wives forward to share power. Everyone
knew Queen Tiye had been formidably influential
behind the throne, but Nefertiti had taken one step
further forward and actually ruled from the throne
when her husband died. Horemheb was determined this
would not happen again and he made sure it was
understood that with the return of the old religious

traditions, the old court protocol was to be meticulously observed. Ankhesenamun was to be seen as the loving wife, the adoring woman, the bearer of the royal blood-line and hopefully, of the royal heir, but was to have no say in government, no life of her own. She was to look beautiful and keep her mouth shut. This was made very plain, and she knew her life depended on how obediently she played this role.

Sometimes she thought of risking everything and speaking out to make Tutankhamun aware that he had power himself and should assert it – that he was being used to implement policies that should not be implemented, appoint men who should not be appointed, and punish men who should not be punished. But she hesitated. Tutankhamun was not ready to make his own decisions. Time and again she saw that he was taken in by appearances and swayed by lies and flattery. At least Horemheb and Ay knew what they were doing and were pursuing a consistent policy. If Tutankhamun took power now they would all be at the mercy of a child's whims and fancies. Much as she loved him, she knew he had not found himself, and until he did, she would bide her time.

But when he did, she thought, Horemheb and Ay better take care!

Tutankhamun grew accustomed to the formalities of kingship and accepted the necessity to be dressed in full regalia, seated on his grandest throne while foreign princes and diplomats filed past, doing obeisance to him and laying costly gifts at his feet. On these occasions Ankhesenamun stood behind the throne and watched in the way she had watched when her parents were alive. With an unerring natural instinct for reading human nature, she amused herself by speculating on the

thoughts of those who came forward. She read their
true status within their own community by the depth
of their bow. She read their hopes and desires and
fears in their eyes as they approached and walked
away. She saw what they expected and wanted from
the king at whose feet they laid their gifts, though
sometimes it was at variance with the carefully
rehearsed speeches they made.

Tutankhamun saw nothing but their symbols of office
and the gifts they brought.

Under the great warrior king, Djehuti-mes III,
Khemet had extended its borders well into the eastern
countries and south, further into Nubia and Kush than
it ever had before. Vassal rulers were obligated to send
tribute to the mighty King of Kings. Amenhotep III,
had ruled more by diplomacy than war, and had kept the
far-flung empire safe for Khemet by shrewd use of
bribe, hostages and diplomatic marriage. But
Akhenaten, his son, had not been concerned to main-
tain the empire and within the chain that bound it to the
Egyptian throne there were now many weak links.
Khemet's power was shifting and crumbling. Almost
more than anything else Horemheb was determined to
shore up the empire and secure it against foreign
invasion and internal disaffection.

On Ay's advice, he invited the rulers of the powerful
kingdoms outside the empire, but now threatening its
security by their own desire for expansion, to visit the
new Pharaoh, hoping the massed armies on parade, the
pomp and ceremony, would impress on them that the
power behind the new King was not to be underestimated.
They knew and he knew it would be more than a social
visit. Behind the scenes there would be discussions; there
would be flexing of muscles; there would be veiled threats,
deals struck and compromises agreed.

Many came, curious to take the measure of the new rule. Some did not.

Among those who came were three Hittite princes. Their father, Suppiluliuma, ruled a huge country beyond Khemet's control and expanding every year by conquest. It was a formidable enemy and had already absorbed many of Khemet's vassal states into its own domain.

The Hittite princes did not come as supplicants. They came as equals and were royally entertained. Gifts were exchanged and they expected to return to the land of Hatti with as rich a haul as they had brought with them.

3

THE LION HUNT

Two of the Hittite princes were tall men, warriors, hard
and formidable. They were on enemy territory no
matter how much everyone pretended that this was a
diplomatic visit between friends, and they did not relax
vigilance for a moment. The heir to the throne had not
come with them. Suppiluliuma had many sons. The
eldest visitor was his second son, Mursilis, and the
youngest was his seventh, Zannanza. The latter was no
more than a young lad not much older than
Tutankhamun and was clearly delighted with
everything he saw. Ankhesenamun watched him in particular with amusement as he ogled the naked serving
girls, the rich and elegant furniture, the elaborate jewels
of the court nobles. When he was greeting
Tutankhamun his eyes never strayed from his necklace,
a winged golden scarab rising from a lake of turquoise
and lapis lazuli lotus blossoms. The Hittite princes had
jewels too, but they were clumsier, rougher, less
delicately and skilfully worked. Zannanza had broad
gold bracelets on his upper arms studded with river-
worn garnets, no necklace at his throat, but heavy rings
on two of his fingers. From his heavily garnet-studded
belt hung a dagger of precious iron with a rock crystal
pommel. If Zannanza's eyes were on Tutankhamun's
necklace, Tutankhamun's were on the dagger at the belt
of the Hittite prince. Ankhesenamun noted everything.
The elder princes were determined to disapprove of
everything they saw, putting down Egyptian finery to
Egyptian decadence, while their young brother was

obviously excited by such luxury, such beauty, and seduced by it.

That night when they retired to their chamber Tutankhamun spoke of nothing but the iron dagger. The blade of the ceremonial adze used in Egyptian funerals for 'opening the mouth' of the deceased was made of meteoric iron sent by the gods from the sky – but the Hittites were said to have found this metal on earth. Indeed the eldest, Prince Mursilis, had an arm band of it decorated with an image of their storm god wielding a zigzag lightning bolt. It was clearly a mark of his status in his father's kingdom. Tutankhamun had seen beads made of the metal before and small funerary objects, but never a weapon.

'I don't care what treasure the Hittites have brought,' he said to Ankhesenamun. 'It is only that dagger I want.'

'I doubt whether he'll part with it,' Ankhesenamun said. 'In their land no one but the royal family may have iron.'

'Their kingdom is nothing to ours,' Tutankhamun grumbled. 'You can see they are almost savages!'

'Don't underestimate them,' she replied mildly. 'They may be different from us, but their father is a force to be respected. He has made the Mittanians and the Babylonians look to their armies.'

'Not one of them could stand up against the Two Lands,' Tutankhamun boasted.

'I hope we may not be put to the test, my Lord,' she said. 'I would say our forces are not yet ready to face up to any one of them. And if they combine . . .'

'Horemheb says . . .'

'Horemheb says many things,' she interrupted impatiently. 'He does not see any way of keeping our country great except by force of arms. You would be better off

taking advantage of the visit of the Hittite princes to
make friends and alliances.'

'I will make friends,' Tutankhamun said suddenly.
'And he will give me that dagger as a friend – not as
King of Khemet!'

Ankhesenamun put her arm around his shoulders and
kissed his cheek.

'You are learning, my brother.'

'You are a good teacher,' he said, and kissed her on
the lips.

The next day Tutankhamun made a point of singling out
the youngest Hittite prince from among the
distinguished guests and suggesting a tour of the palace
grounds.

'I have a collection of animals from all over the
world,' he said. 'There may be some there you have
never seen.'

The prince was pleased to accept and Ankhesenamun
accompanied them. They were all relieved to leave the
formality of the court for a while.

The Hittite stared at everything; the lush gardens and
ponds rich in fish and water plants, the palm trees and
sycamores lining the paths, the slender painted columns
of the shady colonnades, the colourful pavements of
flowered tiles.

Tutankhamun's private zoo was well away from the
living quarters of the palace and a place the boy-King
visited less and less as he grew older and busier. It was
a place he enjoyed, a place to which he could escape, and
the Hittite prince did not realize how privileged he was
to be taken there.

He gazed with amazement at the animals from distant
lands. He had never seen a giraffe before, and several of
the types of gazelle. The animal with which he was most

familiar was the lion. In the iconography of his own
country the lion was the most important. The statues of
gods were carved standing on the backs of lions. His
own father's palace was entered through a mighty lion
gate.

Tutankhamun had inherited a pair of lions from his
grandfather, and the magnificent beasts were housed in
a special part of the zoo behind high walls. Zannanza,
Tutankhamun and Ankhesenamun climbed up alabaster
steps to a viewing platform and looked down upon the
family. Three new cubs had recently been born and the
mother lay in the shade of a tree while they suckled. The
father strode up and down, up and down the length of
the wall restlessly, longing for his freedom.

Zannanza had not seen captive lions before, let alone
lions bred in captivity. The mountains near his home
were dangerous with lions and the lion hunt was one of
the royal sports most encouraged among the princes.

Tutankhamun offered him a male and female cub to
start his own pride and the prince eagerly accepted.
Ankhesenamun smiled quietly to herself to see how
Tutankhamun eyed the iron dagger at the prince's belt
while he made the offer, and how unaware Zannanza
was of the strings attached to the gift.

When they returned to the palace Zannanza broke
excitedly into his own language, no doubt telling his
brothers about the animals he had seen. The eldest
listened gravely and then suggested something that
made Zannanza pale a little.

Ankhesenamun asked him quietly what was being
said.

'My brother suggests the King might like to take us
on a lion hunt while we are here. It is the custom in our
country for princes to be expert in this sport and it is
clear there is such a custom here too.'

Tutankhamun hesitated. Yes, it was the custom, but so far he had not gone on such a hunt alone. He was now twelve years old and it would not be long before he would be expected to prove his manhood in many difficult ways. But he would not like to fail in anything before the Hittite princes, and he was not sure that he would be capable of bringing down a lion unaided yet.

The two elder princes were watching him closely. It was clear their motives for suggesting the hunt were not entirely what they seemed.

Ankhesenamun was about to step in to divert their attention from the idea, when Tutankhamun raised his hand imperiously to stop her.

'We will set off tomorrow,' he said calmly. 'The journey will be long for there are no lions so near the city. Can my friend, your King, spare his sons for so long?'

'Our father, the King, Mighty Lion beyond all lions, would be happy for his sons to learn the ways of the Pharaoh of the Two Lands in hunting the lion.'

There was nothing to be done. It was clear they were determined to test the boy-King out, and if he failed to accept the challenge or failed in meeting the challenge, there would be some insulting and hilarious tales told about the King of Egypt at Hattusas on their return. It was not spelled out, but Ankhesenamun could read the message in their eyes. It was the honour of the Two Lands that was at stake here. She took her husband's hand and gave it a reassuring squeeze.

'Will Prince Zannanza also hunt?' she asked quietly. She had seen in his eyes the same fleeting look of panic as she had seen in Tutankhamun's. It was clear to him that he also would be on trial. He too had not yet been on a full lion hunt at which he was expected personally to bring down a lion. The two were of an age and the

two brothers were amused to pit them against each
other. Ankhesenamun would not have been surprised
had they taken out wagers on the boys.

The young prince coloured slightly at her question
and then lifted his chin.

'Of course,' he said.

'I will accompany you,' the young Queen said.

'This is not women's work,' Prince Mursilis said
sharply.

'I do not intend to hunt, my Lord,' she said coldly,
having taken a dislike to him from the first, 'though my
mother often hunted with my father. I will come to
watch how the great princes of Hatti conduct themselves upon such a hunt.'

Zannanza looked as though he wished she would not,
but Prince Mursilis nodded curtly and said, 'So be it.'

And so the arrangements were made.

Mursilis made it quite clear that he wanted an exciting
and challenging hunt. Ankhesenamun wondered if he
was as determined to travel so far to the south not
because he was in search of the wildest places and the
most dangerous lions, but because he wanted to take the
measure of the whole country. She could not believe
that the Hittites would ever invade Khemet itself –
though they might feel encouraged to attack more of the
Egyptian vassal states if they felt they could get away
with it. It was true Egypt had once been invaded and
conquered by the Hyksos who were an Asiatic people.
She was proud that the first kings of her own dynasty
had been the ones to rid the Two Lands of them. For
all she disliked Horemheb, he was a good and wary
general, and if need be Khemet *would* be defended, and
any invading force *would* be flung back.

As they travelled south, first by boat and then by

mule train and horse, she observed Mursilis. He
was strong and hard and arrogant. There were several
scars on his muscular arms and one beneath the left
breast. He was a man of action and impatient with his
young brother who spent time talking about art and
music with herself and Tutankhamun. She intercepted
a look that passed between the two elder Hittite princes
once when Zannanza was telling her how much he was
hoping to train for the priesthood and leave the court of
his father.

'Will you serve the fearsome storm god Teshub?' she
asked.

'No,' he said, lowering his voice as though he did not
want his brothers to hear him. 'Hebut, the Mother.'

'What does your father think about that?'

He flushed and looked to see if his brothers were
listening. Not for the first time Ankhesenamun received
the impression he was afraid of them.

Mursilis laughed harshly.

'Whatever he wishes, his father grants him,' he said.
There was such bitterness in his voice it was clear that
Zannanza, the son of a favourite wife, was a favourite
of the old King and the others resented how much he
was indulged. 'He will look into the mirror of Hebut
and dream his life away.'

'A mirror mirrors life. Will he not see himself
clearly?' she said softly. 'Will he not know himself for
what he is – while others who do not look into her mirror,' she added pointedly, 'delude themselves about
themselves?'

Mursilis shrugged and turned away pretending to be
bored with the talk of a woman when there were better
things to be done.

Ankhesenamun caught Zannanza's eye and read
gratitude there. She liked him. He was not a weakling as

his brothers implied. He would be a strong man one day too, but with an inner strength the other two seemed to lack.

They made camp at last in a district well known to be the haunt of lions. The guards who had come with them were experienced in lion country and lost no time in organising things so well that, within the camp, they would be quite safe. Having come this far, driven on by her interest in studying the Hittite princes and a desire to be with Tutankhamun in his hour of trial, Ankhesenamun suddenly began to realize what she had done. Here she was – several days journey out of reach of the comforts of her everyday life, set down amongst dangerous and hostile mountains, each rock potentially harbouring death. Why had she done it? This very moment she could be sitting on the terrace at home, sipping cool wine, and watching the birds winging home before the dark.

'I have come,' she told herself, 'to see that my husband is not driven to his death by these reckless fools.' She well knew that when boys were trying to prove their manhood they often lost all sense of proportion and caution. She looked at Tutankhamun, exhausted from the journey, yet strutting about ordering food and wine, prepared to carouse all night to prove something to the Hittites, not remembering for an instant that he would need all his wits about him in the morning. As she watched the wine sacks emptying she knew the elder princes of Hatti were deliberately wanting to make the young King drunk, wanting him to fail in the morning. Whether they intended his death or just his disgrace she was not sure, but suddenly she realized that this was not a game; this was a dangerous situation and if she did not do something to help her husband she might not have him much longer. Zannanza

had wisely slipped away to bed, refusing wine. But
Tutankhamun – challenged by the Hittites – was
determined to outdrink them.

Ankhesenamun slipped aside to where the provisions
were kept and quietly slit open the wine skins and prized
off the stoppers of the flasks. Into the dark earth flowed
the precious liquid, Ankhesenamun saying a prayer for
her husband as though it were a libation to the gods.

When more wine was called for there was no more to
be had.

Mursilis and Hattusilis were up at dawn ready to start,
while Tutankhamun was still fast asleep. Ankhesenamun was just considering letting him sleep on and
keep them waiting when he stirred and opened his
eyes.

'Senamun,' he said drowsily, still under the influence
of a half finished dream. 'Do you think I will live the day
out?'

'Why not, my Lord?' she said, though she too had
wondered just that. 'You have hunted before and you
will hunt again.' She had intended to carry his quiver of
arrows as she often did when he went after wildfowl –
but he would not let her.

'You must not come with us,' he said, rising. 'You
must wait here.'

'I will come, my Lord.'

'No. You must stay.'

'Is that what the Hittites want, my Lord? Or is it your
own wish?'

He did not reply at once. He was splashing cold water
from an alabaster bowl into his face.

'My own wish,' he replied firmly, properly awake at
last.

'It is not *my* wish,' she said sharply.

'In this you must obey me,' he said. 'It is too dangerous.'

'I can shoot an arrow as well as any man!'

Nefertiti had seen that her daughters learned many skills most people considered not suitable for women. 'When it comes down to it,' she used to say, 'one can rely on no one but oneself. Learn to look after yourself. No one else can do it as well.' There were times at target practice when Ankhesenamun had outshot Tutankhamun. But she had never killed. She had never shot at a living creature.

'I know you can,' he said. 'But it will shame me to have my nurse at my side.'

'Surely not *nurse*, my Lord!'

'There are times you forget you are my wife, Senamun, and treat me like a nurse does her child. Last night for instance. I could have handled more wine.'

'I emptied the wine as a sacrifice to the gods, my Lord – as priestess – not as nurse. I prayed for your safety today. Later you will thank me.'

'I thank you now,' he said a little wryly, putting his hands to his aching head. 'Senamun . . .' he paused. His face was momentarily anxious and afraid.

'What is it, Lord?'

'Nothing.'

She took him in her arms and kissed him. They could hear the Hittites talking loudly and impatiently outside the tent. They were eager to be off, and, though they spoke in their own language, a certain note in their laughter made Tutankhamun think they were jeering at him and expecting him to back out of the expedition.

He pulled away from her and strode out of the tent. At twelve years old he was tall for his age. He was certainly more of a man than when he married her, but his shoulders were not even as broad as those of

Zannanza and his waist was as narrow as a girl's. She knew she could not go with him – yet he needed her.

The brothers insisted that the four of them went alone. No beaters. No trackers. No guards. No fall-back safety precautions. It was clear that Tutankhamun and Zannanza must face the ordeal alone if they were to prove themselves. The elder brothers showed no sign of fear and were scornful when it was suggested that they should not go alone.

'If the King of Khemet needs his army to hunt a lion, let him bring his army,' Mursilis said with a curl to his lip. 'We hunt alone in Hatti.' After that Tutankhamun could not bring himself to order the guards to accompany him.

They travelled a long way from the camp, the two men leading, the boys following somewhat unwillingly behind, silently in sympathy with each other and gathering strength from each other, though no words were spoken between them.

The burning orb of the sun rose higher and higher in a sky as blue and as clear as sapphire.

'Incomparable Aten, Father of my father, Lord of the Horizon . . .' whispered Tutankhamun, the words of a prayer to the Aten he had learned in the nursery rolled over and over again in his mind like pebbles in a stream. He was not even aware of them. It was as though one part of his mind was thinking them while quite different words were chasing each other in other parts of his mind. He did not know if he was more afraid of death or of disgrace. For a great king it had to be disgrace. Death would bring him immortality, but if he were disgraced he might fall back into the Void and cease to be. Indeed, it would be as though he had never been – for there would be no memories.

Such terror seized him at this thought, he hurried away from the others and hid behind a rock so that they could not see him shaking. He had never really thought about his life until this moment. The events of each day had occurred and he had experienced them – but he had never taken a step back and wondered who he was and 'why' he existed at all. He had never noticed Life itself – nor pondered how peculiar, precious and mysterious it is. Now – when he thought he might lose it – he began to value it.

Worried suddenly that the others might suspect he was hiding because he was afraid, he pulled himself together and emerged – walking as casually as he could – adjusting his kilt.

It was almost noon before they came upon the lions.

The place was like a natural amphitheatre with a flat area, almost circular, covered with tough bushes and ochre-coloured dry grass. There was a thorn bush, bare of leaves, the long white thorns very visible, to one side. Surrounding this almost completely were huge tumbled chunks of red rock at the foot of an arc-shaped hill. In the sparse shade of the thorn tree a lion and lioness were lying at ease, two newly born cubs playing at their side. In the absolutely still air the smell of the human predators had not reached them.

Tutankhamun went rigid and cold. Not only was he afraid, but he had no wish to kill these beautiful and peaceful beasts. He thought to say as much to Mursilis and turned to where he had been a moment before. But Mursilis was not there.

As though they had pre-arranged their strategy, Mursilis and Hattusilis had taken up positions on the rocks overlooking the drama about to be played out below them, leaving the two startled and unprepared boys on the same level as the lions. Then, simultaneously, they loosed an arrow each and killed the cubs. With a roar of rage the big male rose to his feet, turned and saw the young intruders fumbling to fit arrows into bows. He sought no further for the enemy and leapt forward. Tutankhamun loosed his arrow first and it struck home but did not seem to slow the massive beast down. Wild with anger and pain it sprang towards Zannanza. Tutankhamun tried to throw his spear but it fell short. Terrified, but seeing what danger Zannanza was in, he picked up a rock and hurled it with all his might. It struck the male in the eyes and for a moment blinded him and deflected him from his path. Seconds later the spears of the elder Hittite princes found their mark, and with a sound that curdled Tutankhamun's blood, the king of beasts fell dead at their feet. Zannanza was backed against a rock, white with fear, his small iron dagger held out in front of him ready to plunge it in to his attacker if need be.

But all was not over. The lioness who had been attending, heartbroken, to her cubs while her mate sought vengeance on the brutal murderers, had now turned to see what was happening.

As the two elder Hittites were congratulating themselves on their kill, the lioness sprang at Tutankhamun.

When Ankhesenamun heard the story later she could not believe that two such experienced hunters as Mursilis and Hattusilis had forgotten the dangerous presence of the lioness, and indeed had not shot the cubs deliberately to create a situation in which the two boys would be killed. Tutankhamun's courage and presence of mind had probably saved Zannanza's life, for his brothers' spears might well have been too late for him. Now, in his turn, Zannanza probably saved the life of Tutankhamun. The lioness was upon the King when Zannanza leapt upon her and drove the dagger home.

At this moment a new factor entered into the situation.

An hour after the party had left in the morning, Ankhesenamun had had such a premonition of disaster that she had disobeyed her husband and sent trackers and guards out to follow him. If they had not arrived at the moment of the lioness's desperate leap and taken over from the young Hittite prince, both he and Tutankhamun might yet have died. In the confusion Mursilis and Hattusilis managed to appear busy, but one at least of the trackers was not taken in, and reported back to Ankhesenamun that when they came upon the scene, the two elder Hittite princes were not lifting a finger to help the King, while the younger was risking his own life.

All day Ankhesenamun paced about the camp. She wished a hundred times she had gone with the men she'd sent off to find Tutankhamun. But she had been stung by his reference to her as 'nurse' and did not want to shame him in front of those hard and cynical men. As the first star appeared and the evening fires were lit to keep off the night chills and the marauding nocturnal beasts, she was almost frantic. What if the guards had not found him? What if they were all separated and lost somewhere in this wild terrain? What if . . .? Her thoughts ran on and on and though she prayed to every god she knew her agitation did not abate.

At last she heard a rock slipping on a nearby knoll and rushed to get a better view. In the rapidly dimming light she could make out a column of figures approaching and rushed towards them, scuffing her toes on rocks until they bled, tearing the fabric of her skirt on thorns.

When she was near enough she saw that the guards at

the front of the column were carrying the bodies of two lions, a male and a female. Mursilis and Hattusilis walked beside them and, when they saw her, brandished their bloodied spears triumphantly. But she scarcely noticed them. Her eyes were scanning for her husband.

At the rear, trackers bore two makeshift stretchers, and on them lay the two young boys.

Though she had as yet been told nothing Ankhesenamun knew it all. With a scream she rushed at Mursilis and Hattusilis and, cat-like, drove her nails into their faces.

'Wear these scars!' she shrieked. 'And never forget that you will pay for this!'

Astonished, the two men fended her fury off with their arms.

'Lady! Lady!' they shouted. 'Your husband is alive. His attacker is dead. Why do you treat us so?'

Sobbing, she turned away from them and flung herself on Tutankhamun, covering him with kisses.

'I'm all right,' he whispered hoarsely, in quite considerable pain. 'The dagger . . .' he muttered. And she saw he was clutching the iron dagger in his hand. It was covered in blood. She looked across at Zannanza, surprised.

The young prince was very pale, but he nodded.

'He saved my life,' he said. 'The dagger is his.'

4
THE SACRED EGG OF RA

By the time Tutankhamun was sixteen the court had long since left Akhetaten, the Horizon of the Sun's Disc, and Akhenaten's beautiful city was falling into ruin. From the palaces and the great houses of the officials and nobles everything had been stripped, either by the owners themselves when they moved away following the court of Tutankhamun, or by looters who moved in as soon as the flotilla of ships carrying the King left the quayside. Within moments of the palaces and houses being left they became like dead carcases prey to scavengers. As surely as a man's soul leaves his body at death, so does the life-force, the soul, of a building depart as soon as a decision is made to desert it. Nothing was left of Akhetaten – the vibrant, musical, happy city – but dry stones that could not hear or speak.

The city's death had been as sudden and dramatic as its birth.

Not much longer than twenty years before the whole area had been semi-desert, a level plain, walled in the east by a ridge of mountains and bordered in the west by the river. Akhenaten, fired by his dream to start a new life and a new religion uncorrupted by centuries of misunderstanding and misrepresentation, had chosen to build his new capital there. He had set up his boundary stela and within months the foundations were laid and a vigorous workforce guided by eager and talented artists and architects had created a glittering city, pure and virginal, and ready to house his great ideal.

Ankhesenamun and Tutankhamun had grown up in

this city among lush gardens fed by canals, in light and airy palaces, tiled with green and flowery scenes. They had stood beside the King, the Divine Channel of the Aten, in the great Sun Temple and presented offerings to his god. They had swum in the lakes; sailed on the river; played ball in the vast gardens.

After the bloody riot when a restless population had been stirred up to a frenzy by the cunning of the first prophet of Amun and had done unthinkable deeds in the fair city, including the murder of Nefertiti and her eldest daughter Merytaten, Horemheb had extended a long, hard hand and kept such a grip on the city that he virtually squeezed all the life out of it.

For the first two years of Tutankhamun's reign the court remained nominally at Akhetaten, though the actual time the young King and Queen spent there was very little.

Ankhesenamun suspected it was Ay, who had long held power in the royal circle, and could not easily be overthrown, who kept Akhentaten's religion going for a while. In Tutankhamun's name the other gods were reinstated throughout the country, but the worship of the Aten was not at first forbidden as Akhenaten had forbidden the worship of Amun in his last years.

The Aten, a god symbolized by the disc of the sun, had not been an invention of Akhenaten. It had existed as a divine force since ancient times. Initially all that Akhenaten did was to bring it to the fore as Hatshepsut had brought forward the already existing god Amun. Later he became more and more convinced that he could only free his people from the dark hold of a corrupt and powerful priesthood by insisting that they should have no other gods *but* the Aten, and no other High Priest but himself. In the last years he had been locked in a struggle to the death with the priests of Amun.

They had won. He was dead. And within three years his religion was declared anathema, his city dismantled, his name hacked out wherever it was found, his successor told that his father had been a force for evil and he must publicly disassociate himself from him.

Horemheb finally clamped down on the worship of the Aten when a group of dissidents toppled a newly carved statue of the god Amun from its place in the courtyard of the great Temple of Amun at Ipet-Esut. No one saw it happen and no one knew who had perpetrated such blasphemy, but in the earth beside the fallen god the sign of the Aten was crudely scratched – the sun's disc with the long rays of the sun ending in hands holding the *ankh*, the sign for eternal life.

He persuaded Ay that the time had come to end any allegiance to the Aten.

'If we let the cult co-exist at this stage,' he said to Ay when he protested at the severity with which the General intended to enforce his decision, 'we are inviting disorder and chaos. Later, when the cult has no strength, we can allow the Aten to have priests again.'

The priests of the Aten fled, as recently the priests of Amun had done.

The court shared its time between Men-nefer in the north and Waset in the south, and the city of Akhenaten became a ghost town, haunted by memories and inhabited by the poor who could not leave, wild dogs and jackals, and an occasional ragged priest in hiding who would not give up his faith in the pure light he had been inspired to see under Akhenaten's guidance.

Such a one was Hapu, a member of an illustrious family. He was named after his great-grandfather who had been a high official at the court of Djehuti-mes IV, indeed had been instrumental in insuring that that king had come to the throne over other claimants.

It was his great-grandfather Hapu who had persuaded the most influential priests and officials to use a dream the young prince had as a sign from the god Ra-Harahkti that he was to be king. The story went that Prince Djehuti-mes was out hunting on the plain of Giza, and there at noon he had lain down to rest in the shade of the huge head of the sphinx. He was soon asleep and dreaming. It seemed to him that Ra-Harahkti appeared to him in the form of a great sphinx and told him that if he were to clear away the sand that had blown over his body for centuries and reveal his form again to the world in its full glory, he, the prince, son of a minor wife of Amenhotep II, would become Pharaoh of the Two Lands.

Troubled, the prince had told the High Priest of Amun-Ra, Hapu, about his dream. Hapu advised him to obey the god and clear the sand away from the sphinx. This he did.

At the next great festival when the statue of the god Amun-Ra was being carried in procession a dramatic, and apparently divine, intervention in the course of history occurred. The priests carrying the golden god in his golden solar boat stopped the procession beside the young prince. They claimed later that they had been impelled to do this by the god himself. In spite of their efforts to prevent it the statue tipped three times towards the young prince before it 'allowed' the procession to move on.

Prince Djehuti-mes was named royal heir on the strength of this and in due course became Pharaoh. He erected a stela between the paws of the sphinx to commemorate the event. Hapu was not forgotten and he and his family enjoyed considerable royal favour. The

same Hapu's son, Amenhotep-son-of-Hapu, was responsible for most of the great and beautiful buildings of the
next Pharaoh, Neb-Maat-Ra, Amenhotep III, grandfather of Tutankhamun, and was indeed so close to the
throne and so brilliant in everything to which he put his
mind, that the Pharaoh allowed a statue of him to stand
in his own 'Mansion of Millions of Years' to insure that
he would accompany him throughout eternity. Only
Imhotep the architect of King Djoser nearly two thousand years before had been granted such a privilege.

The young Hapu who now lived in the shadowy ruins
of Akhetaten, had once been an honoured priest of the
Aten, one of Akhenaten's most dedicated converts. He
interpreted the instructions given to the prince by the
sphinx to mean that any true pharaoh must clear away
the dead matter that is obscuring the true meaning of a
revelation from the Divine, and reveal it to the world.
To him this was exactly what Akhenaten had set out to
do and he, Hapu, was not about to abandon that mission
just because it had become difficult and dangerous.

Day after day he greeted the rising of the Aten's orb,
praying to Akhenaten himself who, though dead, was
still the channel through which Hapu believed the god
would communicate with the earth. He placed flowers
and what food he could find in the dying city on the
appropriate altar in the Temple of the Aten. Akhenaten
had built an altar for each day of the year and although
Horemheb's soldiers had desecrated them, Hapu found
a way to clear and consecrate them again.

One night he thought he saw the figure of Akhenaten
passing his open door. He leapt up from his bed and
rushed out into the street. A full moon illuminated
everything with an eerie silver light. The figure of a man
was just disappearing round the corner of the street.
Hapu told himself it could not be his king because his

king was dead, but nevertheless he felt impelled to follow. What if it was the *ka* of his king? What if . . .!

When he reached the corner the figure was just passing round a further corner. And so it went on for some time. Hapu became more and more determined not to lose sight of the man, more and more convinced it was not just one of those men who had remained in Akhetaten after the court had left. It was almost as though the man paused deliberately at each corner to make sure that Hapu was following him before he went further. The distance between them was too great and the light too uncertain for him to be sure it was the king, but the overall shape of the figure was very similar. Yet more than the shape, Hapu *felt* the king was calling him to follow him. He *felt* that he was following the king.

They came eventually to the deserted palace and passed through the empty hole where once the hinged gates had been and the guards had called out their challenge. This night there was no one to bar his entrance and he passed straight through.

At this point the figure he had been following disappeared. Hapu ran down the cracked path in the direction he thought he saw him go, but there was no sign of him. Frantically Hapu ran hither and thither through the neglected garden and then climbed the steps and entered the palace itself. Even though it was now only a shell he felt nervous. What presumption to enter the 'house of the king'! Although Hapu knew that Tutankhamun was now Pharaoh – he could not come to terms with it. Akhenaten was his king and always would be.

He almost tiptoed through the halls and corridors and courtyards, passing through the shadows of the columns of the colonnades, pausing beside the lily ponds that were now too dry for lilies, touching with awe the beautiful tiled walls the vandals had not smashed. In his curiosity about the palace, for, out of respect for Akhenaten, he had never ventured into it before, he almost forgot the man he had been pursuing.

Suddenly a shadow moved and Hapu came to a stop, his heart skipping a beat.

'Who is there?' he asked hoarsely, his voice sounding huge and echoing in the empty building. Shafts of white light were coming through the high window slits and falling like the Aten rays across the courtyard he was now in. He began to tremble. The atmosphere seemed highly charged. More silent than silence. He felt strange – as though he was drifting off from himself.

There was no answer. The shadows were still again.

With his heart pounding he took a step forward. And then another. And another. Cautiously he moved towards the place where he thought he had seen the movement.

How strange that it was so very dark in this corner. Suddenly he nearly fell forward and stopped himself just in time. The paved floor had given way to a hole. Cautiously he knelt down beside it and felt its rim with his hands. He could see nothing in the pitch darkness but he could feel a step below the level he was on.

'Stupid!' he thought. It was not so strange after all to come upon steps in the palace. The building was built on many different levels.

Carefully he moved forward again, feeling the edge of each step with his toes before he trusted his weight to it. The stairs were narrow and steep and went down a long way. He could feel the walls close on either side. The place reminded him of a tomb.

At last he reached the bottom and it seemed to him he could just make out a faint greenish glow somewhere

off to the left. Thankful that at last he could see
something, however indefinite, after the pitch blackness
of the stairwell, he made for the glow. He found that it
was coming from a crack beneath a door. He was now
so anxious to know what could be causing it, he could
not have stopped had a thousand spirits from the dead
barred his way. With trembling and sweaty hands he
pushed at the door. It swung open and he was suddenly
almost blinded by brilliant green light

He stood amazed – blinking and rubbing his eyes.

In a small chamber with no windows, on a black stone
plinth, was a huge green crystal egg emitting powerful
and beautiful rays of green light. There was no one or
no thing else in the chamber. There was no lighted torch
or lamp to be reflected from or through the crystal to
explain its light.

Ancient texts about the green Egg of Ra came to his
mind – the green Egg from which the Sun-bird hatches
– the green Egg from which all living things are
born. . . .

He fell down on his knees in awe.

The green Egg of Ra was not part of the Aten worship
and yet it was here now in the heart of Akhenaten's
palace. Hapu could not understand it.

He felt himself impelled to bow to the ground. The
cold dusty stone pressed on his forehead.

Rays of incredible light seemed to be penetrating his
body. He felt that in some way he was being skewered
by light shafts. Fear and bewilderment were getting in
the way. He knew he was experiencing something
immensely important yet he was struggling to free
himself from it, terrified of being taken over by
something he did not understand.

'I'm not ready,' he whispered. 'Please . . . please . . .
give me time . . .'

The intensity of the rays seemed to lessen. It was as though he had been held and was now being released. He slumped forward full length on the stone floor.

He lay there for a long time, too afraid to open his eyes.

At last he felt calm.

'Now, my Lord,' he said aloud in a steady and reverent voice. 'I am ready.'

He lifted his head. He lifted his body.

He saw nothing but the moonlight falling through the open door of his sleeping chamber. On the table was the familiar flask of water and the papyrus rolls he'd managed to rescue from the House of Life before it was destroyed by the soldiers.

He pulled himself to his feet for he had been lying face down on the floor of his chamber. He stared around him.

He was shocked and disappointed. It had all been so vivid. It could not have been a dream. It could not!

When the day dawned he hurried to the palace. He passed through the broken gates unchallenged. He attempted to find his way back to the stairs leading to the underground chamber. He hurried through corridors and halls and courtyards. He retraced his steps many times when he thought he had taken a wrong turn. The palace was flooded with sunlight now and everything looked so different. He felt himself to be lost in a labyrinth.

At the end of the day he was exhausted and had not found what he was looking for.

He spent a sleepless night tossing and turning on his narrow bed, fitfully watching the open door and hoping that the mysterious figure of the previous night would return to lead him.

Day after day passed. Hapu could settle to nothing but his search for the green Egg. He became desperate, obsessed. He neglected the rituals of the Aten he had so carefully kept up after Horemheb's decree. He slept little and ate almost nothing. He had never been so sure of anything as he was that he had not dreamed the green crystal egg. He cursed himself for being such a coward that he had refused to accept whatever it was that was about to happen to him that night.

At last he thought he had found a solution to his problem. If he could only speak with Queen Ankhesenamun, the last remaining daughter of Akhenaten, a young woman who had lived many years in the palace at Akhetaten and, as the King's wife, probably knew many of its secrets. If anyone alive could tell him if there was indeed a hidden crypt under the floors of the palace where the green Egg of Ra was kept and where it was, it would be she. Those who had built the palace might know of the crypt, but he had no idea who they were. They were probably this very day busy working on buildings to the honour of Amun-Ra, and if he came to them asking questions about the palace at Akhetaten, he might well be arrested. That the green Egg had not been sent back to Yunu, the great temple at the centre of the Ra cult, indicated that it had not been found by Horemheb's men. That it was hidden underground and not displayed in one of the major halls or in the temple itself, indicated that Akhenaten had wanted it kept secret.

But why? He had forbidden all artefacts and images of other gods. Admittedly the green Egg was connected with Ra, the sun god of Yunu, but there had been no mention of it in the liturgies of the Aten, nor anything about it in their training as priests of the Aten. He had not even known that it was missing from the temple at Yunu.

The more he thought about it, the more questions came crowding into his mind.

He felt very strongly that the experience he had had – and bungled – had been of great significance. The *ka* of the pharaoh had led him to it and had expected something of him regarding it. He had let him down by fear and hesitation and it seemed he was not going to be given a second chance.

It would not be easy obtaining a private audience with the Queen, but he was becoming increasingly convinced that doing so was his only hope of solving the mystery.

There were no longer boats or barges drawn up at the quay at Akhetaten. Tall masts no longer bobbed and swayed. Men no longer shouted, heaving heavy loads on and off the decks. In the city's heyday this was a busy place, a place where children gathered to watch the stir of arrival and departure; a place where crowds pushed and shoved to get a better view when some great official arrived from afar. He himself had taken up a vantage point, interested to see how they heaved the huge slabs of stone for the temples off the barges and on to the land. Now the only boats that came to Akhetaten were the boats of those who came to despoil it. The stone, that had been brought here with such effort, was now being taken away to build some other temple to some other god. The huge pylons were already dismantled, the filling rubble all that was left as the facing slabs were removed. Akhenaten's beautiful reliefs and inscriptions would be smashed up and used themselves as filling for other pylons. Hapu feared it would not be long before the paving stones and floor tiles of the palace were taken and the secret flight of stairs leading to the green crystal egg discovered. He felt so strongly that he had been led to it for some good reason, that he was determined to find it before others did.

This determination drove him to seek passage on a barge going south to Waset, loaded almost to the point of danger with shattered pieces of alabaster from the northern palace. Some of the smaller, finer pieces would no doubt be made into bowls or jars, others into statues of Tutankhamun and the gods. The larger pieces would be infill or maybe trimmed and smoothed for re-use as building blocks. Sometimes the broken inscriptions and reliefs were left intact if the blocks were to be buried face down to make a floor. Hapu sat on a pile of blocks at the stern, his fingers tracing the beautiful words of Akhenaten's love for his sole and solar god, the Light beyond all light, the progenitor beyond all progenitors.

'Ah, my king,' he whispered. 'If I can serve you yet I will give my life. Speak to me. Tell me what I must do.'

The heavy craft turned slightly into a bend in the river, the men heaving on the rudder. A large block of white calcite from Hatnub caught the sunlight where before it had been in shadow. Hapu's eyes were drawn to it. There he saw the familiar scene of the royal family basking in the rays of the Aten, hands at the end of each ray holding out the *ankh*, the sign of eternal life, to the mouths of each one of the royal family – Akhenaten, Nefertiti and their six daughters. It must have been carved before Maketaten died. Now the faces of Akhenaten and Nefertiti and most of the princesses had been hacked out, but the figure of Ankhesenpaaten was still clear and perfect. No chisel had fallen on her.

'I am doing the right thing,' Hapu thought joyfully. 'This is surely a sign that she will help me.'

He had debated with himself for several days before

he had started this journey. Ankhesenpaaten was now Ankhesenamun. Was this political necessity only or were the new King and Queen really behind the savage reaction against all their father's teachings. He must be careful how he broached the subject no matter how many 'signs' he was given. Although he was prepared to die for Akhenaten, he would rather stay alive and bring back honour to his Pharaoh's god.

When they arrived at Waset he slipped off and melted into the crowd. He was no longer dressed like a priest of the Aten, but he could not be sure someone might not recognize him. He was disappointed to learn that the Pharaoh and his Great Royal Wife were at present in Men-nefer in the north. It would be a long while before he could talk to her. He was almost in despair and wishing that he had stayed at Akhetaten and spent the time prising up paving stones.

But then he decided that this apparent setback was to his advantage. There was no way as a private citizen he could gain access to the Queen, unless he was allowed by an official, one of the 'Nine Friends of the King', or close council, to attend the court with a petition. But if he succeeded in this, he would have to speak out before everyone – officials, nobles, priests, and probably Vizier Ay and General Horemheb as well.

It would be better for him to wait for the Queen's return, and prepare a more devious way of reaching her.

Hapu was lucky. Before the next new moon Ankhesenamun was back at Waset. A new wing of her grandfather's palace at Per-Hay was ready for the young couple and the Queen had indicated her desire to be there. Now that she was pregnant Men-nefer did not please her. It was too hot and crowded – the pace of life too fast. In normal circumstances she found it stimulating and exciting – the most cosmopolitan of all Egyptian cities. It was near the fertile lands of the delta and the vast estates of the nobles who served at court. It was also the centre from which and to which travellers from the east came and went. But there never seemed a moment when Tutankhamun was free to be with her. Occasionally they went fowling in the nearby marshlands, but lately even that had become too rare an event. Day after day administrative business had to be taken care of. Tutankhamun no longer sealed documents without reading them, nor accepted everything Horemheb or Ay told him without question. She tried to persuade him to come south with her to the quieter town of Waset, to their grandfather's palace where they had had many a happy time in their youth. Tutankhamun was tempted, but resisted. He said she should go ahead and he would follow when he could.

The first time Ankhesenamun had carried a child she had been indifferent to it. But this time she felt the future stirring in her womb and was excited by it. She showed no sign of her delight however, and Tutankhamun seeing her so pale and heavy, was glad she was going to a more restful place.

Without the King in residence Per-Hay was indeed a quiet retreat. Ankhesenamun was soon bored and finding the days dragging too slowly by.

One early dawn, after a restless night, she was walking in the garden when she heard a murmuring from behind a clump of bushes. She paused to listen for a while and gradually became convinced that what she was hearing was Akhenaten's hymn to the Sun, spoken low but with great feeling.

> *'Being afar off, yet thy rays are upon the earth.*
> *Thou art in men's faces, yet thy movements are*

unseen. When thou settest in the western horizon, the earth is in darkness after the manner of death. The night is passed in the bedchamber, heads covered, no eye can see its fellow . . . Every lion is come forth from its lair and all snakes bite. Darkness is illumination while the earth is in silence, their maker resting in his horizon.

The earth grows bright, when thou hast arisen in the horizon, shining as Aten in the daytime . . . The Two Lands are in festival, awakened they stand on their feet, thou hast lifted them up. Their limbs are cleansed, clothes put on, and their hands are upraised in praise at thy glorious appearing. The entire land does its work. All cattle are at peace upon their pastures. Trees and pasture grow green. Birds taking flight from their nest, their wings give praise to thy spirit. All animals frisk upon their feet. All that flyeth or alighteth live when thou arisest for them. Ships fare north and likewise fare south. Every road is opened at thy appearing. The fish in the river leap before thy face . . .'

She crept silently nearer and then, with a sudden increase of pace, rounded the cluster of bushes.

She found there an emaciated young gardener bowing to the east, his head resting on the earth, his hands stretched out ahead of him. Her shadow falling on him, he instantly stopped what he was doing and looked up, real terror in his eyes.

'You may well be afraid,' she said. 'Do you not know that that hymn has been banned and no one may think of it – let alone say it aloud?'

The young man knelt in front of her with his head sunk on his chest.

'I know it, Majesty,' he whispered.

'You could be imprisoned or sent to work in the mines. You could even be executed.'

'I know it, Majesty,' he replied.

'Why do you risk these things for a few words?'

He was silent.

'Why?'

'They are not just words, Majesty,' he said in such a low voice she had to bend down to catch them.

'Indeed?' she said, and looked at him very hard. He was a gardener but his hands were soft and white like those of a scribe or a priest. She had the impression she had seen him before.

'What is your name, priest?' she asked quietly.

He looked up at that and in seeing his eyes she knew that indeed she had seen him before at Akhetaten in the Great Temple.

'Hapu, Majesty. Priest of the Aten.' He answered this time aloud, and with pride.

She looked quickly over her shoulder to make sure that they were still alone.

'You take great risks, Priest of the Aten,' she said sharply.

'I know, Majesty – but my life is of no value in itself. It is only in carrying out the wishes of the Aten that it has any significance.'

'Why are you here? In what way are you carrying out the wishes of the Aten by pretending to be a gardener?'

She wondered if she should call the guard, but he looked so frail she was sure she would be able to knock him down herself if he intended any mischief.

'I intend no harm to your Majesty,' he said. 'I have something I need to tell you.'

'Speak then. Quickly. For soon there will be others in the garden.'

'I saw your father, Majesty.'

She looked at him – startled.

'I swear it was not a dream,' he said quickly. 'He passed my house and I followed him. He led me to the palace.'

'What palace?'

'The Great House at Akhetaten.'

'Akhetaten is dead. My father is dead.'

'I know, Majesty. But I still live there – and I saw your father.'

'You are insane. How could it be my father? How could it possibly be my father?'

'I don't know, Majesty. Hear me out.'

She nodded. Her lips were tight closed. Her eyes dark and intense. She was gazing into his as though she would draw his soul out through them like an embalmer draws out the brain of the deceased.

He told her exactly what had happened that night. When he was describing the green crystal egg and the secret chamber he was watching her expression as closely as she was watching his. He could see that she was intrigued, but he could also see she had not known of it before. He was bitterly disappointed and wondered if he had risked his life for nothing. What if the whole thing had been only a dream after all?

They could hear someone approaching down the path beside the lily ponds.

She put her finger to her lips.

'Don't leave the palace,' she whispered, 'until I've had a chance to talk to you again.' And then aloud she said, 'These bushes must be cut back. I want more colour here. Find me some colourful flowers.'

He bowed low, and then they parted.

Ankhesenamun thought a lot about what Hapu had told her, swinging from disbelief to conviction that what he believed had happened, had indeed happened. It was not unknown that the souls of people walked the earth after they were buried. She pondered and pondered who might possibly know something about the presence of the Sacred Egg and decided the only one might be Nezem-mut, the sister of Nefertiti. They had all suspected that Nefertiti had secrets from Akhenaten in the last years. Most believed they were other lovers. But she herself believed they were more connected with forbidden magic. If anyone had brought the green Egg to Akhetaten, it would not have been Akhenaten, but Nefertiti. But why should *he* be so concerned someone should find it?

Ankhesenamun had never been very close to her Aunt Nezem-mut, and was not sure now how to approach her on the subject. She had always lived in the royal palace and had been part of the royal family's life since Ankhesenamun could remember, but she had been strangely disengaged from it. She had been there to confide in, but no one had felt compelled to confide in her. Ankhesenamun herself did not even like her. She was heavier in build than Nefertiti and sometimes wore a very sullen expression. In some ways she had blossomed since her beautiful sister's death, appearing frequently with Ay and Horemheb as though she was party to their decisions. Ankhesenamun had often wondered why she was not married with children of her own. Nefertiti's younger daughters had always been something of a preoccupation with her and she was incensed when she suspected Ankhesenamun had sent them away. Indeed she was not the only one. Horemheb had tried to find out where they were, but so far Ankhesenamun's vehement insistence that they were dead had been accepted, if not believed, by Ay and Horemheb. Nezem-mut was not so easily convinced however – and there was no doubt there was very bad feeling between the two royal women.

How could she approach her? Ankhesenamun knew there would be no way Nezem-mut would condone the continuing practice of the Aten liturgy. Hapu must be protected from her.

'I had a dream,' Ankhesenamun said to Nezem-mut while they were sitting together on a cool terrace watching the sails go by on the river. They were in Nezem-mut's quarters – her aunt somewhat surprised by her sudden visit. 'I dreamed there were secret passages and rooms under the floors of the Great Royal House at Akhetaten.'

Nezem-mut said nothing but continued to gaze out at the river. Her face was slightly turned away and Ankhesenamun could not read her expression. A servant padded softly up to them and refilled their wine bowls.

'I wondered if there was any truth in the dream,' Ankhesenamun continued, disappointed that her first statement had drawn no response. And then, when there was still no reaction she decided to be more direct. 'What do you think? Do you know of any such passages and chambers?'

'There are always parts of any building that are kept private,' Nezem-mut said. 'Ay, and of people too,' she added silently, her mind occupied with her own thoughts.

'But there was a chamber I saw – in my dream – deep under the earth, that had no access. The floor above the stairs that led down to it was paved over. It was sealed over like a tomb.'

'Perhaps it was a tomb,' Nezem-mut said casually. 'A secret lover murdered . . . an unwanted infant . . .'

'A huge green crystal egg . . .' Ankhesenamun added pointedly.

This at last brought a reaction. Nezem-mut's expression changed and she looked directly at her niece.

'You saw a green crystal egg?'

Ankhesenamun nodded.

'A huge one. Like the one that used to be in the Temple of the Sun at Yunu.'

Nezem-mut was looking so piercingly at her now, her expression so stern, the young Queen decided to retreat a little.

'It was probably only a dream,' she said placatingly. 'Some dreams mean nothing.'

'You *saw* it?'

'Only – only in my dream. Do you think there *is* such a thing in the Great House?'

Nezem-mut did not answer.

'I thought father had had the Sacred Egg from Yunu destroyed. He certainly ordered it.'

'If he ordered it to be destroyed, then it was destroyed.' Nezem-mut's voice sounded strange. She was speaking one set of words, but was thinking another. 'Amun-Ra probably gave you the dream so that you could bring to light the infamy of the heretic and blasphemer who gave such orders,' she said.

Ankhesenamun bit her lip. This was not her intention and she was sure it was not the intention of the *ka* of Akhenaten when he appeared (*if* he appeared!) to Hapu. Strange how Nezem-mut who had been such a close member of the family should go along so vehemently with Horemheb's lie.

'Why would it appear in my dream so precisely in a hidden place in the palace – if it had been destroyed?'

'Who knows,' Nezem-mut shrugged. 'Dreams give only hints and clues – often bizarre. They lead us to find truth for ourselves. They do not give it to us direct.'

'Nezem-mut is wiser than she appears,' Ankhesenamun thought, 'but I know she knows something about the Sacred Egg.'

'Do you think mother . . .?'

'No,' snapped Nezem-mut before she could finish her sentence. She stood up. 'Enough of dreams!' she said. 'We both have things to do.'

Ankhesenamun looked at her. She was definitely agitated though she was trying to hide it.

'If you know where the secret hiding place is, surely . . .'

'There is no secret hiding place! There is no Sacred Egg! Your dream was given to you purely to remind you of your father's infamy. The Sacred Egg of Yunu was the most precious possession of the sun god. Through it the earth was renewed – reborn. If it were found intact that would be the greatest event of Tutankhamun's reign. It would cause rejoicing throughout the world. It would wipe out all the desolation and sorrow caused by your father's actions and restore the Two Lands to pre-eminence. The souls of our dynasty would stand before Osiris in the Judgement Hall unstained by Akhenaten's crimes against the gods . . .'

Nezem-mut's voice was growing stronger and louder every moment almost as though she were on a platform haranguing a crowd – or speaking with the voice of an oracle.

'She knows where it is. She knows!' Ankhesenamun thought. 'Why is she pretending?'

Nezem-mut was pretending because she wanted more than anything in the world to find that Egg. With that one act she would insure her place in eternity and in the affections of General Horemheb whom she adored. She

had a good idea where it might be if it still existed and
if the dream was a true dream. Nefertiti must have
brought it to Akhetaten secretly without Akhenaten's
knowledge. In those last years she did many things
against her husband's precise instructions. Perhaps she
feared the destruction of the Egg was going too far.
Perhaps she foresaw a time when the full and ancient
worship of the sun god Ra would be restored and they
would have need of it. Who knows what was in her
devious mind. Nezem-mut both loved and hated her
sister. She was a complex and disturbing character – a
woman with powerful strengths and powerful weak-
nesses. 'But she is dead,' Nezem-mut told herself
exultantly. 'And I am alive. My time is still to come.'

Ankhesenamun could see that there was nothing
more she could glean from Nezem-mut at this stage.

'If she knows where it is,' she thought, 'she will go to
it. I'm sure of it. And when she does either Hapu or I
will be there.'

Hapu returned to Akhetaten as soon as the Queen told
him what she suspected about Nezem-mut. She told him
to wait and watch and never leave the palace. But when
he was there he found he could not remain idle. He
started tapping all the paving stones in the building with
a heavy stick – listening intently – hoping to hear the
difference in tone that would tell him the area beneath
the floor was hollow.

As he did so from dawn till dusk his mind wandered
on to many things. Queen Ankhesenamun herself was a
puzzle to him. He had seen her before at Akhetaten
when her father and her mother were alive. The other
princesses were warm and friendly and full of fun – but
Ankhesenpaaten had always seemed to be apart from
them – cold and distant. He had been afraid to approach

her – yet this time she had made him feel at ease. She had heard him speaking the hymn to the Aten, yet she had not called the guard. Was it possible that she, who had seemed so bored and impatient with all the Aten rituals when she was a child had now, when it was forbidden, taken up its cause?

The river flowed past the stricken city of Akhetaten as it always had, the sun rose and set. 'Only people change,' Hapu thought. 'Only people pretend to be what they are not.'

One day, resting from his labours and feeling considerably discouraged because of the lack of progress, he was sitting on the river bank watching some water weed drift by when a heron that had been standing on a rock nearby, motionless, suddenly flew up with a startled flurry, then winged away to the north barely skimming the water with its long, grey, arrow-like body. Hapu turned his head to see what had frightened the bird and saw a boat from the south drawing in to the deserted quayside. He had been so absorbed in his thoughts he had not even noticed its approach. He watched curiously, sufficiently distant from the activity to be sure he was not noticed – an undistinguished figure sitting on the bank, his legs dangling over the water, half hidden by some reeds.

The boat was unlike those that came to take away the building blocks. It was small and neat, of the kind used by nobles and high officials, with a cabin made of woven papyrus stalks. He withdrew a little further behind the reeds, but made sure he had a clear view of the vessel.

There were two men crewing and they were first off, tying the boat to the quayside, putting a long plank in place for the passenger or passengers to walk across. Then came two children. No. Not children. Dwarfs. Hapu caught his breath. There were two dwarfs often

seen with the Lady Nezem-mut. They were among her
personal attendants and she rarely went anywhere
without them. They had been in her employ for many
years.

Hapu waited excitedly for the Lady herself to emerge –
but she did not. The dwarfs waited patiently on the
quayside while the sail was stowed and the boat was
made safe, and then they called out some instructions
and one of the crew members returned to the cabin.

'Now she will come out!' thought Hapu. But the
sailor returned with only a large box, awkward in size,
but obviously not heavy. It was handed to the two
dwarfs, who each took hold of a handle and began to
move off. Hapu scrambled up from the river and
followed them, keeping a safe distance, darting and
dodging, convinced now that they had been instructed
by the Lady to fetch the crystal egg. Of course, she
would not have come for it herself! For her, or any of
the royal family, to be seen visiting the forbidden city,
would have been to risk too much. It puzzled him at first
that she should have sent two men so unmistakably part
of her entourage, but then he understood that she would
have to send someone whom she could totally trust. If
questioned no doubt they would say that they had been
sent back to fetch something their mistress had left
behind by mistake.

It was interesting she had not told Horemheb. If she
had he would have been here already with soldiers standing by to escort the precious object back to Yunu. She
was behaving as secretively as whoever it was who had
hidden it in the first place.

The men did not walk straightaway to the palace.
They wandered about the city commenting on this and
that, remembering the golden days when their mistress
was the sister of the Divine Nefertiti. They looked

frequently over their shoulders and Hapu got the impression they were making sure they were not being followed before they turned towards their real goal. He had to use all his cunning and his considerable knowledge of the nooks and crannies of the crumbling city to keep out of sight.

At last they stopped their deception and entered the Great House. Like a shadow Hapu followed them, padding on bare feet over the dusty tiles.

It seemed they had been given clear instructions, for once inside the building they walked quickly and surely towards a particular place. Hapu was chagrined to notice that they stopped where he in fact had intended to work that very day. If only he had not sat dreaming by the river that morning he might have found what he was looking for before they did.

From the box they took a few tools and with sure and determined action prised up the paving stones. Hapu was amazed to see how strong and muscular these small men were. The heavy stones were shifted with apparently very little effort.

Hapu hid behind a pillar and was in an agony of indecision. What should he do? His dream had been proved to be a true dream, but someone else other than himself was taking possession of the sacred crystal. Why had Akhenaten come to him and led him to this place unless he wanted *him* to take possession? What did this secrecy on Nezem-mut's part mean? Would Akhenaten disapprove of her finding it? Should he make himself known to the men, knock them down and take the Egg? If he had the Egg what would he do with it? Akhenaten had ordered its destruction, and then in the form of a wandering *ka* he had asked him to find it. But he had not told him *why*! He had not told him what to do.

Hapu began to feel that surely the intention was for

him to destroy it. Perhaps Akhenaten had felt that it was because this powerful focus of the ancient religion still existed – and indeed existed at the centre of the Aten cult – in Akhenaten's very House – that the religion of the Aten had been undermined and destroyed. Hapu began to feel more and more that the Sacred Egg of Yunu had to be smashed to pieces as Akhenaten had originally commanded and that is why he, the last loyal priest of the Aten, had been told to find it – and indeed had found it.

The two men had lit a lamp they had also taken from the box and had disappeared into the hole they had made. Hapu waited a while and then ventured forward and peered over the lip. At first he could see nothing but the first few steps and beyond that total darkness – but then he saw a flicker of faint light. The lamp was being carried down a side passage and the light was reflecting off the wall at the end.

Hapu seized the heavy bronze crowbar left behind by the men and, with beating heart and not much thought, climbed down the stairs. They were much narrower and steeper than he remembered in his dream. At the bottom he heard a strange noise. The men were talking and the sound of their voices came back to him as hollow and wordless rumbling. He was fired with eagerness to reach the Egg and destroy it before it could be taken away. He believed now that destroying it would topple Amun-Ra from his pedestal and bring back the clear, pure light of the Aten. He believed he had a sacred duty given him directly by the *ka* of Akhenaten to perform this act.

He hurried down the passage in the direction of the sounds and the flickering of faint lamp light.

He came to the chamber where the two men were and stood in the entrance looking in. The great crystal Egg was there on its black plinth as he had seen it – but it was much smaller than he remembered it – and it did not glow with green light. The only light in the chamber was from the earthenware lamp laid down on the floor in one corner.

The men had their box open and were pulling out some lengths of finely woven linen – no doubt to wrap the Sacred Egg in so that it would not break when they were carrying it up the stairs. They looked up, startled, as he loomed in the doorway.

'Stop!' he commanded and held up his hand. He had never felt so powerful. He towered above the small men in the chamber. He gripped the heavy metal crowbar in his right hand.

For a moment it seemed as though he had stopped time itself. Everything was still. Even the flame of the lamp burned steady and straight.

It was the elder of the two men who spoke first, shattering the illusion.

'Who speaks thus to the companions of royalty?'

'I speak with the authority of the Aten, the Living Sun.'

The man's lip curled.

'Stand aside in the name of Amun-Ra. You are hindering the work of those commanded by the god himself.'

'By the Lady Nezem-mut!' Hapu corrected him scornfully.

The two men glanced at each other briefly and then moved forward on either side of the plinth, watching Hapu like a cat watches a mouse.

He stepped forward and brushed one aside with an imperious gesture. He had not intended to hurt the dwarf but the man went flying across the chamber and landed against the opposite wall with a scream.

Hapu barely paused. He was filled with zeal. He saw nothing of the Egg's great beauty – thought nothing of the ancient wisdom that it represented. He saw only that it was the enemy. Generations would bless him for this! His pharaoh and his god would gather him to their side and heap rewards upon him! The hated power of Amun-Ra would be destroyed forever!

And then – it seemed to him as he gazed into the crystal that it flared up like green fire and became huge. It filled the chamber with blinding light. He covered his eyes with one hand and struck out blindly with the other.

At that moment the second dwarf flung himself at his legs and toppled him to the ground, while the other started to kick his head. As suddenly as the light had come it went, and he was no longer a superhuman avenger facing a supernatural enemy, but a thin young man lying on a dusty floor being kicked and pummelled with amazing ferocity. He flailed out with his crowbar, but could not make contact with his assailants. From his position on the floor the weight of his weapon was a disadvantage and it soon fell from his hand as he tried to protect his face and head from the merciless blows. No words were spoken. With silent efficiency and extraordinary strength Nezem-mut's familiars reduced him quickly to unconsciousness.

As he fell into darkness it seemed to him he saw the face of Akhenaten looming out of the shadows behind them. He appeared to be peering down at him, sadly. He had failed, and no one knew what ills would result from Nezem-mut's possession of such a powerful cult object.

5
THE SECRET

When Hapu became conscious again he thought he had
gone blind from the blows to his face. He was in utter
darkness and lay where he was for a long time, aware
only of the throbbing in his head and a growing terror
in his heart. Never to see again! How he had taken the
faculty of sight for granted! He had seen blind people
but he had never dreamed how dark the darkness was
that they were in. Then, when he remembered where he
was, another fear joined the first. What if the two men
had sealed over the stairwell again? He would die here,
slowly and horribly, buried alive.

He started to shiver uncontrollably. Why had
Akhenaten led him to this dreadful end? Why had he
not helped him to overcome the two dwarfs and destroy
the Sacred Egg? Why? Why? Why? He began to wonder
if the figure in his dream had not been sent by
Akhenaten at all – but by some malignant *ka* – intent on
his destruction. Akhenaten himself had always warned
that it takes such skill to distinguish between good and
evil when one is dealing with matters of this world, and
even more so when one is in contact with the shadowy
beings of the Otherworld, that it is best to avoid contact
altogether. He offered himself and Nefertiti as the sole
agents through which the supernatural could communicate with the natural world, believing that they,
and only they, had the strength and wisdom to do this
safely.

But it was not so easy, Hapu thought. Whether one
liked it or not, or whether one tried to avoid it or not,

one *was* in contact – one's whole life was played out among a crowd of beings, visible and invisible, in the body and out of the body. Influences, whether one was aware of them or not, were at work from every level and realm of existence. Surely to be aware and cautious and learn to distinguish between good and evil in the supernatural as in the natural realm, would be safer in the long run.

Thinking these thoughts now made Hapu pull himself together. The physical world was not all there was to life. If his eyes could not see, his other faculties could. If he wanted to survive – and not only survive, but progress through the many exciting realms of being – despair was not to be tolerated.

He struggled to his feet and felt around him with his hands. The walls were rough: the plinth at the centre was still there but the hollow that had contained the great crystal egg was empty. He worked his way around the walls until he found the entrance and then began to retrace his steps back along the passage by touch.

What would Nezem-mut do with the Sacred Egg? Hapu remembered the surge of light and power he had experienced from it. He knew that objects which had been used in a certain way for a long time seemed to acquire certain 'habits' whatever their original nature might be. A cult object steeped in the atmosphere of a temple, reverberating continually to the hum and chant of particular hymns and prayers might well continue to reverberate in that particular way long after the rituals that surrounded it had ceased. Not only that – but cult statues and symbolic objects from potent religious contexts were often used by the great spirit-beings of the Otherworld, the 'gods', when they needed to make themselves known in a physical sense. The crystal egg might well originally have been no more than crystal

mined from the earth, but when it was shaped in the
workshop of the Temple of Ra to represent symbolically
the Cosmic Egg from which all life emerged in the First
Time, and the continual regeneration and renewal of the
golden Phoenix of Life, it became something more. It
gained power in people's minds. Its own energy was
enhanced and increased by the energy of the minds of
those who believed in what it stood for. In this way it
could have become an environment suitable for a bodiless being – it could have been 'taken over' by a spirit-
force as an abandoned shell is taken over by a hermit
crab.

As such – it could do great good – or harm.
Akhenaten evidently believed it would be harmful. If it
was indeed he who had sent Hapu to find it, Hapu's task
was not finished. Blind or not he had to fulfil his
mission.

With greater determination and courage than before
he moved forward, bold enough now to take his hands
from the wall. He walked without stumbling and found
to his unspeakable joy that the dark was less dark.
The stairwell had not been re-sealed, and he was not
blind!

Nezem-mut was excited about the present her two loyal
companions had brought her. They did not mention
their encounter with Hapu and the brutal beating they
had given him. They were convinced he was dead and
anticipated no further problems from him.

She had no doubts that she could trust them, but
nevertheless made them repeat the vow they had already
taken not to reveal what they had been seeking in the
City of the Sun's Horizon, nor what they had found.
She herself repeated the curse she had spoken in the
event they betrayed her. Fire would consume them from

within. They would die by fire and their names would
be erased from history. They would not see the face of
Osiris, nor walk in the Field of Reeds.

She had no intention of making it publicly known just
yet that she had the sacred object. An instinct had made
her seek it out, and an instinct made her keep silent
now. There would be a time when it would be clear that
it would be to her advantage to reveal her secret, and
until that time she would keep it for herself.

Ankhesenamun noticed that her aunt was behaving
differently and wondered about it. She seemed unwill-
ing to meet Ankhesenamun's eyes, and dropped her own
whenever they were together. In fact she seemed to be
avoiding her niece as much as possible and spending
almost all her time closeted in her own quarters. Nezem-
mut was very well aware it was almost impossible to
keep anything from the Queen – but she knew how
important it was in this case to try.

Ankhesenamun was anxious to hear from Hapu and
wondered if the changes in Nezem-mut had anything to
do with the Sacred Egg. She was in an awkward position. Even though she and Tutankhamun were now
well established as King and Queen, and their puppet-
masters gave them more freedom than before, she knew
there was rarely a time when their actions went
unobserved. She could not go herself to Akhetaten –
though she longed to do so.

All she could do was wait and watch as she had always
done.

She had noticed that Nezem-mut's close companions,
the dwarfs, had been missing from Per-Hay for a few
days – but they had been reported travelling south from
Waset in a boat – not north towards Akhetaten. Her
spies had failed to notice that they had changed boats
further upstream, and were still waiting for them to

return from the south, when in fact they had already returned from the north with their precious load.

At last Hapu appeared.

'A gardener insists that you have sent for him, Majesty,' one of the court officials, Pa-nab, announced with decided distaste. 'He is not even the Head Gardener, but a . . .'

'Never mind,' she interrupted. 'I sent for him. Bring him to me at once.'

She was reclining on a couch in her garden pavilion. Her child was due soon and she was feeling very tired and hot. She dismissed the two women who were fanning her, but resisted turning her head to watch for his approach.

She heard the steps of the official's sandals on the alabaster path, and his impatient sighing and grumbling. She could not hear Hapu's footsteps but she heard him being reprimanded for approaching Her Majesty without proper respect.

'On your knees,' the officious little man hissed. 'Crawl on your belly!'

At this she turned her head and saw Hapu with one eye closed by a huge bruise, and cuts and abrasions on his chin and cheeks. It was obviously painful for him to kneel on those swollen knees, but he was about to obey when the official impatiently pushed him to the ground. She saw him wince.

'That will be enough,' she said coldly to Pa-nab. 'I wish to question this man in private. Leave us and make sure we are not disturbed.'

With one last disgruntled look at the commoner hunched over before the Queen, Pa-nab began to back away.

'I'll make sure the guards . . .'

'No. I need no guards. What could this poor creature

do?' She gestured with some disdain at the thin and damaged body before her.

'He might . . .'

'No. He might not. Leave us!' When Ankhesenamun wanted to be imperious there was no one more imperious than she. Her voice was like a whiplash.

As soon as he was out of sight, her face and voice softened.

'Rise Hapu, Priest of the Aten, and son of a distinguished father. What have you to tell me?'

Slowly and painfully he rose to his feet.

'The Egg . . .'

She raised her finger swiftly to her lips.

'Careful,' she said, 'speak that only I might under-stand. In this palace I would not be surprised if even the flowers had ears.' She smiled wryly and indicated that he should stand nearer to her.

He flushed – ashamed that he had been so clumsy – overawed to be so close to such a beautiful and powerful woman. He could smell her scent. He could see the rise and fall of her breast and the jewels that lay in six long strings across it.

He found he could not speak.

She waited patiently and then used a sharper tone.

'Speak!'

He threw up his hands as though he did not know where to begin to tell her all that had happened.

'Has it been taken?'

He nodded dumbly, miserably.

She bit her lip with annoyance.

'By the Lady we spoke about?'

He nodded, and said something in a voice so low she barely heard.

'Not by her dwarfs?' she cried, suddenly aware that she and her spies might well have been outsmarted.

He nodded – shamefaced. Who would have thought they could be so cunning and so strong? He had always thought of them as though they were pets Nezem-mut kept by her because she had no children of her own. He remembered their eyes looking into his. They were the eyes of nobody's pet. They were the eyes of nobody's children!

He told the Queen as best he could. Her quick mind filled in the gaps. So! Nezem-mut had the Sacred Egg yet had not revealed it! What was she going to do with it?

Ankhesenamun's mind was so busy she scarcely heard Hapu's fumbling words vowing loyalty to her and her father forever. She heard, but did not take seriously, his vow to find the Egg and destroy it.

It was certain her father wanted it destroyed, she knew, but it intrigued her that Nezem-mut was keeping its acquisition secret. What did she hope to gain from it? And she, if she herself had it in her possession, would she be able to milk some dramatic advantage out of it?

She knew that it was so central to the worship of Ra – and thus so important to Amun joined with Ra as the god Amun-Ra, that Horemheb would be very keen to claim its return as a sign that the gods who had been displaced by Akhenaten were fully back in power. Its reinstatement would no doubt be the occasion for a massive evangelical drive under the guise of a celebration. She would not be surprised if the Egg was taken to the Temple of Amun-Ra at Ipet-Esut and not returned to the Temple of Ra at Yunu. It would be used to strengthen the power of the priests of Amun over the priests of Ra. The magical, miraculous crystal, imbued with energy and power since ancient times, would become part of Amun's treasure and would reinforce *his* status.

If she were to have it in her possession – if *she* were
to restore it to its place in the world – she would make
sure it was returned to Yunu. She would make sure it
reinforced the worship of the Sun – strengthening *that*
priesthood against the growing arrogance of the
priesthood of Amun. How quickly the men who had
been cast out by her father were back in power. They
had come crawling out of their hiding holes like wood-
lice when a log is lifted. Some had been executed by
Horemheb after the massacre, and some by her father
in his purge of all other gods . . . but many had gone
underground and had now returned. They were already
demanding more than the King should give them.
Tutankhamun was no longer the green boy he had been
when he came to the throne – but he was still no match
for some of these men. He granted far too much land,
far too many privileges and riches, on too small a
justification. He resented taking orders now and could
not be pushed about so easily as he had been when he
came to the throne. But on the whole he was an easy-
going young man and preferred hunting and sailing to
long hours of decision-making and politics.

Horemheb's choice of Zais for High Priest of Amun-
Ra, for instance, was not challenged by him although it
was not based on any considerations connected with
religion. He was a man who had proved himself a
vigorous and efficient collector of tithes and taxes, and
was a good organiser and administrator. Such a man was
necessary to administer the huge estates given to Amun-
Ra by the Crown, to control the thousands of priests
throughout the country, and to supervise the labour
force and acquisition of materials required for the
extensive temple building programme Horemheb envis-
aged. As priest he was required to be able to quote by
rote many hundreds of ritual texts, but most of these he

had mastered during his early training as a scribe – for to rise to any kind of responsible official status in the Two Lands it was necessary to have trained first as a scribe, spending long hours in the House of Life copying texts. Horemheb himself had trained with the same master scribe as Zais and it was through this connection he became aware of his abilities.

It was the king's prerogative to appoint officials and ordain priests, but in Tutankhamun's case the appointments were virtually made by Horemheb or Ay, the young King setting his seal to them without question, often relieved to have the decisions made for him.

At the appointment of Zais only Ankhesenamun made a point of protesting. She claimed that he had 'sly' eyes and that he could not be trusted. There was no evidence in his past to justify her accusation and Horemheb overrode her objections firmly. Tutankhamun hesitated to put his seal for a while and then gave in. So Zais, a tax collector and the son of a tax collector, took his place among the most powerful men in Khemet at the head of what Horemheb hoped would become once again the most important religious cult in the country. His mansion rivalled the palace of the King, with reception halls and courtyards and several magnificent garden terraces running down to the river bank. He even, like the King, had a private quay to which and from which his private boats could come and go.

When it had come to the appointment of the High Priest of Ra at Yunu however, Horemheb left the choice to the King and Queen because he knew that they would choose a man they liked, a man noted for his unworldliness and religious dedication – a man who would be no match for the tough and wily Zais. They chose, just as Horemheb had expected, Ra-mes, a man too young

for the job but who had a fine grasp of the
mystical subtleties behind the formal catechism of the
cult.

> *I am Ra. I pass by – being complete.*
> *I belong to the Flame, which is the soul of Fire.*

He had no illusions that the words meant literally what
they said, and his discourse on them lasted the good part
of a day. Ankhesenamun never tired of listening to him,
though she could see that in the worldly sense he could
not hold his own.

Almost the first thing Zais did when he was made
Chief Prophet of Amun-Ra was to increase the number
of estates that belonged to the god and increase the
taxes that everyone who lived on the estates had to pay
to the god – that is – to him. Wealth poured into the cof-
fers of the temples of Amun while the peasants grew
more and more resentful as more and more of their hard-
won produce went to feed the rapidly increasing number
of priests, while less and less was left for them. Ra-mes,
on the other hand, at his appointment established healing centres at each of the temples under his jurisdiction,
and his priests lived no more luxuriously than the
peasants who worked the estates of Ra.

Zais was frequently at court, frequently in the company of Horemheb, frequently delivering pro-
nouncements from oracles that were somehow always to
his advantage. Ankhesenamun grew tired of his fat,
obsequious smile, his superior glances at a colleague or
at Horemheb when she or Tutankhamun said something
that apparently amused him. She got the impression
that she and the Pharaoh were being humoured like
troublesome children when they tried to exercise their
god-given right to rule.

The oracles of Ra, however, were confined to the temples themselves, a matter between the supplicant and the priest who divined the answer to his or her question – no problem being too small for the priests of Ra to consider. When Ra-mes came to court they could be sure of some good and lively conversation, and some pleasant and stimulating hours.

Ankhesenamun believed now that if she could somehow get possession of the Sacred Egg of Ra she could use it to strengthen the position of the priests of Ra. If she could have restored the worship of the Aten she might well have wanted to do that – but she was a realist, and knew that that dream had failed. The next best thing would be to make sure that no one priesthood ever became as strong again as the priesthood of Amun had become before her father's reforms. The ancient balance should be kept. Her country needed all its gods – but needed them each to perform their special and separate roles. Amun must never be allowed to reign supreme again!

In one of Nezem-mut's chambers was a large silver bowl often used, when filled with water, for scrying. The crystal egg fitted into this perfectly as though it had been designed to do so, and then, both it and the crystal wrapped tightly in seven fine veils of muslin, were returned to the box in which the dwarfs had brought it from Akhetaten. The box, undistinguished in itself, was placed on a table of ebony and ivory. Nezem-mut then carved the words of a fearsome curse on its lid – a warning that anyone who lifted it without permission from the Lady Nezem-mut would be consumed by the monster Apep and cease to be. Around the sides of the box she carved several strange signs that even she could not read, but which she had once seen on a temple

artefact. She had been told that once these signs were
in place no one would be able to see the object they protected. She was not sure if this meant that the intruder
was stricken with blindness or whether the object
literally disappeared from view – but she decided to use
them. It was true she could still see the box with the
magical signs in place – but this she put down to the fact
that it was in her possession and therefore the protective
magic did not apply to her.

The only people who were allowed into the chamber
were the two dwarfs, Heh and Ipi, and they only when
she herself was present. Her women and her personal
attendants were curious, but too afraid to pry. They
were well used to the Lady having secrets and knew
from the past how swift and merciless her punishment
would be if any dared disobey. To her the Egg was the
key to Horemheb's approval and she could think of
nothing but using it in the most effective way possible
to that end.

The small chamber in which it rested was kept locked
and she herself scarcely went near it. An instinct told
her to treat it with extreme caution though she, like
Horemheb, was not prone to experience religious awe
and tended to think of the gods and everything connected with them as a convenience rather than as
something numinous and beyond comprehension. One
asked them for favours and one received them. She
almost believed in them – but not quite. She talked
about them, prayed to them, made offerings and
obeisance to them, but would have been extremely
surprised if they had actually manifested to her or
performed a miracle for her that could not be explained
any other way.

However, the crystal Egg of Ra was a famous and
valuable object, redolent of ancient mystery and secret

rites. She was curious to see it. She had barely looked at it when the dwarfs had delivered it to her so anxious was she to find a protected place for it.

Now, some days later, she decided to examine what she had. Soon enough it would be gone and she would probably never have another opportunity to see it. Sacred objects were kept deep in the most inaccessible parts of the temple, seen only by the highest order of priests and by Pharaoh himself. Horemheb was away in the north and would not be back in the Waset until after the inundation had subsided. There was nothing she could do to further her plan at the moment but keep the crystal safe.

Carefully she unlocked the box, whispering the counter spell to the curse just in case . . . One by one she removed the wrappings. 'Like an embalmed body,' she thought, 'waiting for resurrection.'

At last she reached the crystal egg itself resting in its silver cup. As the sunlight from the window caught the green crystal she was moved by its beauty – so clear at one moment and yet as she turned it into the light there seemed to be areas a deeper shade of green. Reflections from the silver bowl shone against minute cracks and planes within the rock to make a shimmering web of green and silver light. She leant closer trying to make out a shape she thought she saw, but it disappeared as soon as she was near and she had the strange feeling that she herself was passing into the crystal, being absorbed into the web, floating freely in a sparkling sea of light. It was as though she were drowning and yet felt no fear . . .

At that moment some sound in the physical world disturbed her concentration and she jerked back into her ordinary consciousness. She found herself looking at the green crystal egg with amazement. She was annoyed that that beautiful feeling had passed and tried hard to return to it. But it would not come again.

It was not long before Ankhesenamun knew exactly where the precious crystal was kept and was in something of a quandary as to what to do about it. Although her mother's sister had her secrets and her eccentricities, she was closely bound to the sadly diminished family. She had been an integral part of Ankhesenamun's childhood and although in the last years of her parents' reign Ankhesenamun had thought herself detached from everyone around her and had watched events as though they did not concern her, now that those people and those events were past, she felt nostalgic for them. Tutankhamun had been so young. Ay so busy. Ankhesenamun felt that only Nezem-mut was left who remembered the good times before everything went wrong. Only Nezem-mut remembered the intimate details of the golden years of Akhetaten. In fact they had seen more of her than of Nefertiti in the end. She had always been available when they needed her. No mother could have been more devoted to her daughters than Nezem-mut was to her nieces. Poor Merytaten so believed in the goodness of everyone that she would not have survived as long as she did had Nezem-mut not been there to take her in her arms to comfort her when disillusion and despair all but destroyed her.

Tears came to Ankhesenamun's eyes when she thought about Merytaten. She had loved her sister more than anyone – more even than her mother and her father. Merytaten had never done anyone any harm. Why should she of all people be beaten into the ground by the howling mob? She herself would have been better prey for them. Her death would have been no loss to the world!

Ankhesenamun stood up and paced about the room.

She had to stop thinking about how Merytaten had died. Whenever it came to mind she was filled with such anger and hate she could hardly contain it.

She forced her mind back to Nezem-mut and the green Phoenix Egg of Yunu. But, still under the influence of her memories of Merytaten's death, her noble intentions of using the symbolic object to keep the balance between the two major cults of the Two Lands gave way to thinking of how it could be used for revenge against the priests of Amun who had murdered her gentle sister.

She knew Nezem-mut must have her reasons for seeking out the crystal and keeping it secret once she had found it, as no doubt whoever had originally hidden it in the palace at Akhetaten had had their reasons. Ankhesenamun did not want to become the enemy of Nezem-mut by taking it forcibly, but she did not trust her aunt not to use it for the benefit of the Amun priesthood.

Ankhesenamun visited her aunt, sweeping in to her quarters unannounced, surprising the two dwarfs at a game of sennet, and Nezem-mut at combing the hair of a small pet monkey. The dwarfs leapt to their feet at once and bowed. The monkey squawked and jumped from his mistress's arms to the cosmetic table, sending small, fragile bottles crashing and spilling precious oils and unguents.

'What brings you here, niece?' she said somewhat sharply, annoyed at the disturbance.

'I apologise, aunt,' Ankhesenamun replied quickly. 'I felt restless. I wanted company.'

Nezem-mut looked hard at her. She knew why she had come. 'Hoping to catch me out with the Great Egg,' she thought grimly. 'But no one catches Nezem-mut!'

'Heh! Ipi!' she said, clapping her hands, 'take this

creature out!' She pointed at the monkey who was now
jumping from chair to table to chair, chattering noisily
and excitedly. 'Ask Hatnufe to bring cool drinks and
then leave us. The Queen and I need privacy.'

Ankhesenamun watched the two small men trying to
catch the very active young monkey that did not want
to be caught. The scene was chaotic and bizarre – Ipi
on the table knocking over still more jars and bottles
while trying unsuccessfully to reach up to the window
where the mischievous creature now was – Heh hopping
up and down shouting instructions. They looked so
comical she was hard put to remember Hapu's grim
story of their well coordinated and ruthless violence
against himself.

'It's a good disguise,' she thought. 'They are probably
more effective as bodyguards for Nezem-mut than any
number of soldiers might be. No one would think to get
them out of the way before attacking her.'

Servants came running in wondering what all the
commotion was about and soon the mayhem increased.
Ankhesenamun was convinced that Heh and Ipi were
deliberately stirring it up and keeping it going, clowning
clumsily about, knocking over things, reducing the
room with its costly furniture to a shambles. She looked
across at Nezem-mut and thought for a moment she
glimpsed something like fear in her aunt's eyes. She
wondered at the power the two exercised over her.
She remembered how Nezem-mut had watched their
excesses many times in the past with nothing more than
an indulgent smile, as a mother sometimes watches the
naughtiness of her spoiled children. But there was no
indulgent smile now. She was watching them destroy
her pretty room and Ankhesenamun wondered if she
was powerless to stop them.

Ankhesenamun went to the door and called the

guards. Within moments, at her command, the two
were held firmly down. The young Queen met their eyes
and read a truly terrifying malevolence there.

Nezem-mut was flushed and shaken. She ordered the
guards at once to release her companions, but they
looked to the Queen. The monkey was now sitting
quietly watching the scene with bright and beady eyes,
having thoroughly enjoyed the chase. Ankhesenamun
pointed at him.

'Remove him!' she commanded. And he was removed,
quickly and easily.

She then looked back at Heh and Ipi who were still
held sullenly by the guards.

'We were only obeying orders,' they whined. The
malevolence of their hearts was now well hidden. They
were once again pretending to be harmless and amusing
freaks.

'Ah, yes,' she said coldly. 'Release them,' she told the
guards. The two dwarfs were not liked in the palace and
Ankhesenamun noticed that they were pushed over
roughly as they were released. With a gesture the Queen
indicated that all those who had come rushing into the
room should now leave.

'What a fuss over nothing,' Nezem-mut said. 'There
was no need to call the guards.'

Ankhesenamun looked pointedly around the room.
Just about everything in it was broken.

'That naughty monkey!' Nezem-mut said, shaking
her head. But she knew and her niece knew, it had not
been the monkey who had done the bulk of the damage.
'Why?' she was thinking, now very worried. 'Is this a
sign they are turning against me?' She thought about the
precious crystal and wished that Horemheb were coming back sooner. She had wanted time to explore its
mysteries, but now she feared the dwarfs' knowledge of

her secret and what they might do with it. The quicker she could hand it over to the General the better.

'You should not keep wild animals indoors,' Ankhesenamun was saying, looking at the dwarfs who were picking up bits and pieces and pretending that they were trying to mend what they had broken – though they were still clowning by putting together obviously incongruous pieces. 'They should be in cages!' She added with bitter emphasis.

'Oh, that monkey is usually very well behaved and gentle.' Nezem-mut deliberately misunderstood the intention of Ankhesenamun's words. It would not be easy to dismiss the dwarfs from her service. They had served her too well and too long and knew far too much about her.

Ankhesenamun took her aunt's arm and led her out into the courtyard where a green and shady garden seemed like a safe haven after a storm.

'Tell me, aunt,' she said quietly, her arm linked affectionately through Nezem-mut's. 'Have you thought much about my dream?'

'What dream, Majesty?'

'That strange one about the crystal Egg of Ra,' Ankhesenamun said patiently, knowing that all games have to be played by rules or not at all.

Nezem-mut was silent, wondering if Ankhesenamun would be a good ally if the dwarfs turned dangerous and disloyal. 'No,' she thought. 'The thing to do is to move it so that not even Heh and Ipi know where it is.'

'No,' she said aloud. 'I'm sorry.'

'That was your chance to be honest with me,' Ankhesenamun thought grimly. 'You are deceiving a royal Queen and a close friend. What are you plotting?' She knew where it was – for to hide something in a room that is locked is not to hide it at all.

'It was no dream,' she said aloud, withdrawing her arm and moving round to confront her aunt. 'As well you know.'

Nezem-mut dropped her eyes.

'What do you mean?' she muttered.

'You have the Sacred Egg of Ra in your possession.'

'How can you say that!'

'How can you lie to me?'

Nezem-mut looked up and met her eyes at last. She was just about to say something when they heard a sound. Heh and Ipi came out into the courtyard and were approaching. Ankhesenamun flushed with annoyance.

'Do you have no privacy, aunt? Are those creatures ever with you?'

Nezem-mut was relieved to see them.

'They are not creatures, niece,' she said sharply, and then louder, so that they could hear, 'but very loyal companions.'

'They are not what they seem. Be careful,' Ankhesenamun whispered and turned to go. She knew she should confront them – but she did not feel up to it now. She was suddenly very tired and longed to sit down. The whole incident had been very disturbing. She felt pain in her back and was afraid for the child in her womb.

At that moment they noticed that behind the two dwarfs was one of Tutankhamun's messengers.

'Pharaoh,' announced the messenger after the requisite number of bows, 'commands the presence of the Lady Nezem-mut.'

'Now?' asked Nezem-mut, startled.

'Yes, my Lady.'

Nezem-mut looked at Ankhesenamun.

Ankhesenamun shook her head. 'It is not my doing,' she said. 'I know nothing of this.'

It was unusual to be summoned by Tutankhamun so formally. Ankhesenamun was curious too, but all she could think about was how lucky the interruption was for her. Now she would be able to get to the crystal before Nezem-mut had a chance to change its hiding place. She was already regretting that she had alerted her to the fact that she knew the Egg was in her possession.

Nezem-mut was hesitating, torn between a royal command that could not be disobeyed and a fear that if she did not go to the hiding place of the crystal very soon it would not be there when she did. She looked from the dwarfs to her niece in an agony of indecision. Which, if any, could she trust?

Then Nezem-mut looked at the messenger.

'Tell the King that I will be with him soon,' she said. 'It would not be fitting for me to attend his Majesty dressed as I am.'

'There is nothing wrong with the way you are dressed,' Ankhesenamun said quickly. 'I am sure this is not a formal occasion. It would not be fitting to keep the King waiting!'

The messenger bowed to indicate that he agreed with the Queen. Unwillingly Nezem-mut turned to go with him. She looked anxiously at Heh and Ipi.

'I am sure your attendants should go with you,' Ankhesenamun said.

'I don't think . . .' Nezem-mut began, but they looked so eager at the prospect she changed her mind and agreed that they should accompany her. That left Ankhesenamun alone. 'Even if she finds it,' Nezem-mut thought, 'the curse will deter her. She will never risk it while she is carrying the King's heir.'

Ankhesenamun and Hapu found the door locked as they

had expected, but Hapu had brought tools to open it. Ankhesenamun herself broke her aunt's seal.

Inside they found the table of ebony and ivory and the box with the fearsome curse upon the lid. Hapu hesitated to touch it but Ankhesenamun commanded him to pick up the whole box unopened. As he did so he looked surprised.

'What is it?'

'It is very light, Majesty,' he whispered. 'I don't think there is anything in the box.'

Impatiently Ankhesenamun stepped forward and lifted the lid. Inside were several layers of cloth, but no crystal egg.

She frowned. The door had been sealed.

'I swear those dwarfs have it!' she muttered, and then doubled up in excruciating pain.

'What is it, Majesty!' cried Hapu.

Her face was distorted with pain and she was on her knees clutching her belly. Beads of sweat had appeared on her forehead.

'Majesty!' gasped Hapu.

'Help me!' she cried, and clutched him by the arm so tightly he later found bruises there.

'The curse!' he gibbered.

'No! No!' she sobbed. 'Not the curse! Not the curse!'

As suddenly as it had come the pain seemed to pass. Pale and shaken Ankhesenamun pulled on the young priest's arm to raise herself.

'It is my child, Hapu. It is coming. Help me to my quarters. Call the physician!'

When Nezem-mut, slightly dishevelled and out of breath, arrived before her King she found him in one of the garden arbours. With him was a tall, distinguished,

middle-aged man, a face lined but not unhandsome, a
well-fed stomach protruding somewhat over his tightly
tied, crisply pleated, white linen kilt. At her approach
he turned at once towards her and watched her every
step with close attention. She could see as she came near
that he wore the necklet and the bracelets of a nomarch.
He was an important man, the ruler of one of the forty-
two districts of the Two Lands, no doubt in Waset to
bring tribute and report on the affairs of his nome. His
face was familiar though she could not put a name to
him. More than likely she had seen him at one of the
huge state occasions when all the nomarchs attended
Tutankhamun – perhaps even earlier at Akhenaten's
court. His close attention now embarrassed her. She
wished she was dressed more suitably for meeting such
a man. She did not even have a wig, but her own natural
hair was flowing round her shoulders.

She ignored him and bowed low to the young
Pharaoh. Tutankhamun was lounging on a low chair,
apparently feeling very happy and relaxed. He told her
to rise at once.

'No need for such formality today, Lady,' he said. 'It
is a time for celebration.'

'Majesty?' She raised her eyebrows, thinking back to
her conversation with Ankhesenamun – not at all sure
that there was cause for celebration.

'You have met the nomarch Tefnakhte before, I
think?'

Nezem-mut looked at Tutankhamun's companion.

'I believe so, Majesty.' She remembered him now. He
was the governor of the nome in which Akhetaten was
situated.

'He has brought Pharaoh an important petition.'

'Indeed?' Nezem-mut was puzzled that she had been
called rather than Ankhesenamun for such an event.

'Do you want to hear what he has so earnestly requested?'

Tefnakhte was smiling at her, his eyes pleasantly wrinkled at the sides as he looked into hers.

Nezem-mut bowed her head. She did not really care what he had requested and could think of nothing but returning to deal with the problem of the sacred crystal.

'He has requested – no, pleaded for – .' Tutankhamun's eyes were sparkling, the two men were obviously sharing a secret in anticipation of it also pleasing her. 'Marriage with you.'

Nezem-mut looked startled and not as joyful as they had expected. A slight shadow of uncertainty crossed the nomarch's hitherto confident face. Nezem-mut caught her breath and her thoughts began to race. The man was not unpleasing, and his position in the Two Lands was a good one, but – but ever since Prince Djehuti-kheper-Ra, Akhenaten's half-brother, had told her that the priests of Amun had said she was to marry General Horemheb, she had waited, sometimes patiently, sometimes impatiently, for the handsome General to make his move towards her. She knew he was interested in her for she often caught him looking long and thoughtfully at her. But for some reason he said nothing about love or marriage, and deliberately moved away when she tried to get too close.

'He is so busy re-organizing the country,' she told herself. 'He has so many responsibilities – so many difficulties to deal with. As soon as things have settled down . . .' But things now were as settled as they were ever likely to be and he still made no move to take her. What should she do? Settle for someone else whom she cared for less?

'Lady Nezem-mut!' Tutankhamun was saying sharply. 'What do you say?'

She tried to pull herself together.

'I am sorry, Majesty . . . my Lord . . . You must forgive me.' She was stumbling, trying to find words to give her time to think before she committed herself one way or another. 'This . . . this is a surprise. I need . . . I must have . . .'

Tefnakhte raised his hand.

'My Lady, say no more. I understand completely. Pharaoh has graciously given me permission to approach you. Now I will wait until you are ready to give me an answer.'

'Neither of you is getting any younger,' Tutankhamun interrupted impatiently with the tactless of youth, disappointed that what he had thought was such a good idea was greeted with so little enthusiasm by the woman he thought to benefit. 'The marriage will bring honour and comfort to both of you. Why is there hesitation?'

'Not hesitation, Majesty, caution,' Nezem-mut said hastily.

'What if I order it?'

'Majesty, the Lady is surprised – no more. There is no need . . .'

Before he could finish his placatory speech they were interrupted by a commotion – one of the Queen's attendants was struggling to get through to the King, held back by Tutankhamun's zealous guards.

'Majesty,' she shouted above the hubbub – straining against the arms of those who held her. 'The Queen . . . The Queen . . .'

Tutankhamun looked up impatiently.

'What is it?'

'The Queen is giving birth!' she shouted. This was not how she would have liked to bring such momentous news, but the physician had told her the Queen was in danger, the labour was not going well, and she must bring the King to her immediately. The stupid guards and attendants had refused to let her through, the King having given orders that he was not to be disturbed once Nezem-mut was with him.

Tutankhamun jumped to his feet – everything else forgotten.

'Where is she? Take me to her!'

They had waited seven years for an heir. Ankhesenamun had had two early miscarriages and had carried one other child to six months before it was stillborn. This was the first time it seemed that she might actually come to full term. Although this was earlier than they expected, he had felt the child kicking in her womb and knew that even so early it was possible for a child to be born and to live.

Meryt-mut, Ankhesenamun's attendant, shook herself free of the now uncertain guards and turned to run – Tutankahmun following her, and Nezem-mut close behind.

Tefnakhte stood gazing after them, not sure what he should do under the circumstances. It seemed he had been totally forgotten – even by the servants. The garden was deserted. He stood irresolute for a while and then walked about the pathways enjoying the luxurious growth, dreaming of a time when he would not only be governor of a district, but closely related to the royal family, with the royal palaces always open to him.

Ankhesenamun was in great pain, seated on the birth chair, women fussing round her, the physician counting her contractions and suggesting when she should push and when she should relax. Sweat was streaming from her. As far as she could tell there were no non-painful periods, yet the physician kept speaking as though there

were. She tried not to scream. A Queen did not scream.
A Queen did not curse the gods for devising such a pain-
ful way to bring life into the world. She desperately
wished she could have more privacy. So many people!
All staring! All waiting for the moment the future
Pharaoh would arrive on this earth.

She had hated giving birth the first time and she
hated it now.

'Push!' urged the physician.

She knew priests had crowded into the chamber.
Most of the gods were represented, but the pride of
place was given to Bes, the hideous, half-comical
monster who was there to frighten bad spirits away from
the newborn. The priest of Bes wore a mask and danced
around the bed waving his short little arms. He
reminded her of Nezem-mut's dwarfs, and remembering
them, she remembered the curse on the lid of Nezem-
mut's box. Silently she prayed to the Aten, her father's
god. How much she longed for the long healing rays of
the sun, and the soothing balm of a quiet temple with
no histrionics. The first time she had given birth there
were only her parents, the physician and two attendant
midwives present. Her agony now was a public
spectacle!

'Go away!' she shrieked at them. There was drum-
ming. Hathor's sistrums were rattling. It was as though
she was at the centre of a macabre dance and in and out
of the misty shadows came figures of good and evil
fighting for the control of her child.

'Push!' shouted the physician.

And as though all the veils between the realms were
torn open and all the hidden things were revealed,
monsters howled and raged and tore at her.

'Push!' shouted the priests of Amun and Mut.

'Push!' shouted the priests of Ptah and Sekhmet.

'Push!' shouted the priests of Djehuti and Seshat.

'Push!' shouted the priest of Bes louder than them all.

She pushed and pushed and seemed to rip apart. She heard screaming . . . crying . . . but as though it was a long way away . . .

She saw Tutankhamun's face floating in a sea of blood . . . and then she saw nothing more.

When she recovered consciousness, she could tell by the long faces of the attendants that the child was dead.

She turned her face to the wall, and tears flowed silently down her cheeks. So much pain and effort – for what?

6
THE PRIZE

Heh and Ipi were convinced that with the miraculous powers of the green crystal Egg of Ra they would be able to grow taller and had taken the crystal to a hiding place of their own. They cared nothing for the curse because they believed that with the magical object in their possession they would be able to counteract any force that might threaten them.

'When we have shown what it can do to ourselves,' Heh said excitedly to his companion, 'there will be no end to the power we will have over people who want to benefit from it.'

'Instead of servants we will be masters!'

'Instead of masters we will be gods!'

They had taken it to a cave well hidden in the mountains west of Waset. It was just to the north of the Temple at Serui – that strange derelict temple abandoned during the time of the Thutmosid kings and further defaced during the reign of Akhenaten. It was quite a stiff climb up to its entrance but the more inaccessible the safer the two conspirators believed it would be.

Their first session with their prize proved to be fruitless, but they decided it was because they did not have the right incantations, the correct texts of the ancient spells. Before they returned to the cave they sought out a priest they knew, Hesy-Ra, who had once been a priest of Ra at Yunu but was now a priest of Amun-Ra at Waset.

With careful probing and the pretence that they had a serious scholarly interest in the ancient texts of Yunu,

Heh and Ipi learned a great deal about the Sacred Egg. They learned that whatever power a man had it was magnified by the power of the sacred crystal. If the man was evil the crystal would become a force for evil. If he was good, if his motives were pure and unselfish, the crystal would become a force for good. It could destroy. Or it could heal.

'It is very important that it does not fall into the wrong hands,' the old priest said. 'There is a belief among the priests of Ra at Yunu that it was not destroyed by Akhenaten, but that it was spirited away by the god himself and will return to earth when it is needed.'

'What were the kinds of spells the priests used for healing?' Heh asked.

'It depended on what was wrong.'

'What if a leg was broken. Could it be mended?'

'Oh, yes.'

'What spell would be used?'

Hesy-Ra stared into space above the dwarfs' heads, and recalled hesitantly the words of an ancient spell.

'Would it be possible to make a person shorter – or taller?'

Hesy-Ra looked at them. He could see the yearning in their eyes. They were men like other men – yet were often treated as less. They must long for the luxury of passing unnoticed in a crowd.

'I don't know,' he said.

'But if the god willed it – would it be possible?'

'There is nothing the god cannot do if he wills it,' the priest said confidently.

'What kind of spell would be used . . .?'

'The words of the spell are nothing without the crystal. It is the crystal into which the god's spirit comes to work his magic that makes it all possible.'

'So it is possible then to make a person taller?'

'When I was at the Temple of Ra at Yunu we never had occasion to make anyone taller,' he answered thoughtfully, intrigued by the challenging thought. He began to scratch around in his memory. 'There was an ancient text – from the time of Imhotep I believe – that gave a man the power to be what he most wanted to be. I suppose if what one most wanted was to be taller . . .'

Heh and Ipi tried not to show their excitement – tried not to look too eager. They waited. They could see Hesy-Ra was interested enough himself at this point to trust him to recall the words if he indeed had ever known them. Slowly, in fits and starts, they came. Archaic in construction, the ancient sentences scarcely made sense any more, but Heh and Ipi marked every word.

A day or two later, word perfect in the ancient spell, they confronted the miraculous crystal Egg in its secret hiding place.

It was propped up in the darkest recess of the cave so that even if someone found the opening they would be unlikely to find the sacred artefact. For the purposes of their experiment they moved it forward, cupped in a natural hollow in the rock, waiting for the brief moment when the sun shone directly into the mouth of the cave and onto it. They stationed themselves on either side of it, almost holding their breath as the sun's light crept nearer and nearer. As it touched the crystal they both started chanting. For a moment the green crystal seemed to float in a cup of light provided by the sun, and then its aura of light suddenly expanded and swelled so that it seemed to fill the cave with dazzling filaments of green. The two men caught up in the web, began to tremble, wondering what they had started. Ipi tried to break free but felt himself to be held tight. He began to

scream. Heh shut his eyes and kept saying the words of
the spell over and over again, *willing* himself to grow
taller. He felt strange, lighter – he felt as though he was
floating above the earth. He did not even hear his companion screaming or witness his struggles. He felt enor-
mous – like a giant. He felt he had expanded so much
that his shoulders were pressing against the roof of the
cave and he had to bend his head. Larger and larger he
grew until he felt his expanded body was pushing
against the walls of the cave. He could hear the rock
beginning to crack. He suddenly feared that he would
bring the mountain down on them if the expansion and
the pressure continued.

He opened his eyes and stared around him in
astonishment and not a little disappointment.

He was the same size as he had originally been. So was
the Egg. So was Ipi. The sunlight had moved off them.
The cave was dark. He blinked and rubbed his eyes. He
looked at his wizened limbs in disgust.

Ipi was whimpering. 'What happened? What
happened?'

'Nothing!' snapped Heh. 'That is the trouble.
Nothing at all!'

'I felt peculiar . . .'

'You are the same size. I am the same size. What is
the point of the stupid thing?'

He felt like smashing the Egg. What kind of hoax was
the god playing on them? He did not want just to *feel*
large – he wanted to *be* large!

'Perhaps . . . perhaps . . . it is not enough just to
do it once. Perhaps it has to be done several times and
then . . .'

'And then crocodiles will fly!' Heh said bitterly.

'It's worth trying again.'

Heh strode out of the cave and stood with his back

to the Egg gazing out over the landscape – the yellow-gold rock of the mountains around them – the dusty causeway from the derelict Thutmosid temple with its reeded-over canal – the distant black land where the farmers were busy planting the crops – the gleaming tips of the obelisks of Ipet-Esut and Ipet-Resut.

Ipi carefully returned the Egg to its hiding place. He too was disappointed. But not as much as Heh. He was glad to have survived the ordeal intact. He was not that sure that he wanted to change his size. There were certain advantages to being the size he was. His main interest in the spell working on them was that it would indicate the power of the crystal – the power they would be able to tap for their own use whenever they wanted.

Horemheb had returned to Waset when the waters of the Great River returned to the cavern beneath the earth at Suan. Gradually the fields were reappearing, covered now with rich black silt. The farmers were busy repairing the dykes, clearing the irrigation canals, making sure that every drop of water that could be encouraged onto the land during the long dry season, had easy access. At this time of year there was very little other work going on. Men who had been busy on the great building projects of Pharaoh returned to their homes to help their families prepare for the growing season. Even parts of the army were disbanded to provide extra help for the farmers.

Work that had begun on Tutankhamun's tomb in the silent valley of Meretseger ceased. Piles of chippings and tools were left where they were. Only one chamber was complete and in that there were already two members of Tutankhamun's family – two stillborn infants in rich and elaborate coffins. Not far from it another, smaller, tomb was being prepared for Ay, father of Nefertiti,

brother of Queen Tiye, Master of Chariots and Vizier
for three kings. Ay already had a large tomb carved out
and decorated for him in the eastern mountains behind
Akhetaten. The mighty hymn to the Aten was carved on
its walls. But it had been abandoned when the cult of
the Aten became anathema, and the beautiful reliefs of
Akhenaten and his family reaching up to receive the
blessing of the rays were defaced.

Workmen downed tools on Horemheb's tomb in the
north at Men-nefer too. This was the one time of the
year when survival in this world took precedence over
survival in the next. If the preparation for the crops was
not done right at this point, famine would later
decimate the country. Egypt's power and status largely
depended on its rich and fertile land, the land that could
provide food when other countries were starving.

Ankhesenamun had taken some time to recover from
the shock of losing her child and was moody and silent
a great deal of the time.

At first, when she discovered the loss of the crystal,
Nezem-mut was convinced that Ankhesenamun had
taken it. She interpreted the infant's death to the curse
she had put on the box and swung from suffering
agonies of guilt that she had brought about the death of
the future king of the Two Lands, and anger that her
niece should have dared to contemplate stealing the
sacred object. She ignored the fact that the information
about its existence in the palace at Akhetaten had come
from Ankhesenamun in the first place, so, technically,
it was she who had stolen the crystal. She fumed – but
could do nothing while Ankhesenamun was so ill. It did
not enter her head that the dwarfs might have it. If it
had – she might have noticed certain things about them
that would have saved them all a lot of trouble later.

* * *

As Ankhesenamun recovered she found herself turning
more and more towards the forbidden cult of the Aten.
She had never really understood her father's obsession
with his ideal. The Aten had always been one of the
great throng of gods or spirits who hovered over the
Two Lands, the invisible forces that pulled this way and
that. When the second king of her dynasty, the first
Amenhotep, died his death was described with
reference to the Aten:

> *'His Majesty passed through life in happiness, the*
> *years in peace, He ascended to the sky, He united*
> *himself to the Aten, He became blended with him out*
> *of whom He had come.'*

And Tutankhamun's own grandfather, Amenhotep III,
called his special barge after the Aten, the sun's disc. So
why did her father suddenly pick this one out from the
others? Why did he go to so much trouble and cause so
much disruption in the country by insisting on this one
over all the others.

She understood the political reason. The priests of
Amun were growing too arrogant and powerful. They
were becoming richer than the king and trying to dictate
what should be done and not be done by the king. She
understood he had uncovered a particular source of cor-
ruption when he encountered Djehuti-kheper-Ra for the
first time, the youth who was later revealed to be his
half-brother, but who as a child was kept virtually a
prisoner by the priests of Amun and manipulated into
pronouncing false prophesies. Her father had forbidden
oracles knowing how blindly men followed them. He
had forbidden magic, knowing how it could be misused.
One by one he had eliminated the other gods because he
believed so passionately in the truth behind the ancient

texts that he could not bear to see them disregarded. As a young boy he had winced to hear meaningless words pronounced solemnly and ceremonially. He swore that when he became Pharaoh, no one in *his* temples would speak without knowing to whom they spoke or what they were saying. No priest would teach without understanding what he taught, or pray without believing there was someone there listening to the prayers.

He had tried at first to infuse life into what was already there – but frustrated at every turn by a priesthood that had grown used to the easy and privileged life and was not about to give it up, he began to believe that the only way was to sweep all the old cults away – temples and everything – and start again. He even built a new city on virgin ground to be the centre for his revolutionary ideal. He chose to represent what he believed to be the great moving force behind existence, the ultimate and only one, the source of all things – by the image of the sun's orb, its rays reaching out from the unimaginable centre of spiritual energy to give eternal life. Because he had seen what a corrupt and irresponsible priesthood could do, he chose to announce that he and only he was the channel through which this pure light flowed to earth. He later modified this to include Nefertiti and his daughters – but the priests of the Aten were the servants of Akhenaten – and had no power to interpret the will of the Aten to the people of the Two Lands.

Because there was no structure to hold this dream but his own heart – when he died, the dream died with him. It was not difficult to reinstate the old religious network and Horemheb lost no time in doing it. He was a man who liked order and if precise but meaningless rituals kept the people obeying rules and doing what was necessary for the country, that is what he insisted on

having. He never appreciated the burning inspiration of
Akhenaten. He never understood his desire to see
beyond ritual to the living truth. According to
Horemheb *there was no one there* to listen to the prayers
and hymns – but it was good government to pretend
there was.

Now, when all was lost and it could not be a more
awkward time to believe in her father's dream,
Ankhesenamun began to search it out. At first – when
she lost yet another child – she sank into bitterness and
despair. It seemed to her that Horemheb was right –
there were no living numinous beings, caring and powerful, ever present, yet never seen. They were all fooling
themselves by thinking there were. The sacred symbol
of Ra was a green crystal shaped like an egg – no more
nor less. She felt empty, desolate, desperate and
hopeless.

One morning she woke to see the rays of the sun
filtered through the grid of her high window resembling
the cipher her father had designed to represent his concept of the First and Last, the Ultimate Divinity.

She stared at this phenomenon for some time and
then raised herself off her bed. With her legs swung over
the side she reached out her hands to the rays and stared
thoughtfully at them as the sunlight touched them. She
felt the warmth of the light. But then – what had started
as an idle impulse, ended as a quest. With her mind's eye
she followed the beam up from where it rested on her
hand; followed it as though she were walking up a steep
path, the summit she was aiming towards out of sight.
It seemed to her she passed through the stone grill and
out into the open air still following the beam up and up.
The higher she climbed the more difficult each step
seemed, but she had a kind of desperate desire to find
out where the beam led. The beams no longer satisfied

her. Only the source itself could do that! 'Horemheb is
wrong,' she thought. All we know here and now may be
illusion. All we have here and now are the separate
beams to which we give the names and the images of
gods. But the beams cannot exist without a source of
light. Akhenaten was right – the source is what matters,
the sun's orb itself is the most fitting symbol for
divinity. It is *that* that we must seek! We must not be
sidetracked by subsidiary phenomena. However real
they are in themselves, their reality can never be more
than a secondary or derivative reality.

For the first time since her illness she felt strong
again. She called her women and dressed in her finest
clothes. She set off to find Tutankhamun whom she had
avoided since the death of his heir. She was filled with
zeal. It seemed to her that all her life she had drifted.
Everything she had done had been at the behest of
someone else or because she was resisting the behest of
someone else. She felt now she had found direction. She
knew what she wanted to do and she knew she had the
strength to do it.

The question of Nezem-mut's marriage to Tefnakhte
was shelved for a time while Ankhesenamun was ill and
the funeral of the infant was occupying everyone's
attention. He had lived in Ankhesenamun's womb and
was thus a traveller in and out of time as much as anyone
else. He was given magical spells and talismans to protect him on the journey through the Otherworld, and all
the gods were invoked to guide and help him. When at
last the ceremonies were over and the diminutive coffin
of gold and glass the colour of lapis lazuli, carnelian and
turquoise was stowed away, the funeral feast over, and
the mourners departed, Tutankhamun returned to the
question of Nezem-mut and Tefnakhte. It had been the

idea of his mother Kia and on his last visit to Men-nefer
she had pressed him hard to implement her suggestion.

Kia did not see much of her son living as she did at
the palace in Men-nefer. Officially the town had
returned to being the administrative capital of the Two
Lands a few years after Akhenaten's death as it had
been in the old days, but Tutankhamun and
Ankhesenamun were never very happy there and spent
most of their time in the south at Waset.

Men-nefer of the white walls was a huge, sprawling
town, much noisier and busier than Waset, built on low-
lying ground that often stayed damp and marshy long
after the waters of the inundation had subsided. In certain seasons the incidence of fever rose alarmingly. It
owed its prominence as a city to its geographical position at the junction of the many rivers that flowed across
the delta lands, thereby having access to the various
trading ports on the coast. It was also convenient for the
overland route to the East, yet not so near that it was
in danger from invaders. By being a great port on the
Nile itself, it was within easy reach of the southern
nomes. On an escarpment at the edge of the huge
western desert lay The Great Place, the place of burial
at Sakkara, where the ancestors of kings and nobles
silently watched over the city of the dead and of the
living. Towering over this was an immense stone
pyramid rising to the sky in steps like the first mound,
designed, it was said, by Imhotep, the architect and
right hand of King Djoser, more than a thousand years
before – Imhotep who was now worshipped as a god for
the wonderful achievements of his lifetime and the
miracles he had performed since his death. Many of the
most important nobles and officials of the court
prepared tombs for themselves as close to this great
work as they could. Horemheb himself had often visited

the necropolis during Akhenaten's reign to see how his own tomb was progressing, employing the best artists in the region to carve reliefs on the walls of the small temple and the burial chambers. Maya and Nakhtmin, two high officials and close companions of Tutankhamun, were also preparing to house their *kas* there after separation from the body.

To an Egyptian preparations for the afterlife were a natural part of this life. They saw no end to life – only change from one mode of living to another, each mode having its particular joys, dangers and sorrows. One prepared for each phase of life – including that of death when the body is put away safely and the other aspects of one's being take over. To keep the body in a pre-served state meant to keep one's connection with this world. It would act as a kind of gate through which one's *ka* could come and go.

Kia had a tomb prepared for her at Akhetaten, as had Ay. But now that Akhetaten was no longer a place for the living, it could also not now be a place for the dead. Tutankhamun suggested she choose a place for her Mansion of Millions of Years at Sakkara, but she refused. She wanted to be buried in Akhenaten's tomb in the eastern cliffs of Akhetaten as befitted her status as his widow, in spite of the fact that the tomb had been wrecked and ransacked and was now derelict.

'I will be the haven to which he returns,' she had said, remembering that he had so often turned to her for com-fort, rather than to Nefertiti, when he was near to breaking point.

'It is impossible,' Tutankhamun had said. 'Horemheb would never allow it.'

'Oh – so Horemheb is Pharaoh now, is he?' she had replied sarcastically.

Tutankhamun flushed. 'No. Of course not. If that is where you want to be – that is where you will be.'

But no work on her burial chamber was started at Akhetaten in spite of his promise.

The paths of Nezem-mut and Kia did not often cross, but when they did the meeting was never amicable. Nefertiti had always been annoyed that Kia bore Akhenaten a son when she did not, and Nezem-mut lost no opportunity in carrying on her sister's jealous belittlement of the woman. It was after one of their many confrontations that Kia complained to Tutankhamun, and he decided that Nezem-mut must be excluded from the royal circle.

'What makes you think you should have a royal tomb at all?' Nezem-mut was reported to have said scornfully to Kia one day after hearing about Kia's request for a tomb at Akhetaten. 'If all the minor wives of kings were housed in royal tombs there would be no room for the kings themselves.'

'I am the widow of a king and the mother of a king,' Kia said with unusual spiritedness.

'I know,' Nezem-mut had replied impatiently. 'But General Horemheb has good reason to want Akhetaten forgotten. You are asking too much of your son to expect him to bury you there.'

'I will not forget Akhetaten – nor will my son.'

'If you do not – both you and your son will be forgotten.'

The next time Tutankhamun broached the subject of Nezem-mut's marriage was in front of Horemheb.

'Surely you have had time enough to consider the matter?' he said impatiently when she hesitated once more.

Nezem-mut looked at Horemheb who stood impassively by. Nothing in his expression gave her an indication of

what he was thinking. She was in an agony of indecision. She had lived a full and interesting life at court.
When she had felt the need she had taken lovers to her
bed, but up to now she had never felt the need of marriage. She had assumed for a long time she would be
Horemheb's wife one day – but here he was condoning
her being handed over to someone else without a hint
of protest. She tried to derive comfort from the fact that
he did not meet her eyes, but stared at a scroll of papyrus
he held rolled up in his hand. Did this mean he was
thinking deeply about the implications of what
Tutankhamun proposed, or was he thinking about
something else altogether? Nezem-mut bit her lip. She
had been feeling more and more uneasy about the
dwarfs lately, and if they, her closest companions, were
not to be trusted any more, perhaps it was time to seek
someone else to rely upon. She had liked what she had
seen of Tefnakhte but . . .

'Majesty, I do not want to marry the nomarch,' she
said, looking hard at Horemheb. 'I see no reason to do
so.'

'There are many reasons,' Tutankhamun replied,
annoyed. 'Not least that I have requested it.'

'The Queen, the Great Royal Wife, the Daughter of
Ra, is my niece,' she said proudly, straightening her
shoulders and looking pointedly at Horemheb, trying to
will him to look at her. 'Whoever marries me will gain
great power in the Two Lands.'

'The nomarch Tefnakhte is worthy of such power,'
Tutankhamun replied.

'*Such* power, Majesty.'

At last Horemheb looked up and, for a brief moment,
met her eyes. His gaze was penetrating and thoughtful,
as though at last she had succeeded in attracting his
attention.

Tutankhamun was about to reply angrily when he was interrupted. He had set his heart on this match, having grown tired of Nezem-mut being almost always present. Nefertiti had not been close or kind to him as a child, and Nezem-mut was the sister of that strong and formidable woman who had filled his infant heart with such unease. He had always felt that he did not and could not measure up to what she expected of a king or of a king's heir. Nezem-mut did not resemble her sister too closely, but there was a family likeness that was to him a constant reminder of his early years as King when he felt so awkward and inadequate. His resolution to move her away from the court had been strengthened by his mother's dislike of her – again largely a transferred hatred – for Nefertiti and Kia had never come to terms with each other. Ay, her father and Chief Vizier, had thought the nomarch would be a good match for his daughter, but Tutankhamun had deliberately not consulted Horemheb, anxious to make at least this decision by himself.

It was Maya, his friend and Master of the King's Treasury, who had been announced, having been away in Nubia for some months. Tutankhamun was glad to see him and eager to talk to him.

'There is to be no more hesitation, Lady,' he said firmly. 'The matter is settled.'

'Majesty . . .'

But her protest was lost as Maya bustled in, greeting the young King warmly and affectionately. Within moments they were deep in conversation about the animals Maya had brought back for Tutankhamun's beloved zoo. In particular Maya spoke about a young lion cub cut from its mother a few moments after her death. Since birth he had never had any company but human.

'I thought the Queen would like to have him,' Maya said. 'I believe he was born the very day her own son died. It might help her through her time of grief. He is very tame.' Maya had heard how pale and listless the Queen was since the death of her young prince.

Tutankhamun thought this an excellent idea and insisted on going then and there to make the presentation. He had either forgotten the matter of Nezem-mut and Tefnakhte completely, or thought that he had said the last word on it and nothing more was needed to bring about the marriage.

Horemheb and Nezem-mut were left alone.

There was silence between them for what seemed a long time. Nezem-mut's heart and thoughts were racing. There could not have been a better opportunity for them to clear matters up between them. She could not remember a time when they had been alone together and she knew that if Tutankhamun had his way there probably would never be another. But how to begin? She looked at him. He was half turned away from her – his mind on a Nubian tax list Maya had put into his hand just before he left with the King. Nezem-mut could see his face only in profile. It could have been carved in granite, she thought. It was a strong, tough face. A face that did not often smile. She could see the firm line of his jaw and the well proportioned, but not inconsiderable, nose. His body was a warrior's body, firm and muscular with a thin scar-line on his left shoulder and on his right wrist. They did not disfigure him, but rather enhanced the impression he gave of dangerous strength. She saw the concentration with which he read the list. 'Perhaps this is why I find him so attractive,' she thought. 'He is a man of action, stern and strong and violent – yet I know he is also a scholar, a diplomat, a courtier. He would make a good pharaoh,'

she mused, thinking back to Tutankhamun's grandfather who had been so fat and ill during the last years
of his reign, Akhenaten who was feeble of body and full
of crazy obsessions, and now Tutankhamun himself – a
thin youth who swung from being a puppet anyone
could manipulate, to a tyrant who asserted himself over
such matters as her marriage to try to prove he really was
the Pharaoh. She knew he was more interested in the
animals Maya had brought for his precious zoo than in
the official reports on Nubian politics he must also have
brought. Horemheb the soldier. Horemheb the scribe.
Horemheb the commoner – would make an excellent
pharaoh! See with what understanding he read the
Nubian despatches!

Almost as though the vigour of this thought got
through to him, the General looked up at her suddenly,
and gave her a slight bow.

'Forgive me, Lady,' he said politely. 'I should not be
reading these in your presence.'

'Of course you should, General,' she said. 'My life
has been spent at the centre of government. I am well
aware how important such reports are and how urgently
they should be attended to.' She gave an emphasis to the
word 'urgently', implying very subtly a criticism of
Tutankhamun who had allowed his favourite hobby to
take precedence over them.

Did she detect a gleam of interest in his hitherto
impassive face?

'My Lord,' she said. 'What do you think of this plan
of Pharaoh's to marry me off to the nomarch Tefnakhte?'

He took his time to reply. The longer he took the
more hope Nezem-mut gleaned from his silence.

'He is a good man,' he said at last. 'And a woman in
your position . . .'

'There are many good men, my Lord,' she interrupted sharply. 'You yourself, my Lord, would make a good husband for a woman in my position.'

She stared at him boldly, but her heart was anything but bold. 'Have I gone too far? Have I spoiled my chances?' she thought desperately. 'But if I left it unsaid – would it ever be said? Would he ever consider it?' She wondered at the prophecy of the priests of Amun. Had it been a genuine one or were they just trying to make mischief by raising her hopes? If it was genuine – no harm would be done by what she said. If it was false – well – at least she would have sown the idea in his heart and maybe it would take root there. She could not tell from his face what he was thinking – but as he said nothing and a great deal of time seemed to be passing, she grew agitated and reckless.

'I have been meaning to tell you, my Lord,' she said, 'but there has not been the opportunity – that I have found something that would be of great value to you.'

'Oh?' he said, raising thick, dark eyebrows, and looking at her now with interest.

'I intend to present it to my husband,' she said quietly, pointedly.

'What is it, my Lady,' he asked. He knew very well what she was trying to achieve, but was curious nevertheless.

'It would be a pity if it fell into the wrong hands,' she said hesitatingly.

'Do you not trust me, my Lady?'

'I trust you more than anyone else,' she replied quickly. 'More even than Pharaoh himself. Certainly more than the nomarch Tefnakhte.'

'I am sure you may trust Pharaoh and the nomarch Tefnakhte implicitly, my Lady. You do me too much honour and them an injustice.'

Again there was that silence – that tension between them.

General Horemheb broke it by bowing and preparing to leave.

'I am sure your husband will appreciate the gift,' he said calmly, as though he had lost interest. 'And now if you will excuse me . . .'

'Is the Sacred Phoenix Egg of Ra a suitable gift for a wife to give a nomarch?' she asked. Her face was flushed as she made this last bid to bring him to her side. He had already started to move away, but as she said these words he halted and swung round to look at her. His attention was caught at last.

'The Sacred Egg of Ra?'

'Yes, my Lord,' she replied, watching him closely, feeling that now at last, she had the chance to win through to what she really wanted.

'You have it?'

'Yes,' she said, her hesitation so slight he did not notice it. She could not, would not, now admit she did not have it. She was sure it was not beyond her powers to retrieve it from the Queen, specially in her present enfeebled state. That she had not already made her possession of it known indicated that there was still time for it to change hands again – secretly. Nezem-mut was playing for high stakes and was well aware of it.

'It should be returned to Yunu,' Horemheb said at once.

'I thought perhaps it would be better kept here at the Temple of Amun-Ra,' she said slyly.

'Does the nomarch know of this?'

'No one knows, my Lord,' lied Nezem-mut. 'But you and I. Restoring such an ancient and respected sacred object to the Two Lands,' she added, 'will give whoever does it immense power. I would like to give that power to the man I marry. But I'm not sure the nomarch Tef-nakhte . . .'

'Lady, I think you should not make up your mind too hastily.'

'But what if Pharaoh is insistent?'

'Let me speak with Pharaoh,' Horemheb said, now very evidently hooked on her bait. 'We must consider what is best to be done.'

She smiled.

'Yes, my Lord,' she said sweetly, lowering her large, dark eyes at last, acting the part of a compliant and sub-missive woman without shame. 'Whatever you advise.'

He strode away from her, visibly excited.

7
THE POWER

Maya was right about Ankhesenamun and the lion cub. Within moments of receiving the gift her cheek was against his soft cheek and she was calling him by every kind of endearing name. He lay on his back for her and she rubbed the silky fur of his belly and he purred like a kitten. Looking at her shining face, so different from the face he had seen when he arrived, Maya wondered what she was thinking. The cub had entered the earth realm as her child had left it and it was possible that she believed the spirit of the royal prince was in the cub's body. He wondered if he had done the right thing by telling her the exact time of its birth. He had thought it was an interesting coincidence – but no more than that. He had not meant the animal to take the human's place.

Tutankhamun, however, was delighted. For the first time in a long while he saw Ankhesenamun happy, and that was enough for him. It did not even enter his head that there was something too intense and strange about the way she was reacting to the lion.

The cub and Ankhesenamun became inseparable. She had a collar made for him of gold with a lotus of turquoise and *djed* of lapis lazuli and a bracelet identical but smaller for her own arm. A fine, but strong gold chain linked them together as they walked in the garden. Like a child again she rolled on the paved alabaster floors of the courtyard with him, and he slept on a cushion beside her whenever he wanted to sleep.

When Nezem-mut came to confront her about the green

crystal Egg which she still believed Ankhesenamun had, the Queen and the cub were curled up together on a rug in the flickering shade of a sycamore tree in the garden of the palace. Both were asleep. At Nezem-mut's step the animal opened an eye at once and cocked an ear, but he felt so secure within the arms of Ankhesenamun, he did not bother to growl.

Nezem-mut was forced to call her name before the young woman stirred. The sun blazed down on the garden. It was noon and very few people were about. Even the gardeners had retired to avoid the hottest hours of the day. Nezem-mut could feel sweat trickling down her arms. She had deliberately chosen this time knowing that she and the Queen would be less likely to be disturbed.

'Senamun,' she repeated, using Tutankhamun's private version of her name.

At last the Queen moved, sighed and rubbed her eyes. Nezem-mut could see that her eyes though open were still seeing the dream landscape out of which she had been so suddenly drawn. She tightened her arm involuntarily round the little animal as though to protect it from whatever danger might be threatening.

Gradually she awoke and drew herself up to a sitting position. The little cub was awake too and nuzzling against her as though looking for milk.

'Ah – Nezem-mut,' Ankhesenamun said – not entirely pleased to see her aunt. She had sunk so low into despair over the death of her child that she had done nothing more about the Sacred Egg. But that very morning she had been thinking about it again and wondering what she could do to retrieve it. She had seen nothing of Hapu or the dwarfs since that terrible day and indeed had not even wanted to think about them.

Now the thoughts came crowding back, and a shadow crossed her face.

Nezem-mut studied her closely. She believed she had recovered sufficiently to be called to account for her actions.

'I am glad to see you well, niece,' she said stiffly.

'I am glad to be well, aunt,' Ankhesenamun replied, equally stiffly.

'I see you have a new companion.'

Ankhesenamun nodded and continued to stroke and fondle the little animal, avoiding looking directly at her aunt. She was well again, but not sure she was ready for a difficult confrontation. There was an uncomfortable silence for a while and then Nezem-mut decided to go straight to the point.

'There is something we need to talk about, niece.'

'Indeed?'

'You know, I think, very well what I mean.'

Ankhesenamun looked up at her now and her eyes narrowed like those of an angry cat. As though sensing her change of mood the lion cub growled threateningly.

'You took something that was not yours,' Nezem-mut said.

'No, aunt. *You* took something that was not yours!'

'It belongs to neither of us but to the land of Khemet – and it should be returned.'

'Yes, it should be returned.'

Nezem-mut waited, expecting Ankhesenamun to continue. When she did not, she spoke up impatiently.

'Niece, do not play games with me! You opened the box. You took what was inside. Where is it now?'

Ankhesenamun looked at her coldly.

'I opened the box, but I took nothing – for there was nothing to take. If you want the Sacred Egg of Ra – to return it to its rightful place,' she added pointedly, 'you should dream a dream – or if that fails – ask the dwarfs who have served you so well for so long.'

Nezem-mut looked startled.

'Yes, my poor aunt, you have been betrayed.'

'They would never. . . !'

But she knew they had. She knew they had for she had felt the difference in them. She cursed herself for being such a fool to have wasted all this time waiting for Ankhesenamun when the crystal was probably within her grasp. She would teach those treacherous thieves a lesson they would never forget! How could they – after all she had done for them! The sons of peasants – they had lived like princes in luxury. They had been honoured as few people apart from the royal family were honoured. There was nothing she had not done for them. Nothing that she had not given them!

Without another word she turned on her heel and hurried away. Ankhesenamun watched her go – wondering if she should follow – trying to bring herself to take action, to be decisive, to find and reclaim the sacred artefact for Ra.

'I am the god who resides in the Egg of the First and the Last. I am the god who rises from the horizon and swims in the shining sky. Who sends light to illumine all things and whose like is not found among the gods . . .'

Nezem-mut called Heh and Ipi to her audience chamber. There was no doubt when they saw her that she was very angry. She was sitting bolt upright on the most elaborate and uncomfortable chair in the room, the one she used only when she was receiving strangers and wanted to appear haughty and impressive.

The two men stood before her. They were no taller than they had been, but their stare was so confident and arrogant, they appeared taller. She looked at them and realised that for all the years she had had them at her side she had not known them at all. They had shared jokes at the expense of others; they had gossiped and passed the time of day; they had spied and brought reports to her on anyone she wanted to know about – but she had never looked into their hearts – she had never listened to what was behind what they had to say.

'You are thieves,' she accused them. 'You have stolen from me – your friend, your benefactress.'

'Surely not, my Lady,' Heh said smoothly.

'Surely so, dwarf,' she answered sharply.

Heh's eyes seemed to spark with sudden fire. She had never in all their time together called him that.

'We have taken nothing that belongs to you,' he said icily.

'You have taken the Sacred Egg of Ra.'

'We were not aware that that belonged to you, my Lady.'

'What have you done with it!' she almost shrieked, forgetting that she was trying to appear dignified and authoritative. She leant forward, thrusting her face close to his, gripping the arms of the chair until the bones of her knuckles showed white.

Heh and Ipi glanced at each other, and she did not miss the flash of triumph that passed between them.

'If you don't tell me this instant,' she raged, 'no punishment will be too harsh for you!'

'If you punish us, Lady,' Heh said calmly, knowing his strength, 'you will never see the Egg again.'

She bit her lip, and forced herself to sit back in her chair. Her heart was beating fast and she could feel her anger like an ill-tasting liquid welling up inside her throat. She felt nauseous. She knew now she had taken the wrong approach – but her desire to possess the crystal at this moment was almost unbearable. She had promised it to Horemheb – and he – though nothing had been spelled out – must surely have understood that he would not receive the Sacred Egg if he did not marry her.

'I do not want to punish you, Heh,' she said through tight lips, forcing her anger under control. 'I would prefer to reward you. What do you say?'

'We cannot return it, my Lady.'

'Cannot? Or will not?'

'It is not advisable. It has great power and we have learned how to control it and use it. If someone without this knowledge were to attempt to take it from us he or she would be destroyed.'

She looked at him in astonishment.

'Are you threatening me?'

'No, my Lady. Just explaining how it is.'

For a while there was silence in the room while Nezem-mut considered the turn events had taken, and the two men watched her, amused, knowing that there was nothing she could do.

There was a slight sound to the left and the tension was so great they all spun round to see what it was. A cat who had all this while been sleeping on the top of a high cupboard had now leapt onto the table. Heh moved towards it to pick up a jar before the contents were spilled. The cat took one look at him and let out a high-pitched screech. All its fur rose as it arched its back. There was no doubt that it was terrified of him. With a kind of howling shriek it fled from the room.

Nezem-mut looked at Heh in some alarm. He seemed unperturbed.

'You see, my Lady, the holders of the Sacred Egg of Ra cannot give it up.'

She herself was afraid of him now. Ipi was standing a pace or two behind him and seemed less in control than Heh. But Heh had a power she had never encountered before. It was clear she had been very unwise to promise what she could not deliver.

'The General Horemheb is very anxious to find the Egg of Ra,' she said. 'And I am very anxious to present it to him.'

The dwarfs had been intimate enough with her to know of her secret longing for the General.

'Ah,' thought Heh. 'Here we have it!'

Aloud he said, 'My Lady, we will gladly use the power of the Egg on your behalf. Tell us what it is that you want.'

Nezem-mut hesitated. She knew what she wanted more than anything in the world – but she was afraid to say it. The Egg itself was nothing to her. It was for her only a means to an end, and if she could achieve that end without the actual possession of the Egg she would be content to do so. The reaction of the cat to Heh had shown her that it would not be easy to get the Egg back if Heh did not want to part with it.

'The Egg has the power to make someone desire someone,' Heh said slyly.

'It has?'

'If the right spells are cast. If someone knows what he is doing.'

She looked at Heh thoughtfully. She read in his eyes that he knew of her desire for Horemheb. She read in his eyes that he would help her to arouse that same desire in the General's heart. 'Why not?' she thought. 'Why not?' She was sure Horemheb could force the dwarfs to give up the Egg if he knew they had it – but if he did this before he married her – what hold would she have over him? No, she must either use the Egg to bribe the General as she had planned, or use it through Heh to entrap him.

'Heh, my friend,' she said, using a very different tone
from the one she had used before. 'You know my heart.
Can you help me to achieve its desire?'

'Surely, my Lady.'

'You will not regret it. I will make it worth your
while.'

'I know, my Lady.'

She wished he did not look so smug. She looked forward to a time when that expression would be different.
Together, Horemheb and she would enjoy bringing him
down.

Hep and Ipi were not long gone from the chamber of
Nezem-mut when they were called into the presence of
the Queen.

Ankhesenamun was thinner than when they had seen
her last and not only because she was no longer
pregnant. Shadows had come to nest in her eyes and her
cheeks were almost gaunt.

She too was seated when they entered bowing. Beside
her feet the little lion cub was lying peacefully asleep. As
they approached it awoke and, like the cat, showed signs
of fear. Growling – it retreated behind the Queen's
skirt, one anxious and wary eye all that showed of it.

She lost no time in accusing them of theft and
demanding the return of the Egg of Ra immediately.

'We are no thieves, Majesty,' Heh replied boldly.
'We have been chosen by Ra himself to guard the Egg.'

'So?' she said sarcastically. 'And how did the Great
God make his wishes known?'

'By dreams and signs, Majesty.'

'Oh yes,' she thought. 'That is an easy lie to use. I
have used it myself.'

'At first we would not listen,' he continued, his
expression one of studied innocence. 'We could not

believe that such unworthy vessels should be chosen for such a mighty task. But . . .'

'But you soon persuaded yourselves that, unworthy as you are, the Great God had chosen *you* rather than Pharaoh or the God's Wife, Ankhesenamun, royal Queen of Egypt with generations of sacred blood in her veins?'

'Yes, Majesty.' He met her eyes boldly and stared unblinking into them.

'I too have had dreams and signs, sir. Now, who is to say which of us has the most authentic dreams and signs – the *true* dreams and signs direct from the living god?'

For a moment the confident stare faltered. Ankhesenamun was not to be as easily manipulated as Nezem-mut. Her reasons for wanting the Egg were not as simple nor as selfish as her aunt's. 'What does she desire most?' Heh pondered. 'What can I use against her?'

'Ra has given *me* the Egg, Majesty,' he said smoothly. Ipi looked at him, surprised. Surely the Egg had been given to both of them? 'No doubt it would have come into your hands if you were meant to have it.'

'It *will* come into my hands, sir. This very day. I have not yet told Pharaoh of your theft. But before Ra enters the boat of stars tonight he will be told and his wrath will be dangerous and mighty.'

'If Ra chooses – even pharaohs may be unseated from their thrones,' he said quietly – menacingly. 'Kings and queens may be destroyed by the wrath of Ra as easily as other men and women.'

'Ah, sir, you threaten me?'

'Not I, Majesty. But Ra has chosen me as his vessel and as his spokesman.'

'He has chosen you as his fool!' she snapped. 'You will not live long, dwarf, and you will face the gods with a heart that will not balance against the feather of Truth. Apep himself will show you which of us has had the true dream, the true sign!'

Heh's face was distorted with rage. He was shaking as he tried to hold it in check. She too was taut as a bowstring, trying to keep her dignity – knowing that if she let it go she would achieve nothing, but lose everything.

'Go from my sight now,' she commanded bitterly, 'but if the Sacred Egg of Ra is not brought to me by the time the sun rises tomorrow you will enter the Void – nameless. Your existence will be wiped away and no record of you will survive; no shred of your past will draw you back to earth; no god will know you.'

Without a bow Heh turned and strode out of the room, Ipi stumbling at his side, white-faced as he thought of the horrifying curse that had been pronounced upon them.

'Should we not . . .?' he suggested timidly.

'No!' snapped Heh. 'Come – we have work to do.'

That night Ankhesenamun lay unsleeping while Ra progressed through the twelve realms of the night, wakening the spirits of each in turn, inspiring them into life. The Two Lands slept – the stars wheeling silently over a dark and silent earth.

Tutankhamun slept peacefully, unaware of the dangerous forces that were gathering around him – disappointed that his Great Royal Wife had again turned away from him, her troubled face indicating that it would not be worth his while to persist. He longed for her to come back to him – but meanwhile he could sleep with his other, lesser wives. 'I'll give her a little more time,' he thought. 'Just a little.' He forgot that time is like liquid in a jar – the more we pour, the less we have.

Around midnight Ankhesenamun began to feel

frightened. She could not explain her fear. Her palms began to sweat; her heart to beat too fast. She turned her face this way and that to peer into the shadowy corners of her room, wondering if someone – or something – was lurking there. She could see nothing, but the fear grew. The little cub was growling as though it too sensed danger. She clutched its little body close to hers, trying to comfort herself by comforting it. She sat up, straining her eyes to see into the darkness. She wanted to light the lamp, but she would have to cross the room to do it and it would take time. Who knew what nameless horror might reach out and touch her! She decided to call for her women attendants who slept in the next chamber, but found that no matter how loudly she shouted, no sound came out of her mouth. The lion cub was silent too now, trembling as much as she, burrowing into her for protection.

'Coward,' she whispered with dry lips. 'Lions are supposed to be brave.' But not even the whisper sounded in the totally silent room. Was it her imagination or had it grown darker? There was always moonlight or starlight shining through her windows and there had been a short while before. But now there was none. It was as though all light-giving sources had been snuffed out and she was alone in absolute darkness.

'Not alone,' she thought, desperately clutching the animal until it could hardly breathe. 'Not alone!' She tried to force herself to visualize the blazing light of Ra at this very moment starting its return towards the Two Lands. She tried to visualise her father's image of the great life-giving force, the Aten, above her as a disc of fire itself too bright to gaze upon but emanating rays that could be experienced by the human mind. But to her horror she could not see even those things with her inner eye. Even there she was in darkness, stone blind.

Worse than losing physical sight she had lost her capacity for inner vision. She had lost the faculty that enabled her to 'see' beyond seeing.

The morning came at last and Ankhesenamun emerged from the night white and shaken, knowing that Heh would not give up the sacred object and yet, if she did not take control of it soon, they would all be in deadly danger. She had promised to tell Tutankhamun, but he had left on a hunting expedition long before she recovered sufficiently to drag herself from her room.

In a panic she sent for Hapu and told him what had happened and demanded that he find where the dwarfs were keeping the Egg.

'Don't try to take it,' she warned. 'Just come right back to me and tell me where it is.'

Hapu had been searching ever since they had discovered it was missing and was not very convinced he would be able to find it. But realizing now how urgent the matter had become gave him an added incentive. He believed it was also possible that Heh and Ipi would become more and more careless as time went by and as their arrogance grew. Hapu knew at least that the hiding place must be somewhere in the cliffs just north of the ruined temple at Serui. He had succeeded in tracing them there, but then lost them again.

He set off at once for the area but after an exhausting morning of fruitless search, he retired to the shade of one of the cool colonnades of the deserted temple. Akhenaten had been particularly violent towards the images of Amun in this place and before him someone else had hacked out other names and other images. Hapu rested his back against a huge stone figure of some ancient king in the form of Osiris. The columns of one whole terrace were faced with these figures, though many were fallen and broken. Most of the faces even of those still standing had been smashed in as though someone was very determined that whoever the king was who erected these to his eternal glory would never return and would never be remembered. Horemheb had ordered that the images and names of Amun were to be restored – but so far nothing had been done. Most of Tutankhamun's workforce were busy on the restoration and extensions he had ordered in the Temple of Mut at Ipet-Resut and the Temple of Amun at Ipet-Esut. Behind Hapu on the wall was carved in low relief the story of a great expedition in five mighty ships. Hapu puzzled for the inscriptions referred to the Pharaoh concerned sometimes as a woman and sometimes as a man. He stared at the fine pictures of a strange land, 'God's-land of Punt'. Where was it? It must have been far, far away. The people lived in strange huts on stilts. Mountains of gold and incense, herds of cattle and wild animals were evidently brought back to Khemet. But more important than all these were the great leafy frankincense trees, some of which still struggled for existence in the gardens of the lower terrace of this temple.

> *I have led them on water and on land, to explore the waters of inaccessible places, and I have reached the Myrrh terraces. It is a glorious region of God's-Land: it is indeed my place of delight . . .*
>
> *I am their wise Lord, I am the Begetter, Amun-Ra; my daughter, who binds the Lords, is the King Maat-ka-Ra, Hatshepsut. I have begotten her for myself. I am her father, who set her fear among the Nine Bows, while they came in peace to all gods.*

Hapu had not heard of the Pharaoh Hatshepsut and
wondered now if she was one like Akhenaten whose
name had become anathema and there had been a
deliberate attempt to blot her memory off the face of the
earth. Yet what has been will always be no matter how
hard men try to obliterate it. There will always be a seed
left under a stone, biding its time, perhaps to germinate
long after those who had thought to destroy it were
themselves long since dead. Hapu stared at the face of
one of the Osirian statues that stretched away from him
on the edge of the terrace. Only one was undamaged. It
was the face of a woman. A woman Pharaoh? A woman
taking on the role of Osiris at a time when Osiris was
the mighty Judge of the Dead, the Father of Resurrection? Nefertiti's usurpation of the throne seemed a
lesser achievement coming, as it did, at a time when the
old rigid rules and traditions had already been violated.

But sleep overcame him before he could ponder further and in his dream he saw the temple in full working
order with priests going back and forth, Hathor's music
echoing against the cliffs, processions carrying palm
leaves, climbing the ramps to the highest terrace of all,
the Holy of Holies, the sanctuary of the Great God
Amun-Ra.

He woke with a start. He would not do homage to
Amun-Ra. Not even in a dream! How ancient rituals
lingered in a place!

The sun was lower and he must have spent more time
than he realized resting in the shade. With renewed
determination he started to climb the northern cliffs
again – seeking for some clue to where he had once seen
the dwarfs disappear.

The rocks changed shape and colour with every movement of the sunlight. Shadows appeared at some times
of the day that disappeared at others. Some rocks were

illuminated as others were shadowed. By great good fortune he was just at the right time to see a particular rock lit up in such a way that a cleft or cave was revealed that he had not noticed before on all the occasions he had been to the area. He clambered towards it at once and as he did so he could see that others had been there before him. The rock was scuffed; the dust unsettled. His heart began to beat fast. He felt he was really very near indeed. He had found the dwarfs' secret hiding place. He had found the Sacred Egg of Ra!

In the dim light of the cave after the bright sunlight he could at first see nothing. He stood for what seemed a long time trying to adjust to the change. But eventually the moment came when he could enter the cave and see reasonably well. He avoided looking back to the brilliant strip of light at the entrance and concentrated on the furthest, darkest part of the cave.

At last he found what he sought. He could see it faintly glowing in its hiding place, and reached up for it. He knew what he was going to do. He was going to take it out of the cave and hurl it down onto the rocks far below. He was going to smash it into a thousand pieces. No matter that he would be disobeying the Queen. *His* king, Akhenaten, had ordered its destruction, and it would be destroyed.

But then he paused. He stared at it, his eyes seeing almost as clearly now as they did in the daylight. How beautiful it was. Perhaps it would be a pity to destroy such beauty. Perhaps Akhenaten would be content if it was in the safe keeping of his daughter. Perhaps he himself had put it in that hiding place in his palace at Akhetaten because he did not want it destroyed after all – but kept safe.

It seemed to Hapu that as he stared at it, it seemed to glow more than it did at first. It seemed larger.

'Why return it to the Queen?' he thought. It certainly should be taken out of the hands of the dwarfs who were obviously misusing it. But would not he, the last remaining priest of the Aten, be the best guardian for it? He could take it back to Akhetaten and keep it safe there. Perhaps with its power, used carefully and wisely, he could re-activate the city and bring back the worship of the Aten to the Two Lands. After all – it was connected with the sun. It would not take much to change the emphasis from Ra to the Aten.

Even as he thought these things with one part of his mind, another part was warning him of danger – warning him not to lie to himself, not to be diverted from his purpose – reminding him that he did not have the qualities of a reliable guardian. Did Tutankhamun or the Queen?

'No,' he decided. 'I will throw it into the valley. No one will ever be able to use it against anyone again.' People should not turn to minor aspects of the Ultimate Deity, he thought. They should not compromise. The Aten blazed out in the heavens unique and supreme. Ra was but a shadowy aspect of the One. To follow Ra, or any of the others, was to follow a mirage in the desert while the real oasis is passed by.

He reached out to seize it, his heart full of iconoclastic zeal. The crystal seemed to flare with green light and grow huge. It looked as it had looked in his dream. He plunged his hands into the light and tried to get a grip on its crystal surface. His eyes were watering. Surely there was something solid there? It seemed like his hands were burning hot as though he was approaching fire and then he touched the ice-cold surface of the crystal.

With a scream he fell back. Pain such as he would never have believed possible coursed through him.

When he regained consciousness he was lying on the
floor of the cave and the crystal, now back to its original
size, was still in place on the stone ledge. He tried to get
up and found to his horror that one whole side of his
body was numb. He could not move the hand that had
touched the crystal, nor any part of his body on that
side. He rubbed his dead arm with his other hand, hoping to get it back to life. But as time passed and no feeling came back to his right side and it would respond to
no effort on his part to move it – he realised that he was
partially paralysed. He tried to keep control of himself
and explore his body logically and carefully to find out
exactly what damage had been done. He was blind in
the right eye and deaf in the right ear.

With desperate and determined effort he dragged
himself out of the cave and down the mountain. Some
peasants found him the next morning at the edge of
their cultivated fields, covered in dried blood –
unconscious – but still breathing.

8
THE WASTE

A few days passed before Hapu had recovered enough to leave the care of the kindly people who had taken him in. He could talk – but with difficulty, the one side of his mouth not functioning at all and words coming tardily from his brain.

He tried unsuccessfully for some time to see the Queen but was prevented by zealous guards who turned him away with increasing violence as he persisted. At last, by luck, the chief gardener spotted him at the gate and recognized him. He did not know what business he had with the Great Royal Wife, but it had not passed unnoticed that she had called him into her presence more than once. He assumed Hapu was somehow in her employ as a spy. The court was full of spies.

He stopped the irate guard kicking him, and helped him into the palace garden. There he listened patiently while Hapu tried to tell him how urgent and important it was that he should see the Queen. He tried to get out of him why he wanted to see her – but in this he did not succeed. At last the man sent a message to Ankhesenamun and when the reply came back at once that she would give him audience, he ordered two of his men to carry him to her while he himself strode ahead – no doubt hoping to be present when the interview took place.

Ankhesenamun was shocked to see Hapu's condition and ordered the men to place him on a couch. He struggled to protest and rise, but she held up her hand and insisted that he stay. She then dismissed the others and cleared the room of everyone but the two of them.

'Hapu,' she said anxiously. 'What happened?'

Slowly, painfully, he told her, his voice rising to something like hysteria near the end as he besought her to find a way to destroy the Egg.

'It is evil! Evil!' he stammered, rising on his good elbow and staring fixedly at her with his one good eye while the other gazed sightlessly in a different direction.

She paced about the room, thinking hard.

At last she stopped beside him.

'It is not evil in itself, Hapu. I'm sure of that. When it was in the Temple of Ra at Yunu many miracles were reported. It was a great force for good. No, it is not evil. It has been misused by evil people and taken on some of their malevolent energy.'

Hapu remembered a time when he had entered an empty house in ruined Akhetaten seeking shelter. He had had to leave before the night was out because he felt so frightened and uncomfortable there. Later he learned that it had been the house of a cruel man who had tortured and killed his own children.

'If the crystal cannot be touched as it is,' she was saying, 'I must go with you to the cave and we must try to cleanse it of their influence.'

Tutankhamun was astonished to hear about the Egg, scarcely crediting the drama that had been going on right under his nose without his suspecting anything about it. At first he was angry that he, her husband and her Pharaoh, had been kept uninformed about the matter for so long, but Ankhesenamun persuaded him that it was partly because she had not realized the gravity of the situation before, and partly because he had been so busy, and she so ill, that a suitable opportunity had not arisen. She stressed that she believed now it was important to retrieve the Egg and cleanse it with the utmost secrecy – but Tutankhamun did not agree. Within moments of his having heard the full story from her he had sent for Heh and Ipi and placed them under strong guard, demanding that they, still under guard, fetch the Egg from the cave and bring it direct to him.

His decisive action took Ankhesenamun by surprise and she could not countermand his orders. But as soon as they were alone she berated him for his foolishness.

'Ordinary soldiers and ordinary weapons are useless against someone who has as much power as Heh,' she snapped. 'Look what he did to me in the privacy of my own chamber! Look what he did to Hapu! You'll never see those guards again and you'll never see the Egg of Ra.'

'Nonsense! It was the only thing to do. You forget I am Pharaoh and I have all the power of the gods behind me.'

Ankhesenamun looked at him as though she despaired of his ever having any good sense.

'The gods!' she muttered bitterly and dismissively under her breath.

He was shocked and she seeing it, tried to explain.

'The gods are forces we don't understand and cannot control. Who knows if a man behaves in a foolish and impossible way, the gods might let him learn his lesson the hard way – yes – even if he is Pharaoh himself!' she added, angry at the smug look on his face. She wanted Tutankhamun to be a great and wise Pharaoh and he had the potential – but he was still so young and still naive enough to believe that what happened in the visible world was all that need be taken into account.

'We ourselves should go and fetch the Egg of Ra away, before they reach it,' she said.

'How can we do that? Pharaoh and his Queen? We are

less free to go where we like and do what we like than
our least subject!'

She knew it was impossible – but she knew also that
it had to be done. She could trust no one else to do it
as it should be done.

At that moment Nezem-mut was announced.

'Dismiss her,' Ankhesenamun said quickly. 'It is
through her that everything has gone so wrong.'

'I sent for her,' Tutankhamun said, 'precisely because
it is through her that everything has gone so wrong.'

Before Ankhesenamun could say more, Nezem-mut
was bowing before them. She could see that
Tutankhamun was very angry.

'Not only do you defy me openly about your
marriage, but you steal from Pharaoh and the gods,' he
snapped. 'I have no patience left for you and I am
considering banishing you from the Two Lands.'

'Majesty!' gasped Nezem-mut.

'Nezem-mut,' Ankhesenamun hastily intervened.
'We believe your dwarfs are misusing the power of the
Sacred Egg of Ra and we need to get it back, soon,
before it does any more damage. We need your help,'
she added ingratiatingly, giving Tutankhamun's arm a
squeeze and hoping he would have the sense to grasp
that this was the more effective approach.

'What help can she possibly give?' Tutankhamun
muttered.

'She knows Heh and Ipi well. She might be able to tell
us something that will help us persuade them to give up
the Egg peacefully.'

'They don't need persuasion. They need a good
whipping!'

'Majesty,' interrupted Nezem-mut quickly. 'Of
course I will do anything to help. I had no idea Heh and
Ipi . . .'

'Let me talk to my aunt alone, my Lord,' Ankhesenamun said quietly but in a tone that had often made him
back down in the past. 'You will see we will soon know
how to achieve our object without any trouble at
all.'

What he would have replied to that they would never
know because a messenger entered with an urgent
matter to be dealt with and Tutankhamun waved the
two women away. They retreated to the courtyard that
led out from the audience chamber and walked beside
the central pool.

'Pharaoh means what he says, aunt. You have a
choice.'

'If I could help, I would. But I have already tried to
retrieve the Egg from Heh and Ipi. It is not easy. They
have become powerful magicians and are determined
not to give it up.'

'We both know what has happened and who is
responsible for it,' Ankhesenamun said sharply. 'Now
we have to forget the past and work together for the
future. You have known them for a long time. Tell me
about them.'

'Majesty?'

'Anything about them. The more I know the more
likely I am to find a way of outwitting them.'

'Heh is the dominant one. Ipi tends always to do what
he says.'

'That I have observed for myself. One is a follower
and one is a leader. So! We have one man to deal with
– not two. Has Heh any particular weakness? Any fear?
Any secret dread?'

Nezem-mut was silent, thinking hard. She had to pretend to help or she would be banished, and to go now
before she had secured the help of Horemheb would
mean disaster. Once Horemheb was hers no one would

dare to order her about. Only this morning Heh had told her the spell was almost ready and if she were to lie down on her bed at a certain time and concentrate her thoughts on Horemheb he would start the process that would lead to her marriage.

'What is it? Why do you hesitate?'

Nezem-mut tried to hide what she was thinking, but Ankhesenamun was too good and practised an observer to have missed the conflict that was going on in her mind. She was afraid of Heh and what he could do – but she was dependent on him for an important favour. Ankhesenamun had long suspected her aunt was in love with Horemheb and so it did not need too much patience and cunning to discover what that favour was.

Nezem-mut was startled when her niece confronted her with what she was sure was such a well kept secret.

'It is not . . .' she started to protest, but her face was scarlet.

'It is, my Lady! There is no shame in loving a man and trying to keep him at your side. But – not at such a cost!' Ankhesenamun disliked and feared Horemheb, but she could see that he might not be unattractive to others. He had long been the real power in the Two Lands and that gave him a kind of glamour. Recently, with her encouragement, Tutankhamun had been trying to challenge his authority and assert his own. With a wife closely associated with the royal family Horemheb might well regain what ground he had lost. She had noticed lately that he was dangerously close to discovering where her three younger sisters were living. Two were established in the houses of nobles loyal to her on large delta estates. The eldest, Nefernefruaten, named after her mother, was living abroad, in Kepel, one of the priestesses of Hathor at the great temple that had been established there. It was generally believed that they were dead and she had managed to keep their whereabouts secret all this time, though she had not intended to keep them away from court so long. Each year she told herself she would fetch them back. But they seemed happy where they were and Ankhesenamun always persuaded herself that it was best for the country that she kept one powerful secret she could use against the General when the need arose. She knew he suspected they were still alive and was trying to find out where they were. She considered it a great victory that he had not yet succeeded. To marry a royal princess descended from the great Amenhotep III would put him in a good position to do away with Tutankhamun and herself, and establish himself as Pharaoh. Ambitious commoners in the past had done just that. Until Tutankhamun was man enough to hold his own against Horemheb, Ankhesenamun felt it wise to keep the princesses safe and hidden. To marry Nefertiti's sister would not be as useful to him as to marry one of Akhenaten's daughters – and that is why no doubt he had hesitated to do so though it must have been obvious to him that Nezem-mut was offering herself. But to marry her would be better than nothing. And he certainly would gain from it.

'I cannot cross Heh until he has done for me what he has promised,' Nezem-mut's voice cut across Ankhesenamun's thoughts. The sense of desperation in the tone was unmistakable. 'Give me one more day,' she pleaded. 'One more day will not alter much for you – but will change the course of my life.'

'One more day might well change the course of all our lives,' the Queen said sternly. 'We cannot, dare not, delay.' And then her tone changed, and she took her aunt's arm almost affectionately 'Nezem-mut, I know you love the General – but to win his love with a magic trick is foolish and dangerous. Heh may achieve a magic spell and the General may say the words you long to hear. But a magic spell cannot change a man's heart. Deep inside he will know it is not his choice to marry you. Let me work on Horemheb – quietly, gently, subtly. My methods will take longer but they will be surer in the long run. I will point out things about you he might not have noticed. I will lead him without his knowing he has been led until he makes the decision to marry you on his own volition. My dear aunt – you have much to give him. He will see that without a doubt.'

'I have no beauty,' Nezem-mut said sadly – all those long years of being under the shadow of her beautiful sister were behind those words. Nefertiti! The very name means: 'The Beautiful One Comes'.

'Of course you have beauty!' Ankhesenamun cried.
'Nefertiti . . .'

'Forget my mother. She was beautiful, yes. But so are you in a different way. I have seen Horemheb look at you! I am sure all that makes him hesitate is that he does not want to presume to ask a royal lady for her hand.' Ankhesenamun hated lying to her aunt – particularly since, for the first time, she realised what a burden of frustration Nezem-mut had been carrying as the sister of Nefertiti. But she needed victory in this matter. 'You do not need Heh,' she insisted. 'Horemheb is yours already. We just have to encourage him a little.'

Nezem-mut's face was a study of conflicting wants and desires.

'Think what damage Heh can do if he does not give up the Egg of Ra! Think what power he will have over you, knowing how he helped you to trick Horemheb. He needs only to remind you of it and threaten to tell your husband and you will have to do everything he asks.'

Nezem-mut went white. Ankhesenamun had at last persuaded her.

'Heh is terrified of giants, and particularly ghost giants,' she said.

'Giants? Ghost giants?'

'Whenever I want to subdue him for some reason I just have to tell him a story about how there used to be giants in a far country over the sea and now that they are dead they can cross the Great Green and come to Khemet. I even told him I'd seen one. I suppose it is because he is so small . . .'

Ankhesenamun was thinking.

'Nezem-mut you have been very helpful and I will not forget it. You will see – the General will ask you to marry him without any spell. Besides – Heh is under guard now – so he probably would not be able to concentrate on the magic ritual anyway.'

'What are you going to do?'

'I'm not sure.'

'Whatever it is – I want to . . . I want to help you.'

Ankhesenamun nodded, but her thoughts were busy elsewhere. She could not trust Nezem-mut. Hapu was crippled and could not be expected to climb the mountain. Tutankhamun did not understand what they were up against. She had to go alone. It was lucky Hapu had described the place in such vivid detail.

She told Nezem-mut that she would call her as soon as she had decided what to do, and returned to her chambers. She dismissed all but Meryt-mut, one of her most faithful serving women, whom she swore to secrecy. Meryt-mut had seen her mistress through many vicissitudes and did not hesitate to help prepare a disguise. Ankhesenamun left the palace with grey hair and a grey cloak, apparently bowed with age. Meryt-mut, pretending that the old woman was her mother, saw that she was safely mounted on a donkey and sent on her way. The Queen did not tell her where she was going or what she was doing, and Meryt-mut did not ask any questions. Ankhesenamun cast a look back over her shoulder and wished she did not have to face this alone.

Once near her destination she dismounted and tethered the donkey. She went the rest of the way on foot, passing villagers and farmers unnoticed in her peasant clothes. By the time she reached the ruined mortuary temple of Hatshepsut there was no one left to see her. She slipped like a grey shadow into the wilderness of rocks to the north of it and searched for the landmarks Hapu had so carefully given her. It was almost evening when she finally reached the cave. The sun would soon be behind the mountains of the west. There was an incredible silence and each pebble her foot dislodged startled her as it echoed against the cliffs. She looked over her shoulder a hundred times, half expecting to see Heh and Ipi and the hapless guards making their way to the same place. But no one came.

Once at the cave she stood for a moment leaning against the entrance, out of breath and exhausted. She was irritated with the heavy grey cloak and would have liked to abandon it – but she had to get back into the palace as unnoticed as she had left.

She could not afford to rest long. She had brought firestones and a pitch torch – but she would rather not use them if she could help it, fearing that they might attract attention.

She found the sacred object where Hapu had said it would be and fell down at once on her knees in the dust before it. She touched her forehead to the ground and said a fervent prayer for the help of the great God beyond all gods that he might read the sincerity of her heart and allow her to return the holy artefact to his Temple at Yunu.

At that moment she heard a sound behind her and looked up.

Heh was standing in the entrance to the cave. Ipi was just behind him holding a torch above his head. There was no sign of the guards.

'Ah!' the dwarf said. 'We have an intruder. What are you doing here, old woman?' In the flickering of light and shade she was thankful her disguise was holding. Should she assert herself as royal Queen – or play the harmless old hag?

In a quavering voice she said she was seeking shelter for the night and prayed by all the gods that he would not harm her.

He moved into the cave. Ipi lifted the torch so that it shone full on the green crystal. In the dim light she had not appreciated how truly beautiful it was.

'You were about to steal my treasure?'

'No. No, sir. I – I did not know there was treasure here to steal. Even if I did – I am not a thief. I do not steal what belongs to another.'

'So you are not a thief?' Heh said, still suspicious. He ordered Ipi to lower the flame until it shone in her face. She dropped her eyes at once and bent almost double, but she was afraid he had had a glimpse of her before she did so.

'Queen Ankhesenamun,' he breathed at last.

She heard Ipi gasp.

Quickly she stood up, towering above them.

'Yes, Queen Ankhesenamun!' she said icily. 'Come to take back what you have stolen. Come to do what all the King's guards could not do.'

She could see his face in the flame-light and his eyes were unbelievably malevolent. The fire seemed to dance on their dark shiny surfaces so that it was hard to believe he was ordinary flesh and blood.

'Lord of the Green Stone,' he began to intone in a huge and hollow voice, and she could feel the crystal behind her growing and growing. The cave seemed to swim in eerie green light. Ipi and Heh were dark and sinister silhouettes. She felt as she did just before a storm when the very air seemed as tense as a lion preparing to spring on its prey.

'Ah, my father,' she whispered. 'Why did we not all listen to you. You had the wisdom to see what would happen if these power-objects fell into the wrong hands. Help me now. Help me. Help me!'

Suddenly Heh faltered and took a backward step. He was looking at something or someone behind her. She did not turn her head, but knew who it was. She acted at once, and in the moment of confusion plunged her hands into the green aura surrounding the Sacred Egg of Ra as Hapu had done, but unlike Hapu, she did not envisage its destruction. She imagined it held high above her head and all the rays of the Aten reaching down to it, bathing it in pure and life-giving golden light and washing it clean of all the miasma laid on it by Heh. Her body was shaking as she imagined herself raising it high. It seemed to her it was the heaviest thing on earth and every muscle in her body ached to lift it – though in fact she was not lifting, or even touching it, at all.

'Ra!' she cried. 'Great God. This is your green crystal. This is your artefact and tool. Let it not be used against your people. Let it be as it was meant to be – a vehicle for your love to reach the earth – the channel of your energy from your realm to ours!'

Heh was screaming. Behind her he could see a monstrous giant – a ghost giant – reaching out long fingers towards him. He stumbled back against Ipi and together they turned and fled, dropping the torch, sliding and slipping down the mountainside, cursing and shouting with terror as they went.

Ankhesenamun was left in the cave, the burning torch on the floor illuminating every nook and cranny. In her hands she held a green crystal shaped like an egg. Nothing stirred in the cave.

Exhausted and shaken, and with hands still trembling, she placed the precious object in a pouch at her waist. She then knelt down again and bowed to the ground, saying a heartfelt prayer of thanks for the help she had received. She could see no one – but she did not feel alone.

Tutankhamun was furious that she had exposed herself to such danger and made love to her, exhausted as she was, in a kind of frenzy, thinking how nearly he had lost her.

'If I do not have you,' he said tenderly, and with unmistakable fear in his voice, 'I have no one.'

In the morning, after a restful and dreamless sleep, she took the initiative and roused her husband with all the old passion.

It was noon before they rose and left their chamber, hand in hand like lovers. They were agreed that the sacred object should be returned at once to the Temple of Ra at Yunu, and they planned to take it there themselves, not trusting anyone else. Tutankhamun was in the mood to listen to her now, having been so wrong in his handling of the dwarfs.

Heh and Ipi were nowhere to be found. It was hard to believe such distinctive looking men could pass unnoticed, but a very thorough search throughout the district proved to be fruitless.

Nezem-mut suspected something had happened

regarding the Egg, and chose to raise the subject in front of Horemheb.

The General was talking about the Hittites and how their King, Suppiluliuma, had attacked Mitanni, effectively slicing off a considerable amount of their land to join to his own.

'The man is growing too powerful, Majesty,' Horemheb said. 'He will be challenging the Two Lands next.'

'We're a long way from the land of Hatti, General,' Tutankhamun said comfortably. 'And he knows we are in a different league from Mitanni. He would not dare shake his fist at us.'

'The Mitannian empire is vast and strong. One would not have thought he would have dared shake his fist at them,' Horemheb said sarcastically.

'Not as strong as Khemet, General. Not even close. We have beaten him too often in battle. Our kings have driven him back, taken his dependencies, humiliated his princes. He knows and we know he has no chance against us. There is no need to fear him.'

'No need to fear, Majesty. But need to strengthen our garrisons in the east and keep a wary eye on him.'

'Pharaoh never sleeps, General,' Tutankhamun said grandly. 'Our cobra eye is on the whole world.'

'Has your cobra eye helped you find the green Egg of Ra, Majesty?' Nezem-mut took advantage of the momentary break to introduce the subject at present closest to her heart.

'She doesn't know we have it,' thought Ankhesenamun quickly. 'She is guessing.'

But Horemheb had taken the bait as Nezem-mut knew he would.

'What is this?' Horemheb asked sharply. He liked to know everything that was going on and indeed secretly thought it was he who had his eye upon the whole world. Was this something he did not know about?

Before she could be stopped Nezem-mut poured out her own, highly coloured, version of the story in which she had found it and brought it to Waset, rescuing it with great effort and courage from where Akhenaten had imprisoned it. She, of course, was the only one with the sense to know that the Egg should belong to Amun-Ra and be kept at Ipet-Esut, and had tried to get it to him knowing that he, above all others, would know what to do with it. But, she added, looking hard at Ankhesenamun and Tutankhamun, it had been taken from her and she feared now for its safety. She begged the General to take matters into his own hands and see that the sacred artefact was delivered into the safe-keeping of the priests of Amun-Ra.

'It seems you have done the Two Lands a great service, Lady,' Horemheb said.

'I did it for Amun-Ra,' she answered piously.

Ankhesenamun let her have her moment. She could see how she was struggling to achieve her original objective in spite of all that had gone wrong with her plan. Ankhesenamun could not help admire her persistence and ingenuity, and pity her desperation. But, she thought, how people lie! It was possible Nezem-mut was even beginning to believe her own lies.

'The Sacred Egg of Ra is to be returned to the Temple of Ra,' Ankhesenamun said firmly, making their position clear before Nezem-mut could stir up any more mischief.

'I agree of course – the Temple of Amun-Ra, here at Ipet-Esut.'

'No, General Horemheb,' she insisted. 'The Temple of Ra at Yunu where it has been since the world began.'

His lips were set in a hard line, but he said nothing.

'Did you ever see the Egg, sir, while it was still at Yunu?' Nezem-mut asked quickly. 'It is a most beautiful object.' And then, without giving him time to reply, she said to Ankhesenamun, 'May we not see it before it goes to the temple? I'm sure . . .'

'I have never seen it, Majesty,' Horemheb interrupted. 'It would be a great privilege to be allowed to glimpse it now.'

Ankhesenamun would have refused and was already opening her mouth to do so, when Tutankhamun clapped his hands to call an attendant and issued the orders for a certain casket to be fetched from his bed chamber.

'Majesty,' Ankhesenamun protested. 'I think it is not wise to expose the Egg of Ra to too many people.'

'The General is not too many people, my love. It will do no harm to show it to him.' Tutankhamun was excited about it and wanted to show it off before it was locked up forever in an almost inaccessible room at the Temple of Ra where only the highest priests and occasionally the Pharaoh himself were allowed to see it. 'The priests of Ra will re-consecrate it and then the General will never have the chance to see it.'

The attendant entered with the casket – a magnificent one of ebony, gold and ivory. On one side was a scene depicting the sacred Benu Bird landing on the first mound that arose from the Void. On the second side there was a scene of the Benu Bird laying its Egg from which all things were born. On the third side the Benu Bird was seen being absorbed back into the Egg it itself had laid. On the fourth the Egg burst open in flames and the Spirit-Bird, reborn, was seen to fly abroad trailing feathers of fire.

The attendant was ordered to lay it on the table and depart.

General Horemheb took a step nearer the table, his

eyes eagerly fixed on the box. Nezem-mut stepped forward too – to stand beside it proprietorially.

Tutankhamun opened the casket and took out the great crystal, setting it carefully on the table cupped in a golden dish.

How long they stood without speaking was difficult to judge – each locked in his or her own thoughts, each under the spell of the ancient, potent symbol. Ankhesenamun wondered how existence really came about – what mysterious energy became suddenly active and Nothing became Something. She wondered what mysterious energy the Egg itself possessed – was it a conscious energy or not? What came first – consciousness or physical form? Tutankhamun wondered if the possession of the Egg would give him the edge over Horemheb. Would he at last be able to control rather than be controlled? Should he delay returning it to Yunu? If Ankhesenamun's description of its power was accurate, it might well be wise to keep it by him – at least until he was truly master of the Two Lands. Horemheb, however, was determined it would be in his own hands before the day was over. What a fool Nezem-mut must be to have let it go! Nezem-mut herself was watching Horemheb's face, trying to decide what ground she had lost, if any, by losing the crystal.

Horemheb broke the silence first, and it was to say categorically that the Egg must go the temple of Amun-Ra at Ipet-Esut. The old temple at Yunu was not suitable to house such a precious artefact these days, he said. 'It has not been fully restored since its destruction. And even if it had,' he added, 'Amun-united-with-Ra here at Ipet-Esut is the God beyond all gods.'

'I disagree,' Ankhesenamun said at once. 'It has always been part of the sacred accoutrements of Ra – never in any way connected with Amun. You, of all people, General, in trying to re-establish the old traditions, the old values, must realize it has to go back to Yunu!'

'The priests of Ra are suspect.'

'How "suspect", General?'

'They were not treated with such severity by the heretic who-shall-be-nameless.'

'Our royal father, General? The Pharaoh, Akhenaten?'

He looked at her quickly. This was the first time she had dared to name her father with pride. Were these young puppets beginning to want a life of their own?

'His name by royal decree has been declared anathema.'

'Not by royal decree, Horemheb!' Tutankhamun, taking his cue from his wife, spoke up boldly. 'By your decree, General.'

'It was your seal upon the decree.'

'It was your hand that guided the seal.'

'When you are ready . . .'

'I am ready, General Horemheb, and have been for some time. I say the name of my father shall be pronounced and the priests of Ra shall have their sacred crystal returned to them.'

It was true, Ra of all the gods, using as he did, the sun as his symbol, had lasted in favour with Akhenaten longer than the others. But in the end – because Akhenaten's revolution was as much political as religious – he, too, was overthrown. The power of their great rivals, the priests of Amun, broken, the priests of Ra tried to reclaim their power and privileges, saying, quite rightly, that Amun had usurped them at the time of the Thutmosid kings and they were theirs by ancient right.

'Power? Privileges?' Ankhesenamun had heard her father cry the day the High Priest of Ra had come to

court. 'Get out of my sight! The only power is the power
of the Aten. The only privilege is the privilege Pharaoh
has – to serve the Aten!'

The Temple of Ra had gone the same way as all the
others and Akhenaten had no doubt taken the Sacred
Egg as a man removes the venom sacs of a snake in order
to render it harmless. Had he meant to destroy it and
had Nefertiti hidden it for her own reasons? Or had he
hidden it – contemplating a time when Ra at least would
be restored? But however it had come to be so carefully
preserved and however it had come to be in their hands
at this moment, both Ankhesenamun and Tutankhamun were agreed that it was a well timed issue on
which to make their first serious stand against
Horemheb.

Horemheb's face had darkened alarmingly, veins
standing out on his neck and forehead as he struggled to
control his anger. He was shrewd enough to sense the
difference in the young couple. At first he had
manipulated their fear and bewilderment. Then he had
exploited the fact that on the whole Tutankhamun was
pleasure-loving and disliked confrontation and strife.
But something had changed – almost overnight.
Tutankhamun looked strong, determined. He was
meeting Horemheb's eyes boldly, challengingly. He was
letting him know he was Pharaoh at last.

Horemheb bit his lip and cast a bitter look at
Ankhesenamun. She stood beside her husband, not
behind as a good wife should. It was clear her strength
had given her husband strength. He should never have
let her live!

'Ra-united-with-Amun shall have the Sacred Egg,'
Horemheb said through tight lips. He saw at once what
they were trying to do – reinstate the power of the
priests of Ra and by doing so limit the power of the

priests of Amun-Ra. They were thinking for themselves. They were playing the power game he knew so well. If he was not careful he would lose his grip on the Two Lands. For a long time he had made all the important decisions in the country while paying lip service only to the King. Now . . .

'We ourselves are taking the sacred artefact to Yunu,' Tutankhamun was saying. 'It will be a royal progress. Every village, every town, every man, woman and child between here and there will know the Sacred Egg of Ra is returning to its rightful home. Proclamations will go out. I myself will hold it up in every temple on the way so that every priest will know that Pharaoh is returning the Egg of Ra to Ra himself. The Temple of Ra will reclaim its full and ancient glory.'

'You will not do this, Majesty,' growled Horemheb. 'It will undo all that we have worked so hard to achieve.'

' "Will not", Horemheb?' Tutankhamun had never felt so sure of himself. Ankhesenamun was proud of him. ' "We", Horemheb? Who is this who dares challenge the King? Who classes himself with the King?'

'I do not presume, Majesty,' Horemheb said hastily. 'But – allow me – as your advisor – as an older man – as one who has had long years of experience in the government of a great empire . . .'

'You may give advice, Horemheb, but you may not command. If your advice is good – we will take it. If it is not – we will not.'

Horemheb felt a nerve twitching in his neck that he could not control. He tried to hold his temper – to appear calm.

'We have worked hard to restore stability to a land reduced to chaos by misgovernment. We have achieved it. Let us not now jeopardise all that work.'

'Am I wrong in thinking,' Ankhesenamun interrupted,

her voice dangerously sweet, 'that one of the main reasons you – disapproved –' and here she paused as though to isolate the word and indicate that it was an understatement – 'of my father was because he chose one god over all the others. By doing so you believed he destroyed the Cosmic Order, the rule of Maat, the subtle and careful balance of all the forces that keep us in existence, that keep us safe and fruitful and happy. He in his turn started what he did because he felt this same balance had been destroyed by the priests of Amun taking too much power and privilege for themselves.' She paused. 'Surely you see we are drifting once again into the situation you yourself say is so dangerous – the monopoly of one priesthood over all the others.'

She thought Horemheb would explode. But he held his tongue. There was a tense silence in the room. 'You will pay for this,' he was thinking. 'Your cleverness will be your undoing, Lady. You think you have helped your husband by teaching him to stand on his own feet – but you have destroyed him!'

At this moment the door burst open and Hapu lurched into the room. His face was like that of a maniac – his eyes staring and wild. Before anyone had grasped what was happening, or the guards who were chasing him caught up with him, he hurled himself bodily on to the Sacred Egg. With a sickening crash, he and the precious crystal fell onto the alabaster floor. Horrified, the others saw a livid lightning flash as though the splitting open of the Egg had released all the energy that had been stored in it. They were flung back against the walls and without exception covered their eyes against the glare. It was at once as though they were caught in a fearsome mountain storm and in a whirlpool being sucked into the Void. Screaming, they buried their heads in their arms and fought to keep upright against a mighty wind.

'How dared we think it was up to us to decide the fate of this . . . this . . .' Ankhesnamun could think of no words to express the awe with which she now regarded the object of their controversy. How dared they presume . . .

With a tremendous effort she forced herself against the wind into a kneeling position.

'Great God,' she whispered. 'Forgive us. We know so little and assume so much . . .'

Gradually the wind died down. The thunder ceased. The light dimmed. One by one they opened their eyes and looked around them.

Hapu was lying sprawled out on the floor. He was dead. Around him were fragments and splinters of crystal. The Sacred Egg of Ra was no more.

9
THE DEATH OF A KING

The controversy over the Sacred Egg of Ra left its mark.
Relations with Horemheb were even more strained than
they had been before. In the past year or two the
General had not spent much time at court, Ay being his
intermediary with the King. Now Horemheb chose to
stay close and supervise matters himself directly as he
had done at the beginning of the reign. This led to more
than one confrontation. Tutankhamun was no longer
the docile child ready to do everything Horemheb
wanted. He insisted for instance in restoring the great
Temple of Ra at Yunu to its former glory, and, although
he could not return the miraculous Egg, he presented it
with some magnificent sun-pillars and statues to make it
the wonder of the Two Lands.

Ankhesenamun came more and more openly to pay
attention to the god Ra as opposed to Amun, and saw
that, from her own wealth, the Temple of Ra received
generous endowments.

'Amun is the Unknown, the Invisible One. He can be
what you wish to make him. But Ra has shown his face.
We know him. We know that he brings light to every
realm within and without, above and below. There are
no shadows in Ra – his temple is open to the sky.' She
had always hated the darkness of the Temple of Amun,
having been used to her father's temple to the Aten,
very similar to the temples of Ra. Every god who had
something to do with the sun – Ra-Harakhte for
instance – Horus in his solar aspect – was given special
attention by the royal couple, and at Ipet-Esut, the

heart of the cult of Amun, his union with Ra was stressed to such an extent that he seemed subsidiary to Ra, where Horemheb had meant Ra to appear the lesser aspect of the dual god.

Ra-mes, the High Priest of Yunu, recommended a young priest of Ra as her personal scribe, and she kept the man, Ra-hotep, at her side most of her waking moments. She seemed to have taken it as a personal mission to strengthen the influence of Ra in all his aspects and weaken the position of the priests of Amun.

Tutankhamun could see that she was trying to restore a balance but was still uncertain of his own role. On one hand he chafed at the power of Horemheb and the priests of Amun to influence events in the Two Lands – himself meekly using his seal at their suggestion. On the other hand it was clear Horemheb and his priests knew how to make things run smoothly and comfortably. If he went against them it was extraordinary how many difficulties arose and how much precious time was wasted. As King no one could be seen to oppose him – but there were an infinite number of ways delays could happen, apparently innocent mistakes could be made and disasters occur. In the end it was always easier to go with Horemheb's ideas than try to impose his own. Perhaps if he had felt strongly enough about the theology of the two gods he would have known what to do – but basically he was indifferent to the subtle differences between the cults and could see no reason, other than the wielding of political power, as to why he should take sides in the matter. He sometimes felt Ankhesenamun exaggerated the dangers of the Amun faction, and accused her of inheriting her father's obsessive nature.

Sometimes – torn between his wife's insistence that he go one way and Horemheb's that he go another – he would storm out of the palace and go riding off into the desert alone, his hunting bow strapped to his back. Usually Ankhesenamun would send some trusted guards after him to make sure he was not in danger – but one day – particularly annoyed herself – it was she who left the room first in anger.

The controversy had arisen because Tutankhamun had insisted that the Temple of the Aten at Ipet-Esut, destroyed at the beginning of his reign, should be restored alongside the temples of the other gods. Horemheb himself had supervised the inscription on a large stela erected at Ipet-Esut.

> *When His Majesty arose as King, the temples of the gods and goddesses, beginning from Suan down to the marshes of the Delta had fallen into decay, their shrines had fallen into desolation and become ruins overgrown with weeds, their chapels as though they had never been and their halls serving as footpaths. The gods turned their backs on the land . . . But after many days My Majesty arose upon the seat of his father and ruled over the territories of Horus, the Black Land and the Red Land under his supervision.*

It continued to assert that this king, Tutankhamun, had made it his duty and pleasure to restore these ruined temples and turn the faces of the gods and goddesses back to Egypt.

But Horemheb vigorously resisted the idea of the restoration of the Temple of the Aten.

'Akhenaten did not invent the Aten, General,' Tutankhamun reminded him. 'Like Amun and Djehuti and Ptah and all the others he has been a divinity since the Beginning. If we are to restore the traditional gods, he too must have his place.'

'I would agree Majesty, and in time he will take up his place again. But it is too soon. Too many people remember the excesses of the Heretic. Some might react for the god and others against. We will have riots and disorder. We cannot risk it.'

'Unless you restore the Temple of the Aten and reinstate him in full dignity – you have not restored the ancient balance you talk so much about,' Ankhesenamun said.

Zais, who had hitherto kept in the background, moved forward now and spoke in a voice of undisguised contempt.

'I see this idea is not Pharaoh's – but comes from the house of his women!'

At this point Ankhesenamun, white with rage, had walked out. Not only was it insulting to suggest that Tutankhamun did not have ideas of his own, but Zais had equated her, the Great Royal Wife, the descendant of a dynasty of kings, with the other, lesser wives . . .

Once in her chamber she paced about anxiously, wondering if Tutankhamun was indeed strong enough to stand alone against the strength and cunning of Horemheb and Zais.

'You dare to speak thus to your Pharaoh and insult our Great Royal Wife?' Tutankhamun said haughtily. 'Take care, priest. Men as powerful as you have found themselves in the fields again – or in the mines – or exiled in some alien land!'

Horemheb's eyes narrowed and he studied Tutankhamun's face. There was no doubt that he meant what he said and he was no longer afraid. Horemheb could feel the tide was turning and if he were not very, very careful he would lose all the power he had.

Meanwhile Tutankhamun was thinking: 'These two must go. Ankhesenamun is right. I'll never be Pharaoh in anything but name as long as they have the power they have.'

'Think well, General Horemheb,' he said aloud. 'Consider your position. If I want the Temple of the Aten to be restored – the Temple of the Aten will be restored – and no one – neither you, nor Zais, nor Ay, nor anyone can stop me. You have been my adviser for a long time and there are many measures that you have instituted and carried out for which I am most grateful and for which Khemet will always remember your name. I have always respected and honoured you. But lately it seems you have tried to overreach yourself. Consider your position, General. You are not – nor ever will be – Pharaoh.'

Horemheb's face was like a mask. No sign of the dangerous rage that was seething in his heart showed on it.

He bowed to the ground as though he had taken note of the King's words and was contrite.

Tutankhamun was elated at his apparent victory over the man who had been more awe-inspiring than any god to him since his birth. But with that feeling came a kind of terror. He was now exposed and alone. *He* had to make the difficult decisions. He had to impose *his* will on this vast country. He both wanted that power and feared it. Ankhesenamun insisted that he was ready for it – but he was not so sure.

Already he was beginning to regret the anger that had sparked between them and to remember all the things Horemheb had done for the country. Ankhesenamun had often pointed out that to be sensitive to all sides of a case was admirable – 'but not if it makes you incapable of making a decision. A pharaoh must be strong, decisive, unquestioning of himself.'

'I will go hunting,' Tutankhamun thought. Strangely, in hunting he never had hesitations or doubts. At first, after that terrible experience with the Hittite princes, he had sworn he would never go near a lion again. But Horemheb had insisted he go hunting and had taught him so much skill that this was now something he knew he could do and knew that he could do well. Even now his memories of Horemheb's strength and courage on the hunt, and the patience and kindliness with which he had helped the boy-King overcome his fears, came back to him, and he regretted what he had said to him. He owed him a lot. But if he felt like affecting a reconciliation it was too late. With icy politeness Horemheb was already withdrawing from the audience chamber – and others were entering.

'No more today!' Tutankhamun cried out to his officials. 'I am going hunting. Alone,' he added firmly. There was only one way he knew to clear his mind of all the webs that seemed to cling to it – a wild, fierce ride over the desert – with no one but himself to consider. There were few lions so near to civilisation these days, but if one came his way – he would deal with it. But if it did not – he would still return to the palace with a kill. He would have conquered something fiercer and more destructive than a lion in his own soul.

Horemheb on the terrace of the palace watched him go.

Ankhesenamun spent the afternoon closeted in her private chambers poring over some ancient texts regarding the sun god Ra and the Aten, brought to her by her secretary Ra-hotep, hoping to find some conclusive argument for the reinstatement of her father's god. It had turned into an interesting quest in which she found many things she had not thought she was seeking. She regretted so many things now about her life at Akhetaten. She had been a child when great things were happening and had only been half aware of their significance. She had been irritated by her father more often than she liked to remember and had hated the brief time she had been his wife. But now, looking back, she realized what opportunities she had missed. Why had she not listened when he tried to explain his passion for the Aten over all other gods? The words had washed over her when he distinguished between the sun's disc, the visible cipher, and the invisible energy of absolute consciousness it represented. She heard the sounds of his words, but not the meaning. Her thoughts had been on other things. Now she struggled with the ambiguous and enigmatic texts – garbled versions of potent myths – and could hardly make sense of them.

'You should not try so hard,' Ra-hotep told her. 'As soon as you analyse sacred myth into its separate parts and look at each part – the meaning escapes. It should be glimpsed like a bird in flight. It should lead the eye upwards. The myth itself is not what matters. It is where it leads you.'

So engrossed was she in following the bird of myth, it was evening before she realized it and the servants had come to light the lamps. Suddenly Meryt-mut rushed in to bring the news that the King had ridden off into the desert earlier in the day and had not yet returned.

'What? Alone?' Ankhesenamun asked in some alarm.

'Yes, Majesty. I heard the Lord Nakhtmin asking for him and when no one could find him I thought you ought to know.'

'When was he last seen?'

'The groom said . . .'

'Why did the groom not stop him going alone?'

'He says the King often goes riding alone.'

'Never! I always send someone with him, riding out of sight. He only thinks he is alone!'

'The groom is new to the stables and did not know that.'

Ankhesenamun gave an exclamation of disgust.

She hurried from the room and ran down the corridors to question the groom herself. She found the stables in a state of confusion. People were in groups talking and arguing. Nakhtmin was shouting at a young man cringing against a wall. The horses were stamping and snorting as though they sensed something was wrong.

Ankhesenamun swept in and demanded silence. Instantly everyone fell to the ground. She felt the fear coming from them like an almost tangible wave of hot air.

Nakhtmin at once told her what he had already managed to glean, and she knew at once how it had happened. She chided herself for leaving Tutankhamun and Horemheb alone together when so much ill feeling was manifesting between them. Of course Tutankhamun would have ridden off in frustration and anger! Of course she should have been there to protect him!

She told Nakhtmin where Tutankhamun usually rode when he was in such a state and he mounted up at once, with several guards at his side. The sun had already set and the shadows of the western mountains were lying heavy on the land. Ankhesenamun demanded a horse for herself – but was dissuaded by Nakhtmin.

'You must be here if . . . when he returns,' he said. 'Trust me. I'll bring him back to you.' They had been friends since childhood and although Nakhtmin now spent a great deal of time away from court because of his official duties, the friendship still held. Ankhesenamun was thankful he was here now. If anyone could save Tutankhamun from whatever had befallen him – he could.

Why did she feel so anxious? Tutankhamun was an able rider, and he had often stayed out later than he

should. But never alone. The desert at night was no
place to be. She shivered. The heat of the day had
passed already, and Set's icy breath was blowing over
her shoulders. Meryt-mut, who had followed her, slipped a wrap around her.

'Majesty,' she whispered. 'There is nothing you can
do here. The King will come soon. Let us wait for him
on the terrace.'

From the terrace nearly all the approaches to the
palace could be seen. It was a good idea and the Queen
allowed herself to be led away from the stables.

But her heart was like a stone weight. She knew
something bad had happened to her husband. She knew
it! It was as though something important had gone out
of the world. She could feel it!

Horemheb joined her on the terrace but she would
not look at him. She would not reply when he spoke to
her. He ordered some of his own soldiers to set off in
search of the King. He ordered the peasants who
worked the fields around the palace grounds and men
from neighbouring villages to be rounded up and questioned. With great efficiency he organized everything
that could be done to find the King. But his face was
cold and hard. He showed no anxiety – no concern.

The first stars came out. The blue of the sky turned
deeper – deeper. No lapis lazuli from the mountains of
the east could compete with it. Lamps were glowing in
the palace; cooking fires in the mud houses of the people. And then – at last – the glow of the moon began to
suffuse the sky. Djehuti, the god of wisdom, in his silver
boat, drifted out from the harbour of the Otherworld,
and set sail across the darkness.

They brought Tutankhamun back at midnight. He was
dead.

10
THE LETTER

Over the next few days the Queen was not seen. She retired to her chambers and shut the doors. No one entered but her faithful woman servant Meryt-mut. In the distance she could hear the women of Tutankh-amun's House of Women wailing. They would set off in groups and wander the corridors of the palace, bare breasted, tearing their hair, sobbing and shrieking. It was expected. Some had loved him. Some had not. But whatever their feelings their futures were now uncertain. Those who had been brought to the Egyptian court virtually as hostages for their fathers' good behaviour, hoped the death of the King would bring about their release and their return to their own countries. Kia, his mother, mourned louder than anyone, genuine sorrow sounding through the well-worn words of the mourning ritual. It was shocking to everyone that Ankhesenamun, the Great Royal Wife, did not join in. Her sorrow was deep and private and she stayed in her chambers, ignoring tradition.

The seventy-day embalming process was begun. High officials from every corner of the empire began to return to Waset to be present at the funeral. Pharaoh's own tomb was not ready for the burial and Horemheb ordered that the small tomb prepared for Ay should be used instead.

The seventy days of preparation for the funeral created a useful hiatus in the business of the Two Lands. Everything apparently stopped. Everything apparently froze as it was – except the funeral preparations.

Everyone waited. An unprecedented situation had arisen. Pharaoh had no sons – not even by lesser wives than Ankhesenamun. He had not named an heir because he had not expected to die so young. The royal line from his father had ended – apart from his sister-widow Queen Ankhesenamun. Her three younger sisters had disappeared at the time of their mother's death and were assumed dead. Whoever was to be king after Tutankhamun would have to legitimize his position by marrying Ankhesenamun. Anyone's guess was as good as anyone else's, and speculation and rumours kept the people busy throughout the long slow days of mourning.

No one doubted that it would be Horemheb's decision in the long run – though there would be a show of consulting Ay and the other senior governors of the kingdom. There would be a council meeting when all were gathered and many a nobleman began to prepare himself, looking into his family lineage and bringing to the notice of anyone who would listen any connection he might have with the royal blood-line.

Zais, High Priest of Amun, became even more important than he already was. Horemheb let it be known that the god Amun-Ra would choose the next Pharaoh and that the pronouncement would be made in the Temple of Amun-Ra soon. This was acceptable to the people. Traditionally, even if the king died with an heir or a co-regent in place, the High Priest of the King of the Gods would make the formal declaration of his accession.

Horemheb knew the matter was urgent. Already he could see rival factions gathering and jockeying for position. He wanted to take the double crown himself and had no doubt he deserved it, being the most powerful man in the country, but – there was murmuring as there had been at the death of Akhenaten, that he had brought about the King's death. Rumours were spreading that lately he and the King had had many serious arguments. Some wondered why he had not already taken the throne long ago – when Akhenaten suddenly and mysteriously died – when Nefertiti and the king's half-brother Djehuti-kheper-Ra were killed leaving only an infant to inherit the throne. He had not even made himself co-regent. Why? Some wanted him. Others did not. One of his greatest skills was judging the mood of the people. Tutankhamun and Ankhesenamun were much loved. If there was any question that he had brought about the young King's death in order to take the throne himself, a commoner, there would be no peace in the land. There would always be the chance of disaffection and rebellion. He did not carry the god's blood, the royal blood, for all he was worthy to be Pharaoh a hundred times more than those who inherited the position legitimately.

Within a very short while he had made his decision, but it needed formal ratification by the council. Ay was very old and would not last long. If he were made Pharaoh, Horemheb would appear totally disinterested and innocent of any plot to take the throne – yet in a short while the prize would certainly be his.

Ay was not a descendant of the great Neb-Maat-Ra, Amenhotep III, the last Pharaoh Horemheb considered to be without blemish, but he was the brother of his Great Royal Wife, the powerful and influential Queen Tiye. He was also the father of Queen Nefertiti and therefore the grandfather of the present Queen Ankhesenamun. His credentials were good.

Meryt-mut brought the news to Ankhesenamun with a white face.

'Ay is to be Pharaoh, Majesty,' she cried. 'And you are to be his Great Royal Wife.'

Ankhesenamun looked shocked. She had been bracing herself to consider suicide rather than giving Horemheb the satisfaction of claiming Tutankhamun's throne through her. How extraordinary that he should not take this golden opportunity for ultimate power! And then she saw through his game and another strategy presented itself to her.

She told Meryt-mut to bring her damp clay writing-tablets and pens immediately. That done – she was to ask Ra-hotep, her secretary, to come to her chamber – secretly and in haste.

Ra-hotep travelled north, the current carrying him swiftly to the delta and the town where he could get a ship to Kepel, the great market port of the East, the sprawling cosmopolitan city to which merchants from all over the world came, citizens of Egypt and Egypt's vassal states mingling in its streets with merchants, travellers, officials and messengers from Mitanni and Hatti and Babylonia. It was here the hardy adventurers who ventured into the dangerous mountains of the Hindu Kush in Afghanistan came to barter the precious blue stone, the magnificent and rare lapis lazuli Egyptian kings prized so highly for their most sacred artefacts. It was here the gold from Nubia was bartered for horses and the men who could train them. It was from here most of the tribute and gifts, the oil that kept the diplomatic channels open between the many and varied countries, were exchanged.

It was here Ankhesenamun's younger sister, Neferne-fruaten, was priestess of the Temple of Hathor. Her name had been changed to Her-ya and no one knew of her connection with the Egyptian royal family but the

High Priestess herself, a very old and venerable woman who kept her counsel. Her-ya herself was happy where she was. As priestess of the goddess of love, she had many lovers and lived in a pleasant atmosphere of music and flowers. The news she heard from Egypt did not encourage her to return. She had really only known Akhetaten as home as a child and if Akhetaten was gone and the gardens in which she had played so happily had returned to dust and desert, her sisters dead or scattered, there was nothing to draw her back. Sometimes she thought about it – but soon dismissed the thought. It was a long time since she had heard from Ankhesenamun, the last time the Queen communicated it was to suggest she returned to Egypt – but warned her that if she did not want to, their communications must cease. 'Horemheb will find you and force you to return,' she said. 'He has spies everywhere.'

Year after year passed. She knew she could return if she wanted to and that very fact somehow removed the urgency. Lately she had fallen in love with a man – a Hittite – one with whom she had originally made love as part of her duty to Hathor, but with whom she now had a personal relationship. The Hittites had long been enemies of her people. She did not care. Lupakkis was a general in the army, distantly related to the Hittite royal family, and full of aggression on their behalf. It was not so much that she loved him as a companion, but that he drove her wild with desire whenever she saw him, and desperate with frustration when she did not. Under his influence she was more determined than ever not to return to Egypt.

Lupakkis had come to her first with nothing more in his mind than to explore a possible source of information. No one but high officials, priests and royalty were allowed into the chambers of the priestesses of the goddess Hathor. The priestesses were not common whores but vessels of the goddess and those who came to her must have weighty problems to put to the goddess, serious prayers that needed answering. The ritual of supplication was long and daunting and only at the very end the priestess accepted on behalf of the goddess the gift of the supplicant's seed. The priestess was sworn to discretion and nothing contained in the prayers and supplications should ever be passed on. But Lupakkis reckoned the priestesses were only human and a clever man might well be able to extract information about enemy countries without their even knowing it was happening.

By chance the priestess on duty the day he came first to the Temple of Hathor was Her-ya. He did not know she was an Egyptian princess, only that she was Egyptian. He delivered his petition and made his supplication, she all the while standing before the statue of Hathor like a statue herself, holding up a mirror to his face that he might see into his own heart while he spoke. In the shadows around the hall other priestesses danced and sang, rattling the sistrum, the sacred musical instrument of the goddess. The music was low at first, barely noticeable in the background, but as the ritual progressed, the music became more insistent, the women moved closer until he was surrounded, the heady scent of flowers and incense making him dizzy. He was led away to another chamber, the walls full of erotic pictures of Hathor and her lovers. Her-ya was lying on a couch watching him closely as he was led forward. He would have been prepared to lie with any old crone to get the information he wanted, but the goddess had been kind and the woman who lay before him was young and extraordinarily beautiful.

But he had not expected an audience. He hoped the

others would depart. If there were witnesses the girl would certainly not speak of things that were forbidden.

Carefully the handmaidens of the goddess removed his clothes, his heavy, studded belt and arm bands, his sword, his necklace, his sandals until he was as naked as the woman on the couch. He felt strange, half drugged by the thick smoke of incense that filled the room and the somnolent chanting of the singers. He felt roused and yet uncomfortable. He was a man used to being in charge – yet here he was like a lamb being led to the slaughter in an environment that was exclusively and potently female. Females were guiding him; controlling him; using him. He wanted to draw back but he could not. Inspite of his anger that his sexuality was being blatantly manipulated and was now out of his control, his desire to enter that place open for him was too strong.

Time and again the women drew him back and prepared him once again to enter. Exhausted and confused as he was he could have sworn there was an element of mockery and amused superiority in their eyes, and with this conviction his anger grew. He was not a religious man and although Hathor was very like the Hittite goddess of fertility, even to the mirror and the music, he had no illusion that he was performing any religious duty. As his anger increased, his passion increased, and he had the satisfaction of knowing that he had wiped the resigned expression from the face of Hathor's substitute and that she was abandoned to an ecstasy that she had not expected and would not easily forget.

At last in dead silence he was allowed to rise.

Silently the women bathed them both and dressed them both. He was guided out as he was guided in, but he knew he had made more than sexual contact with the priestess and would, if he was careful and clever, be able to see her again outside the temple precincts – though this was, of course, expressly forbidden.

Ra-hotep had been bundled out of the palace at midnight with scarcely time to gather what he needed for a long journey.

He had in his possession two clay tablets sealed in clay envelopes – not with the royal seal of Egypt but with a strange design he had never seen before. One was addressed to the priestess Her-ya at the Temple of Hathor at Kepel and the other was completely blank. He had been instructed to wait until Her-ya had read the one addressed to her and then, if she gave him a particular sign, he was to deliver the second to her. He was not to leave until he had a reply to the second letter no matter how long it took to arrive.

He had no idea what was on the tablets for Ankhesenamun herself had written them and sealed them before he came to her call that night, but he was charged that they were of the utmost urgency and importance and that no Egyptian spy must see to whom he was delivering them. 'If they are intercepted, I am dead,' she said. He could see that she was extremely agitated and did not doubt that what she said was true. He longed to ask questions, but his loyalty to her was absolute.

When he arrived at Kepel he did not go straight to the Temple of Hathor but to the small Temple of Ra on the outskirts. If there was someone following him he hoped their suspicions would now be allayed. He was a priest of Ra visiting his appropriate temple in a foreign land. He was given a sleeping cell without question and he arranged his few possessions about it as a normal traveller would. The letters he kept in a pouch close to his body under his robes.

Ankhesenamun had told him about a woman in the town whose practice it was to deliver secret letters to the priestesses. They were no doubt usually from lovers. He was to enlist her help but insist that he had to deliver this particular letter in person. He would offer her more gold than she was accustomed to receiving and impress on her how important it was for the meeting to be clandestine. He was to imply that his master was of very high rank and did not want his name known. She could not be trusted to know that the letter came from the Queen of Egypt – but she could be trusted to do almost anything for gold.

Ra-hotep was not enjoying this mission. He felt the treasure he carried on his person was a burden, and feared robbers. He hated deceit. But the Queen whom he loved and honoured had said her life depended on this and for her he would go against his nature and do what he had to do. He knew the question of the succession was in the balance and guessed that Ankhesenamun's letters had something to do with her safety if somehow there was a struggle for the throne. He assumed that she was preparing a hiding place for herself at the Temple of Hathor in Kepel outside Egypt.

He found the woman, Ba-nakht, easily. Everyone seemed to know her and several seemed to know her trade, for they gave him a nudge and a wink when they told him how to find her.

She was one of those elderly females who like to pretend they are young and by applying too much make-up do nothing but emphasize their age. Under the heavy paint she looked grotesque. Her withered arms were overloaded with bracelets, her sagging breasts with necklaces. Another, older woman, was seated cross-legged on the floor at the door, and Ra-hotep had to answer her questions before he was allowed to enter.

She had no cosmetics on her face. It was lined with wrinkles and her hair was grey – but she had more beauty and dignity than her mistress. Her eyes sparkled with amusement to see how nervous and gauche he was, and she gave him a reassuring smile as she sent him on his way.

Ba-nakht wanted to arrange for the letters to be delivered by one of her servants, but Ra-hotep insisted that they had to be delivered into the hands of Her-ya by himself. It took more gold than he expected to get his way, but at last it was agreed. He was told to wait at a particular corner late one night. One of Ba-nakht's servants was to wait with him to make sure he found the right priestess.

'And then she will go?' Ra-hotep asked anxiously. 'I have to be alone when I talk to Her-ya.'

Ba-nakht considered him with shrewd and narrowed eyes. What was this gauche young scribe up to? He appeared so inept and confused and yet he had surprising determination. She had done her wily best to find out who his master was, but Ra-hotep had managed to keep his identity well hidden.

Ankhesenamun's messenger and Ba-nakht's servant waited for a long time in the shadows of a doorway watching the moonlit street.

'She is expected at that house tonight,' the servant whispered. 'But it looks as though she might have changed her mind.'

Ra-hotep was almost deciding to give up, when someone appeared walking with a light and springy step, a fine haze of white muslin cloth wrapped around her against the night chill.

The servant pinched Ra-hotep's elbow and pointed to her.

The young priest rushed forward.

The woman stopped in some alarm and almost turned to run.

Ra-hotep called her name and she paused, half-turned towards him.

'I have a letter for you,' he whispered, his hand shaking as he held out the first clay envelope inscribed with her name.

She peered at it but could not read the seal in the dim light.

'It is very important,' he breathed. 'A life depends on your answer.' He could sense that she was scrutinizing his face, but he could not see her eyes. It was his face that was in the moonlight. 'I bring it from Khemet,' he added. At this she seemed more interested.

'I will read it,' she said.

'I – I need a reply right away.'

'How can I read it in the dark?'

'I beg you, my Lady . . .'

She was silent a moment, thinking.

'Wait here,' she said, 'if it is so important. I will bring you an answer before the sun rises.' She turned away from him and continued walking down the street. A door opened as though someone had been watching for her and she disappeared into the house.

Ra-hotep looked round to see if Ba-nakht's servant had kept her promise and left. The street was empty. He squatted down, leaning his back against a wall, preparing for a long wait. He was very nervous. The whole long journey from Khemet had been leading up to this. What if something went wrong? What if . . .?

Time passed as this thought went round and round. He wondered how Ankhesenamun would manage to travel to Kepel without being seen if she were on the run from dangerous enemies. He wondered why this young priestess of all the priestesses at the Temple had been

singled out for such an important message. He
wondered why she was visiting this house in the middle
of the night. He wondered what exactly was in the letter
he had already delivered and in the unnamed one he still
clutched in his hand.

At last she came out into the street again. He sprang
to his feet and went to her.

'My friend,' she said quietly. 'Tamarisk never grows
in water. How then do you expect me to plant the seeds
in the Great Green?'

His heart leapt. She had given the sign Ankhesenamun
had said she should.

He handed over the second envelope and it was taken
at once. Her cool hand touched his and she smiled.

'You are sweating my friend,' she said. 'Are you
afraid of me?'

'No – no, my Lady,' he said, embarrassed. 'It is just
that I am a simple priest of Ra. I am not used to delivering secret messages half way across the world.'

'You have done well, friend. Now go to bed and rest.'

'I have to take back a reply, my Lady.'

'I know,' she said. 'You will have a reply – but it may
take some time. Have you lodgings in this town?'

'At the Temple of Ra.'

'That is good. Go about your business there and wait.
I will see that you get your reply. Don't seek me out
again. I will find you.'

At this she began to walk away. He watched her go,
pacing quietly along the street as though clandestine
meetings and secret messages brought all the way from
Egypt were nothing remarkable.

But the letter she had read by lamplight in the house
where she met her lover Lupakkis *was* remarkable, and
as she walked away she was anything but calm. She had

been asked by her sister, the Queen of Egypt, to insure
that the second letter her messenger bore would be
given to a reliable and trustworthy messenger for
delivery to Suppiluliuma, the Hittite King. Did her
sister know she had a Hittite lover? Why would the
Queen of Khemet want to contact the Hittites, long the
enemies of her country – even now causing trouble
among Egypt's vassal states?

The letter she had read had been carefully worded –
not giving much away. She knew the message to the
Hittites must be of utmost importance – but why not
have it go through the usual diplomatic channels? She
had heard of Tutankhamun's death and had been
worried for her sister – but – why the secret message to
the Hittites? She would give anything to read the
second letter – but there was no way of opening it
without breaking it.

Lupakkis arrived at the gates of Hattusas, the Hittite
capital, dusty and exhausted. The city was above him
like an eagle in its eyrie. Impregnable cliffs reinforced
with walls and towers kept invaders out. The huge
bronze doors were only reached by steep ramps set
parallel to the walls and were heavily guarded by soldiers
and by the gods. He made for the smallest and most
southern gate, the one guarded by fearsome sphinxes.
Two staircases led up to this, but under it was a secret
passage, a tunnel that led deep into the heart of the
citadel. He was well known to the guards there – indeed
they were his own men – and he passed through with
little ceremony.

He had hardly rested since Her-ya had given him the
letter from the Egyptian Queen. That it had not come
through the usual diplomatic channels was intriguing
and significant. What secret message was she trying to

convey to the Hittite King behind the backs of her
officials? They were all aware that Egypt was in a very
vulnerable state at the moment, and Ankhesenamun's
position was more insecure than most. Why would she
write a personal letter to the enemy of her people?

He had told no one, not even his closest associates.
Kepel was a place where every nation met. There were
tin traders from Britain and Bohemia; lapis traders from
the Afghan mountains; purveyors of perfume and deli-
cate rhytons from the island of Crete; horse traders
from the steppes; bearers of incense from southern
Arabia and the Horn of Africa and gold and ivory
merchants from Nubia via Egypt. But most of all there
were the diplomats and spies, the messengers passing
letters back and forth between the different kingdoms
and factions – humble letters and boasting letters;
threatening letters and wheedling letters. That Lupakkis
had received an important letter and set off fast for his
home country raised no eyebrows. His servants prepared the luggage and the horses without question. His
friends wished him the protection of the storm god
Teshub. More women than Her-ya shed a tear at
parting from him – but he promised to be back. Her-ya
knew at least that he would not be long. There would
be a reply and he would have to bring it to her, and her
alone.

Ra-hotep waited in the Temple of Ra knowing
nothing of the distant destination of the blank envelope
he had delivered – daily expecting a reply.

Lupakkis demanded to be shown into the presence of
King Suppiluliuma at once, travel-stained and weary as
he was. He refused angrily when various officials and
dignitaries of the court offered to take the letter from
him and deliver it themselves, suggesting that he would

be insulting the King if he were admitted to his presence
in the dishevelled state he was in.

'The King will know why I have done this when he
reads the letter,' he said. 'Get out of my way.'

He strode through the familiar corridors and found
the old warrior relaxing on a couch, women tending
him.

His face was as angry as the storm god himself when
he looked up and saw that his privacy was not being
respected. The servants who had been running behind
Lupakkis, trying to get ahead of him to warn the King,
backed out nervously and flapped their hands
ineffectually, wondering if they would be punished. The
general was a powerful man and not easy to cross. They
hoped the letter he bore was indeed important enough
to turn aside the King's wrath. What could it be? Threat
of imminent attack? Mitanni's powerful wings had been
clipped by the Hittite King and they were ever restless
for revenge. There was always some war or other on the
go, the Hittite kingdom beset on all sides by foreign
powers, and Suppiluliuma constantly on the alert to
protect the trade routes that brought him the precious
tin which was essential for the making of bronze
weapons for his army.

'Majesty!' Lupakkis fell down at once on one knee
before the King. 'Forgive the intrusion, but I have a
letter I think you will want to see.'

'A letter? Can it not wait?'

'No, Majesty. This is no ordinary letter. Dismiss
these women. It is for your eyes alone.'

Suppiluliuma clapped his hands and the room
emptied as though by magic.

'Well, Lupakkis, I would not be ordered about by any
man the way I have allowed myself to be ordered now.
Your letter had better be special. What is it about?'

'I have no idea, Majesty.'

Suppiluliuma frowned.

'It is the way it was delivered, Majesty. I think you
will find it interesting. It was given to me secretly and
I was told it was from the Queen of Khemet – very
urgent.'

Suppiluliuma sat up and reached out his hand. He
took it and turned it over and over, curiously. Then he
summarily dismissed Lupakkis, and as the disappointed
general left the room, he saw the King break the seal and
the clay envelope and draw the contents out. The door
was then slammed shut triumphantly by one of the
humiliated officials, and he saw no more.

Suppiluliuma called a meeting of his sons. Amuwandas
was there, heir to the throne, and Mursilis, his second
eldest son. Telepinus, Hattusilis and Zannanza. Three
others also – for Suppiluliuma was rich in sons.

He held up the clay tablet he had received from
Lupakkis with its closely worked cuneiform writing.

'We have a puzzle here, my sons,' he said. 'I need
your advice.'

'What is it, father?' Amuwandas asked. It was
unusual for a council to be called with no trusted scribe
present, or high official.

'It is a letter from the Queen of Khemet,' Suppiluliuma said.

Zannanza, who had not been particularly interested
a moment before, thinking the meeting would be yet
another council of war, pricked up his ears. He
remembered Ankhesenamun and Tutankhamun well.
He had often thought the experience with the lion had
somehow linked them. On hearing of Tutankhamun's
early death he had shivered – as though the long shadow
of the boy-King's destiny touched his own soul

somehow. Would he too die young? He would not be surprised.

'What she asks is extraordinary,' his father was saying, 'and I cannot make up my mind if it is a genuine call for help or a cruel and devious trap to rob me of one of my sons and cause war between our two great countries.'

'What does she ask, my father?' It was Zannanza, usually so silent among his brothers, who spoke up first.

'She asks for one of my sons to be King of Khemet,' Suppiluliuma said, and sat back in his great chair, his shrewd eyes studying the reaction of his sons to his words, his thick and greying eyebrows hiding his amusement as their expressions ranged from disbelief, through hope, to naked ambition. To be King of Khemet would make whoever was chosen more powerful even than their father!

And then in his deep, authoritative voice, Suppiluliuma read out the letter.

'Queen Ankhesenamun, descendant of a line of mighty kings, Daughter of Ra – to Suppiluliuma, King of Hatti, noble Bull of the Mountains. Since my husband's death sorrow has been my sole companion, despair my bedfellow. Alas! Khemet has no royal sons to take the place of my beloved husband. I am told that I must marry an old man, a servant, and make him King. This I will not do.

King of Hatti, father of many sons, many noble and royal princes – send me a son, a prince, to be King of Khemet, to rule beside me on the throne of the Two Lands that my country and your country will be bound together in peace and prosperity.

To Suppiluliuma, King of Hatti, I will send gifts rich beyond belief, to ease the hurt of parting. To Suppiluliuma, King of Hatti, I send my greetings, my friendship, my vow that he whom you send will be honoured above all men.

If the private contents of this letter are spread abroad may the curse of all the gods of your land and my land fall on your head and the heads of your sons and on your city Hattusas forever.'

Then came the royal seal of Khemet. The seal of Tutankhamun – showing that she was still Queen and had it in her possession.

After the reading there was a stunned silence in the room.

What she was asking was incredible. At that very moment the army of the Hittite King was attacking allies of Egypt in Syria. They were traditional enemies – a dangerous game of aggression and counter aggression always in progress between them. That a proud and arrogant dynasty should invite a foreigner, an enemy, to be its king without being conquered . . . No wonder Ankhesenamun's message had come by such a devious and secret route. No wonder she did not want her diplomatic officials to see what she had written!

'It has to be a trick!' Mursilis said. 'Father, you cannot believe she is serious.'

Suppiluliuma looked thoughtful.

'Father!'

'Trick or no trick – it is a tempting proposal.'

He had always been a formidable warrior and was not slow to lead his people into battle to spread his empire, strengthen his borders, secure the trade routes that kept his country supplied with vital commodities – but he was also a shrewd politician. He had not attacked Babylon for instance, for Babylon was too strong. He had married the daughter of the King of Babylon and made her his Queen. Egypt was similarly too strong to attack – though he often harried her vassal states and

conquered more than one of them. But Egypt would
never send her daughters to be the wives of foreign
kings. It always had to be the other way around. Princesses from almost every country were sent to Khemet
to be kept as lesser wives by the Egyptian kings –
hostages to keep their fathers under control – or, in the
case of the more important ones, friends to keep their
fathers friendly. Now – if he could believe it – an opportunity he would never have dared dream about had
come his way. He longed to accept it.

But there was an uproar from his sons. Only Zannanza was silent.

'You are right,' Suppiluliuma said at last. 'It smells of
treachery. I will write back for proof that the invitation
is a genuine one. I will rush into nothing.'

'We must do more than write a letter, father,'
Mursilis insisted. 'We must send a spy to the court of
this Queen. He must look into her eyes. He must judge
for us what is the truth.'

'What spy could be entrusted with such a mission?
What spy of ours could get so close to royal Khemet?
We have tried for years to place such a spy and have lost
many good men that way.'

'Lupakkis could go in boldly with one message about
the war in Syria, offering peace terms, while delivering
another secret message to the Queen. Lupakkis is a
clever man and can be trusted. He is already partly
involved by bringing the letter to us.'

'And he has a mistress among the priestesses of
Hathor in Kepel,' added Amuwandas. 'He knows the
language of Khemet and their ways. It is clear the Queen
trusts him already or she would not have arranged for
him to be the bearer of her letter.'

'She may trust him – but is she the power in Khemet
now?' Mursilis warned. 'She may not even have written

the letter. It may be a trap by her generals to take a hostage to weaken our Syrian campaign.'

And so the debate went on.

In the end it was decided that a letter delivered into the hand of Queen Ankhesenamun herself would determine whether she had written the one they had received or not. Lupakkis, who was to deliver the letter, would keep his wits about him and determine whether she indeed had the power to impose a foreign king on Khemet or not, and if she had, how she proposed to do it. They all knew there was little time to waste – for once the mourning for Tutankhamun was over, the new king, whoever he was, must be in place or the country would be in turmoil.

Lupakkis was called into the council of princes and given the responsibility. He was reminded of the Queen's curse if he should reveal anything of what had passed between them to anyone at all.

'Even to your mistress!' he was told.

Rested and eager for the task he bowed to the ground, taking the vow of secrecy.

He left Hattusas that night with the King's reply to Ankhesenamun bound to his body, while another letter regarding the Syrian war resided in his pouch.

Never had the days and nights seemed so long to Ankhesenamun as she waited for the reply to her letter. It was more than a rumour now that she was to marry Ay and that the man who had stood at the right hand of three kings – four if you counted Nefertiti's brief reign – would be King himself. Horemheb was anxious for the wedding and the coronation to take place to avoid any chance of restlessness and instability in the country, but the Queen's insistence that the mourning period for her young husband must be respected and her

sorrow was so patently heartfelt, Horemheb granted her
at least this – though he would not retract his decision
that Ay should be the next Pharaoh.

Ay himself was somewhat bemused by the role that
was suddenly thrust upon him. He was a competent and
intelligent man and no one knew more about the intri-
cacies of kingship than he, but guiding and advising in
the background was much easier than standing out in
front.

He tried to talk to Ankhesenamun, but she shut
herself up in her chambers and would talk to no one.
Horemheb assured him that she accepted what was good
for the country, and that her withdrawal was not aimed
personally at him, but was due only to the shock of
Tutankhamun's sudden death.

'Your granddaughter has the royal blood of generations flowing in her veins. When the time comes she will
play her part as it should be played. Give her time to
mourn.'

Ay had no wish to be Pharaoh, but he could see that
with no royal prince of the direct line there could be
conflict among the nobles who claimed some distant
connection with the royal family. Already several
factions were manoeuvring for position.

Nakhtmin and Maya and all the friends and officials
who had served Tutankhamun well supported the idea
that he should be King. He was shrewd enough to know
that his age had something to do with their enthusiasm.
He was not expected to last long, but his reign would
give the Two Lands time to recover from the traumatic
events of the previous reigns. It would be uneventful –
for old men did not court violent change. He had always
been a bridge between extremes, working to modify the
erratic moods of one pharaoh after another. He had
been a sober and wise guide for Tutankhamun and on

more than one occasion had held Horemheb's ambitions in check. Whether he thought the General had anything to do with Tutankhamun's death or not, he never gave any overt indication – but Horemheb sensed a cooling in their relationship, a reticence, that had not been there before. It made him pause for a moment – but then he decided to ignore it. 'The old man is frightened,' he decided. 'This is not an easy step for him.'

Ay had no illusions. He knew that he was only a stopgap for the General and that sooner or later, with the inexorability of destiny, Horemheb would mount the throne and raise the double crown to his own head.

'I wish he would do it now,' Ay thought, 'and save me the trouble.'

He was sad his granddaughter was shutting him out. He wanted to reassure her that she would be his Great Royal Wife in no more than name. He wanted to tell her he knew his choice as Pharaoh was no more than an expedient move to save the peace of the Two Lands and that he would not be there to trouble her for long. He wanted to promise her her privacy. He wanted to promise her anything she desired. He wanted to assure her that only public appearances must be orchestrated for the people – her private life would be sacrosanct.

He paced the terrace outside his wing of the palace thinking back to the time of Akhenaten's reign when Ankhesenamun had been a little girl. He had watched her grow from a carefree infant, happy to play with her sisters, to a bitter adolescent, closed in her private and painful world of disillusion and despair as the shadows of obsession and violence reached the golden city. He had seen her open out again with her marriage to Tutankhamun. There was no doubt she loved the boy and mothered him with all the love the death of her own

children had denied her. Lately she had seemed pur-
posive and happy. They had all noticed her devotion to
Ra, though he had known nothing of the incident with
the Sacred Egg.

Horemheb had warned him that she must be weaned
away from that special relationship with the sun god.

'A healthy country must have a King of Gods as it must
have a King of Men. The balance of all the different
cults must be kept of course – but over all there must be
one authority and Amun-Ra must be that authority.
Why does she quibble? Ra is not denied. He lends his
strength to Amun. He is part of the King of the Gods!'

'Part is not enough for her,' Ay thought. 'As part was
not enough for her father.' She, who took so little notice
of the theological war that raged around her as a child,
had now taken sides. 'She probably supports Ra so
fervently just because we are trying to push him into the
background,' Ay thought. 'She is a natural rebel, and
will always fight to retain her right to believe what she
wants to believe – even if she does not know what that
is!'

Zais, the High Priest of Amun-Ra, prepared for his
role in the funeral, the wedding and the coronation. He
pronounced that the oracle of Amun-Ra had declared
Ay the successor to Tutankhamun – and with this
announcement the fears of most of the population were
allayed, and the hopes of the various nobles were
dashed. If the god proclaimed a man king, the man
became king. If Prince Djehuti-kheper-Ra were still
alive he would have told how these oracles were not to
be trusted, he having been an oracle himself, and
knowing the tricks the priests were party to to impose
their will upon the Two Lands. But Djehuti-kheper-Ra,
the half-brother of Akhenaten, was dead and there was
no one who dared speak up against the powerful priests

of Amun-Ra, backed as they were by the General who controlled the army.

One day Meryt-mut came to Ankhesenamun and asked if she would make an exception to her rule of isolation and admit her aunt Nezem-mut to her presence. Ankhesenamun refused as she had refused every other visitor. Meryt-mut was at her wit's end. She was very worried about her mistress, watching her sink day by day into a deeper and deeper depression.

The time had passed by several days that Ankhesenamun had estimated it would take to receive an answer from Hattusas. She had been outwardly calm at least up to now – but Meryt-mut could see a sudden change in her this day and feared it. In the morning she had flung an exquisite glass bottle of rare perfume against the wall, and insisted that her pet lion, given her as a cub by Maya to help her recover from the loss of her own child, and long since banned from the corridors of the palace because he had become unpredictable and violent, be brought to her.

When the keeper delivered him – nervously – she flung her arms around the creature's neck and wept so desperately that Meryt-mut was afraid for her. She insisted on being alone with the beast for some time and Meryt-mut, the keeper and guards with weapons at the ready, waited anxiously outside the door, listening to the faint sounds of a woman's crooning voice and the low growls of the animal.

At last she called the keeper and told him with a set, pale face, wet with tears, that the lion must be taken to the place where he was originally found and released.

'No one should be kept prisoner,' she said. 'Give him his freedom. Let him choose a wife. Let him have children.'

Meryt-mut watched Ankhesenamun's face as she watched him being led away. She was letting go more than the lion.

After this she sat in her chamber so listlessly, her hands loose in her lap, her chin sunk on her chest so low, that Meryt-mut had no difficulty in persuading her to admit Nezem-mut. The Queen seemed too tired and discouraged even to shake her head.

Nezem-mut was shocked to see how pale and drawn her niece's face was.

'Child!' she cried. 'What have you been doing? Have you been eating? You must look after yourself for the country's sake!'

She took the young woman by the arms and shook her. 'Listen to me. This must stop! Tutankhamun is dead and cannot be brought back. The time for mourning is almost over.'

At this Ankhesenamun looked up and her eyes were so full of anger her aunt recoiled.

'Child!'

'I am not a child, aunt,' Ankhesenamun said fiercely. 'I am not even a woman!'

'What do you mean?' Nezem-mut was shocked.

'I am a corridor of blood. I am an object passed about to make a man a king. Something that has no feelings, no will, no desires of its own. I am an artefact of kingship like the crook and flail, like the double crown and the throne. Kings need me to reign. No one needs me as woman.'

Nezem-mut had entered the chamber full of her own good news, eager to tell her niece. Her mouth fell open and she stared. How could she tell her now that the man she herself most desired in all the world had asked her to marry him! Horemheb had asked her, Nezem-mut, the plain sister of the beautiful Nefertiti, to marry him!

'Nonsense!' she said, but without conviction – knowing that Ankhesenamun was partially right. She had never been consulted about her wishes. She had been married to her father to give him an heir of the royal blood because Nefertiti had only daughters. She had been married to the child Tutankhamun to give his claim to the throne legitimacy. She was now to be married to Ay, an old man, her grandfather, for the same reason. Nezem-mut had never thought about it before – but Ankhesenamun had had no life of her own – ever.

'If you had your choice . . .?' she asked, hesitatingly, 'who would you choose to marry?'

'My choice!' Ankhesenamun said bitterly.

'Yes, your choice.'

Ankhesenamun stood up and walked to the cosmetic table and lifted up the silver mirror Tutankhamun had given her and gazed fiercely at her own reflection. Her face was distorted by the pain she was feeling and the tears that filled her eyes.

'I can never have my own choice. Why do you mock me?'

'But if you had?' persisted Nezem-mut.

Ankhesenamun turned and looked at her.

'It is too late,' she said.

'If Tutankhamun were alive – would you choose him?'

'He is dead.'

'But if he were alive and you had a free choice – would you choose him.'

'No.'

'Who then?'

Ankhesenamun shrugged. 'I am tired of futile games Nezem-mut. You came to tell me something. What is it?'

Nezem-mut's face brightened up. 'You see I used to be as despairing as you are. I loved someone and I thought there was no way I would ever, ever be asked to marry him. But now . . . now . . .'

'Horemheb has asked you to marry him?'

'Yes! How did you know?'

Ankhesenamun smiled bitterly. 'I expected it.'

'I never did! I had tried so many ways! Even that whole trouble with the Sacred Egg was because I hoped to win the favour of Horemheb – but now – without any enticement – he has asked me and I am to be his wife.'

'Ah, yes,' thought Ankhesenamun, 'and his queen.'

But she said aloud: 'I congratulate you Nezem-mut Mudnodjemne, and wish you well. It is good to hear of someone actually achieving their heart's desire.'

'You will too. I know it. Ay is old and although I love him as my father and would hate to part with him – he cannot live long. After him . . .'

'After him . . . who knows?' Ankhesenamun said. Her aunt could not see that she was to be Horemheb's wife only because she too was an artefact that could make a man a king. She was to be stored up in reserve in case she, Ankhesenamun, let the powerful General down and had to be disposed of as Akhenaten had been – as Nefertiti and now Tutankhamun. One of them would survive to be Horemheb's queen – but which one?

She thought about her attempt to frustrate his plan. If only it had worked. If only . . .

Meryt-mut was at the door again.

'You said, Majesty,' she was saying, 'if ever your secretary, Ra-hotep, were to . . .'

'Show him in!' almost shouted Ankhesenamun, her face transformed.

'Surely not her secretary!' thought Nezem-mut. 'Surely not!'

But the young man was shown in and Ankhesen-amun's obvious agitation could not be missed. Meryt-mut ushered Nezem-mut to the door at once, but not before she had seen the Queen take his hands in her own, her face brilliant with smiles.

Her-ya had tried to frustrate the Hittite plan to send Lupakkis as envoy and spy to the Egyptian court. She had drugged him and stolen his letters, giving the one she knew to be for her sister to Ra-hotep who was still unaware that the reply was from Hittite sources. The other she returned to Lupakkis.

When he recovered he was furious at what she had done.

'I don't know what business the Queen had writing to your King,' she said, 'and I do not question her wisdom. But I am not going to be party to a Hittite spy entering the royal court of Khemet.'

'How can we know if what your Queen said in her letter is true if I cannot see her face?'

'The Queen of Khemet does not lie. If she said something – it is true.'

'So you say – but you do not know her. What does a subject ever know of the rulers that rule over them?'

'And how would you – a foreigner and an enemy – know any more even if you stayed a lifetime at the court?'

'I can read a face and know if it can be trusted. A letter gives no message other than the words that are written.'

'Did you read the letter you delivered?'

'No.'

'Did you read your King's reply?'

'No.'

'How do you know therefore what to look for in the face?'

'I know.'

'Can you read my face?'

'Yes.'

'Read it then. *I* do not lie. My Queen is trustworthy. Whatever she said in the letter she sent, she meant.'

'You have no idea what you have done,' he said. 'You have destroyed me.'

'I asked for a reply to be given to *me* – to be sent by *me* to the Queen of Khemet. You betrayed me. You were not going to give the letter to me.'

'My King commanded otherwise.'

'Why should I trust your King if you do not trust my Queen?'

Lupakkis looked at her – annoyed. What was he to do? Go back to Suppiluliuma and say a woman had out-witted him? A woman had taken the letter and exposed him to a fearsome curse and an horrific punishment? Must he say 'sorry' and expect to be forgiven and trusted again with an important mission?

Her-ya was in despair. She had alienated the man she desired – but she knew she had been right to do what she had done. When he told her he was going to Men-nefer as ambassador bearing a letter from his King – she knew that there was something he was hiding. The letter she had received from her sister had left her in no doubt that this was a secret matter between Suppiluliuma and herself, and she would forfeit her life if anyone else at the court knew about it.

She could see that Lupakkis, by losing the secret letter bound to his body, was in danger of a swift execu-tion at the hands of his own people.

'Trust me,' she whispered. 'The letter will get to the Queen and there will be no problem. Your King need never know you did not actually deliver it yourself.'

The look Lupakkis gave her made her shiver.

'You can still go to Khemet if you have to – but only
if you use the usual diplomatic channels. If your mission
is honourable you will be treated with honour. The letter you say you have of general political importance can
be delivered by you. But *my* letter cannot. My letter
cannot be the reason for your going, and I cannot be the
channel through which you go.'

He was quiet for a long time.

At last he stood up – carefully – for he was still dizzy
from the drug she had given him.

'Goodbye Her-ya, priestess of Hathor,' he said
coldly.

He walked out without a backward glance. The words
he had said had a finality about them that frightened
her. But what should she have done? What *should* she
have done!

When Ankhesenamun read the reply from Suppiluliuma
delivered by Ra-hotep she lay down on her bed and
wept. Precious time had been wasted. If she sent a letter
back this very day it would still be almost impossible for
the prince to arrive in time for the coronation. Should
she reply? Should she go on struggling to get the better
of Horemheb? She was exhausted. Everything seemed
hopeless. She had made one dramatic bid to influence
the course of her life and it had been frustrated by the
Hittite King's caution. Whèn had he ever shown
caution before? He was well known for his sudden and
reckless moves. Why now should he choose to
prevaricate? Was she not offering him the fulfilment of
the greatest dream it was possible for him to have? Was
she not offering him a solution to the problem of the
continual and costly warfare over his borders? With two
such mighty empires joined together in amity who
would dare challenge any part of their joint territory?

When she had made the decision to send the letter she had not thought through the whole matter as carefully as she should. It had come to her as a flash of inspiration in her darkest and most desperate moment. Even now she would not be able to explain all her motives if her life depended on it. She had done what she had done partly because she genuinely believed it was a means to bring about a lasting peace between traditional rivals, and partly because she wanted to make a gesture of defiance – an angry reply to Horemheb's arrogant manipulation of her life. She knew that this solution to the succession problem would enrage him more than anything else in the world. Perhaps she also believed that if she brought someone strong in from outside Khemet, whom Horemheb did not know and could not control, she would at last be able to break his stranglehold on Egyptian affairs. She had not forgotten the strength of the Hittite princes she and Tutankhamun had entertained all those years before. She was sure they were men who could hold their ground against anyone. They would be kings in the old sense – in the sense her grandfather, the great Neb-maat-Ra, Amenhotep III, had been king. She remembered listening to him talking to her father when she was a child – telling him that power by marriage and negotiation was infinitely preferable to power by bow and spear. He had reigned long and well. He had fought wars when he thought they were necessary – but war had not been his only reaction to anything that happened. He was strong and just and held the reins of government firmly in his own hands. As she began to build up this idealized picture of him – she suddenly smiled. Even he was not totally in control of his own decisions. She remembered her grandmother, Queen Tiye, and the commonly held belief that Neb-maat-Ra would do anything for Queen Tiye and nothing without her approval. Well, if her Hittite prince was to be a king like Neb-maat-Ra, she would be a Queen like Tiye. She had heard that the Babylonian Queen of Suppiluliuma had great influence in the Hittite court – so they would be used to a reigning queen who was a partner and not simply a breeder of heirs.

She began to recover from her despair and think of how she could convince Suppiluliuma she meant what she said and had the power to implement it. Horemheb might have intimidated her young husband – and indeed herself – on many occasions – but it was she who carried the blood of Neb-maat-Ra into the future. If she was to survive, Horemheb and the priests of Amun must never know that her younger sisters were still alive. Horemheb and the priests of Amun were powerful, but not yet so powerful that the people would follow them against the divinity of the royal blood. She would have the oracle of Ra declare her choice of king was the will of Ra. She would involve the priests of Ra in her whole daring project and they would follow her because through her lay their only chance of retrieving their ancient dominance in the Two Lands.

Horemheb could kill her – but if he did he knew the chaos he dreaded might well return to the Two Lands – two giant cults splitting the country into rival factions. Privileged priests defending their privileges to the death.

Ankhesenamun wiped away her tears and with lips pressed tightly together settled down to compose her reply to Suppiluliuma.

She was told that the Hittites had sent an ambassador to negotiate a deal over the Syrian borderlands Suppiluliuma was attacking. Horemheb almost got away

Daughter of Ra

with handling the audience himself and was indeed in the process of dealing with it, when Ankhesenamun swept into the chamber in full royal regalia and took her seat on the throne. Horemheb fell back in surprise. The woman had changed. Her face was no longer sad and confused, but strong and determined. Haughtily she demanded to know what had been said, and coldly, efficiently gave a judgement.

'Tell your King,' she said, meeting the eyes of Lupakkis boldly. 'We understand his anxiety about the security of his frontier – but there are other, better ways to win security for one's country than by constant and wasteful bloodshed. Tell him to waste no more time. The matter can be settled to both our advantage round the council table. If you will attend me after this audience I will see that you have letters to take back to your King.'

Lupakkis noted that General Horemheb had fallen back at her entrance and that all her ministers and officials were silently hanging on her every word. 'She is in control,' he thought. And that is what he would report back to his King.

11
THE FUNERAL

The embalming period could not last forever and Ankhesenamun had to face the start of the funeral ceremonies for her young husband without having had a reply to her second message to the Hittites. There was not much she could do to delay things longer. The fact that Ay was to officiate at the funeral taking the role of priest and heir to the throne – the part usually reserved for the eldest son of the deceased king – confirmed his position without doubt as heir to the mighty double Kingdom of Khemet.

When the embalmers had finished their grizzly work of preparing the body to last forever, the tent inside the golden hall that had hidden the work from unsanctified eyes was rolled up and the King in his three golden 'skins' was laid on a golden boat-shaped bier under a canopy and carried down to the quayside. The people came from everywhere, crowding and pushing – eager to catch a glimpse of the magnificent procession.

Before he could be interred the King had to make his last visit to the great cult centres of the Two Lands, and for days the royal flotilla sailed down the Nile to the delta and up again, stopping for ceremonies all the way, to end its journey eventually at Waset where the necropolis workers were labouring all hours of the day and night to try and finish cutting and decorating the tomb that had been chosen for him. However, it was clear that the tomb even when completed would be much smaller than it ought to be.

When they reached Yunu, Ankhesenamun made a

point of seeing that the stop-over was longer than usual. She had secret meetings with Ra-mes, Chief of the Seers and High Priest of Ra, over and above the official and scheduled ceremonies, and a great deal was planned. When she and her foreign prince were crowned it would be Ra alone and not Amun-Ra who would perform the ritual and give their reign divine energy and power.

'Amun led our people to war and you and I are leading them to peace,' she said. She quoted from the well-known victory stela of her ancestor Men-kheper-Ra, Thutmosis III, to prove her point that Amun was a boastful god of war.

> 'I have come, that I may cause thee to trample down those who are in Asia; thou smitest the heads of the Asiatics of Retenu. I cause them to see thy majesty equipped with thy adornment, as thou takest the weapons of war in the chariot.'

Horemheb watched her obvious pleasure at being in the precincts of Ra with dissatisfaction.

'When you are King,' he said to Ay, 'the temples of Ra must be dismantled. There is no need for Ra to have separate establishments. He must be seen more and more as only one aspect of the King of the Gods, Amun-Ra.'

Ay said nothing. In the tomb prepared for him during Akhenaten's reign at Akhetaten, the greatest hymn to the sun god ever written was inscribed on the wall. He knew that as soon as he became Pharaoh another tomb would be started for him in the Valley of the Kings in the mountains west of Waset. Would he have the courage to mould the country the way he wanted, or would he give in even then to Horemheb as he had as Master of Chariots, as Fan-bearer on the right hand, even as Vizier? It was a pity this great power had come so late. He was old and not very well. He was tired. The years since the death of his brother-in-law, Neb-maat-Ra had not been easy. He pitied Ankhesenamun, caught as she had always been in the web of political expediency, but he pitied himself also. He had been dignified and politic and wise. He had tried to encourage some things, and prevent others – but inspite of him divine kings had met mysterious deaths, and commoners were dictating the policy of the Two Lands.

'When I am King . . .' thought Ay – but then he sighed. Why did they all fear Horemheb? There was something about him – an iron strength, a powerful conviction that he was right that persuaded you that you were wrong . . . He was a born leader. He claimed a distant relationship to the royal family when it suited him, and on more than one occasion he had used the epithet 'hereditary prince', together with his other already considerable titles – but Ay knew the connection was tenuous indeed. Was Tutankhamun dead because he had crossed him? Ay would not be surprised. If it was so he had every reason to fear him. He too could see what Ankhesenamun had seen. He was being installed as king purely to take suspicion of murder away from Horemheb, and when he had served his purpose he also would be disposed of. It was not so bad for him for he was old and had lived his life – but Ankhesenamun was still so young. Why had Horemheb married Nezemmut, when, if he had waited, he could have married the thrice widowed Ankhesenamun? Ay feared it meant Ankhesenamun too was expendable. Taking up the cause of Ra and opposing the priests of Amun must have sealed her death warrant as it had sealed Tutankhamun's. Ay was not a particularly religious man. He was content to go along with whatever kept the

peace in the land and could not really see why one had
to shed blood over obscure theological points. The differences between the gods were often blurred. But – if
it meant a balance of power – *that* he could understand.

Ankhesenamun spent a long time beside her
husband's triple golden coffin in the Temple of Ra at
Yunu. There were times when the mystical side of her
country's religion had not meant much to her, but she
had come passionately to believe in it this past year. The
Sacred Egg of Ra may have been physically destroyed,
but she still saw it in her mind's eye and in her dreams,
and it still affected her and influenced her life. As she
waited beside him through the full twelve hours of one
long night, it seemed to her the two of them were being
drawn to a mound of earth rising from a great ocean, on
the top of which rested the glowing green crystal Egg of
the first phoenix.

Tutankhamun was afraid and she was leading him by
the hand as a mother leads a child. First they sailed
over the ocean in a golden boat and she told him not
to look down into the water for in the depths lay the
potential forms of all that the gods could imagine –
good and evil – dark and light – horrifying and
beautiful – all as yet uncreated – unborn.

When the boat scraped against the side of the mound
she helped him out. He appeared to be as she had last
seen him – young and vigorous – not encased in funeral
masks and bound with hundreds of yards of linen. His
flesh was gold and his bones were silver.

They climbed the mound and reached the Egg. She
felt very strange – almost as though she were at once
drowning in liquid light, and burning in invisible
flames . . .

She knew it was not yet her time to go – though at
this moment she longed for nothing else. She drew

Tutankhamun forward and saw him disappear into the interior of the Egg, passing through the crystal shell as though it were mist. As she watched she could see him turning and turning as though he were in a whirlpool, a silver vortex. And then it seemed to her there were golden feathers forming in the depths of the Egg and somehow they were beginning to adhere to him. At last he rose on shimmering wings of gold and broke out of the Egg – transformed. She watched him with a breaking heart fly away into the unimaginable darkness that surrounded the luminous Egg. She lifted up her arms – calling and weeping. But he did not look back.

Ay found her on the ground beside the triple coffin of her husband in a deep trance-like sleep.

The royal progress through the Two Lands continued. Lining the great river the people were gathered to honour the passing of their King. Ahead of the procession was the small boat of Maya who was in charge of the funeral arrangements, and directly behind him came the huge royal barge with the canopied bier clearly visible on the deck. At the foot of it stood Ankhesenamun dressed as Isis watching over the body of her brother-husband Osiris. At the head stood Nezem-mut representing another important goddess in the Osirian myth, Nepthys. In death the King would take on the full identity of Osiris – the god of regeneration and resurrection. He would live again.

In acting out the great drama of an ancient and powerful myth, the human protagonists were giving vitality to the truth behind the myth both for their own comfort and the comfort of those who stood keening on the river banks, weeping and throwing dust over their dishevelled heads.

Finally the procession came to Waset and the King

rested for the last time in the palace that had been his favourite home.

That night the men who had not shaved since his death, shaved and prepared themselves for the climax of the funeral rites.

Before dawn the women of the court were in Ankhesenamun's little garden pavilion preparing the garlands and wreaths of flowers to adorn the King, and for the guests at the great banquet that would mark the end of all the fasting and the mourning. Olive leaves, willow leaves, blue lotus petals, cornflowers and wild celery were woven onto circles of papyrus pith. The berries of woody nightshade were threaded onto strips of palm leaf. Ankhesenamun herself cut the mandrake fruit, the fruit of love, to thread onto the great floral collarette that would be laid on the third coffin. The women twittered like a dawn chorus of birds. Ankhesenamun listened to them as she worked silently and thoughtfully on the garlands that were to be worn close to Tutankhamun himself, choosing all his favourite flowers and not only the ones that were charged with significance from the ancient texts. No one saw the private tears that dropped onto the petals as she worked.

At sunrise itself the King crossed the river from east to west for the last time. On the western bank his golden bier was mounted on a golden sled drawn by red oxen and taken towards the great funerary temple of his grandfather, Amenhotep III, passing between the gigantic effigies at the gate and into the vast courtyard beyond. His own funerary temple had been barely started when he so suddenly died, and though workmen had done their best it was still in such an unfinished state that Ay, Horemheb and Maya in consultation decided it was not suitable for use. In choosing his grandfather's temple which had been so brutally vandalized by Akhenaten, his father, and which Tutankhamun, under instruction from Horemheb, had so carefully restored, Horemheb believed an important point would be made. The King now being sent off to join the gods and his ancestors was in his last act on earth rejecting his father and accepting his grandfather. In fact, when Tutankhamun was very young, Horemheb had ordered an inscription in Nubia to be carved on a magnificent red granite lion naming his grandfather as his father.

Horemheb had not been able to exclude everything connected with the time of Akhenaten from the furnishings of the tomb – there was, for instance, Tutankhamun's early throne still bearing the symbolic rayed sun disc of the Aten, that Ankhesenamun insisted on including – but he was determined it would be Amun and the priests of Amun who would make the greatest impression on the population at this time and be remembered in years to come most vividly. No one had ever seen such numbers of priests so magnificently arrayed.

Zais, the High Priest of Amun-Ra, in full and spectacular regalia was waiting to lead them in, the chief mortuary priest of the temple standing down on this occasion to make way for him. Two columns of important mourners passed through the huge cedar doors heavy with bronze strips and gold and silver ornament. One column consisted of the highest officials in the Two Lands, men in white robes with white sandals, known as 'The Nine Friends of the King', led by an impressive figure in a long cape carrying a cane with a pommel in the shape of a figure of the deceased. He was named 'The Mouth of God' and was in charge of all the sacrifices to be performed at the funeral. From his

mouth would issue the commands that started and
ended each phase of the long, long ritual. The second
column consisted of women in white led by the widowed
Queen who was also dressed in simple mourning
garments with no adornments.

Priests walking just ahead of the oxen drawing the
bier poured libations of milk on the ground. This served
the practical purpose of easing the progress of the sled,
and the symbolic purpose of reminding the mourners of
Hathor, the goddess of love and fertility, often depicted
as a cow from whose udders the Pharaoh drew
nourishment.

Behind the bier and the nobles who walked beside it,
came the procession of people carrying the furniture and
the artefacts that had been used by Tutankhamun in his
life on earth and would accompany him into the Otherworld. Who knew but the King's *ka*, returning to earth
to attend to the prayers of his people, might want his
familiar things around him. Although the Otherworld
might not be visible while we are alive in this one, it is
probably all around us. A golden chair may appear to be
empty, but a being of another world may well be
occupying it.

Together with all these familiar objects from his past
were many new and costly gifts from friends and
relations. Maya had provided an exquisite little effigy of
Tutankhamun lying on a sacred bed. He was between
two birds – one human-headed to represent the soul, the
other a falcon to represent Horus – stressing that his
body and his soul were separate and under the protection of Horus. Nakhtmin had provided four beautiful
ushabti, tiny statues of the King, each wearing a different royal headdress to indicate that he would be
ready for any occasion in the Afterlife. Ay had provided
a little box containing a curl of his sister's beautiful

auburn hair. He knew that Queen Tiye had been very close to Tutankhamun when she was alive. Merytaten, though dead herself, played a part in her young half-brother's funeral. A writing palette of hers was laid between the paws of the statue of Anubis, the Guardian of the Dead. Ankhesenamun had been very fond of her sister Merytaten and had used her writing palette herself since her death. It was a sacrifice to give it up now, but she did so as a secret gesture of love for her husband that only she and he would understand – over and above the public and formal gestures she was expected to make.

The ceremonies in the mortuary temple, the Mansion of Millions of Years, lasted four days and culminated in the sacrifice of a bull.

Ankhesenamun took her part as though she were an animated doll. Her face was painted white apart from the heavy lines of black kohl that accentuated her eyes. She neither wept nor smiled but mouthed the ancient ritual texts designed to guide the King through the trials and dangers of the Otherworld until he stood before Osiris – justified – and ready for eternal life. She listened impassively as Zais and Ay as the chief officiating priests spoke their lines, burned their incense, poured their libations of oil and water over the golden coffins.

Horemheb stood aside most of the time and apparently played very little part. Only those of the inner circle at court knew that his will was driving it all, and his dark and piercing eyes were watching for any breach, any sign of deviation from what he had laid down should take place.

Ankhesenamun never forgot his presence. When she could not see him she still felt him there. Once when he came into view she was convinced 'he' as flesh and blood was not there at all, and in his place was a bodiless and menacing shadow.

No word from the Hittites came to her. She had arranged that at whatever time, no matter what was happening, Ra-hotep was to make contact with her if he had a message. But nothing happened. The days passed in a haze of ritual and incense. Ankhesenamun's hopes sank lower and lower.

She looked at Ay. He was not a bad man. She could see that the strains of the long funeral were beginning to tell on him, and his back was bent lower than she had ever seen it. It was not he she objected to – it was Horemheb waiting in the wings ready to take over the role he had been lusting after for as long as she could remember. It was Horemheb who had destroyed her family and with her death would try to wipe the last remnants of the memory of it off the face of the earth. If only – if only her virile Hittite prince would come she would have children to thwart his plans. She would recall her sisters and re-establish the dignity of her dynasty. Ah – where was Ra-hotep? Why did he not come!

At dawn on the fifth day the funeral procession left the Mansion of Millions of Years and set off on the long walk to the Valley of the Kings. The oxen were left behind and 'The Nine Friends of the King' and the viziers of north and south, drew the sled themselves. Columns of men carried long stalks of papyrus, and women carried the lotus – the two symbolic plants of the Two Lands.

Dancers and acrobats and singers dressed in costumes representing the ancient gods and the spirits of dead ancestors accompanied them.

When they arrived at the tomb, the King in his three heavily decorated golden coffins was propped up on a layer of fine white sand brought from the desert where the head of Osiris was supposed to have been found. It was regarded as particularly sacred. Most of the grave goods were carried inside. The workmen who had laboured so hard on the tomb waited at a respectful distance. Their task was not yet finished. When the King had been safely installed in his four golden shrines, and all the ceremonies were over, they would be required to build the last wall of mud-brick and plaster, sealing him up forever in that silent place.

One of the most important parts of the whole ritual then took place. Ay, in his newly acquired role of High Priest and heir to the throne, stepped forward. This moment had already been painted on the wall of the tomb indicating that, in a sense, outside Time, it had already taken place. He took the ceremonial adze with its tiny blade of meteoric iron and prepared for the 'opening of the mouth and the eyes'. During the embalming process the King was of necessity regarded as an object – albeit a royal and sacred one. Now he was to be restored to life. He would be able to see and to communicate with the Earthworld while residing in the Otherworld.

'I have arisen from the Egg which is in the secret land, my mouth has been given to me that I may speak with it in the presence of the Great God, Lord of the Netherworld; my hand shall not be thrust aside in the tribunal of all gods, for I am Osiris, Lord of Rosetjau.'

Ay intoned from the Book of the Great Awakening, and again:

'My mouth is opened by Ptah. Djehuti comes indeed, filled and equipped with magic, and the bonds of Set which restricted my mouth have been loosened.

My mouth is opened, my mouth is split open by Shu with that iron harpoon of his with which he split open the

*mouths of the gods. I am Sekhmet, and I sit beside Her who
is in the great wind of the sky; I am Orion the Great who
dwells with the Souls of Yunu.*

*As for any magic spell or any words which may be
uttered against me, the gods will rise up against it.'*

Ankhesenamun stepped forward on cue and placed
The Crown of Justification of olive leaves, blue lotus
and cornflowers on the golden mask. Kia, his mother,
came next with a great necklace of flowers, and Nezem-
mut followed with another garland.

Earthenware pots were flung against rock and shattered to indicate that the King was now ready to break
off from the Earthworld.

Then the signal was given by Maya that the last phase
had begun.

Chanting spells from the ancient Book of the Great
Awakening, the deceased King in his heavy and
unwieldy mummiform nest of coffins was lowered
carefully down the steep steps to the tomb itself.
Ankhesenamun suddenly cried out and almost fell as she
rushed forward to hold him once more in her arms. The
dust that she had flung over herself in the traditional
way as she walked on her white sandalled feet to the
Valley of the Kings, showered over the gold and turquoise, the lapis lazuli and carnelian.

'O Lord of Flame,' she whispered, 'who guards the
two eyes of the sky – who opens the two eyes of Nut –
bind me a ladder. Make me a way that I may follow the
love of my heart. I am weary of the Heh Gods, of the
Watery Abyss, of the Disappearing One, of the
Darkness!'

Ay held her back gently but firmly. It was the custom
that a wife should try to haul her husband back from the
grave, but Ankhesenamun was playing more than a
traditional role here. He could hear the pain in her

voice, see the suffering in her eyes. It was as though she had suddenly realized she was utterly alone – and she had no wish to go on living.

'You are not alone,' he whispered against her dusty and dishevelled hair. 'I will take care of you.' She pulled away from him and flung herself on the ground howling the names of her beloved – but only those that held him to the Aten or to Ra. Ay looked quickly at Horemheb and saw him meet the eyes of Zais. He saw her death in that meeting.

Zais moved forward and stepped over her prone figure as though she were nothing. The other priests hesitated to do so, and during that hesitation Ay pulled her to her feet.

Dazed, she looked into his eyes as though he were a stranger.

'For the sake of Neb-kheper-Ra make sure you are here to the end. He needs you!'

She set her lips in a tight line and straightened her shoulders. She walked ahead and joined the rest in the small and overcrowded tomb. She looked around her in dismay. This was not a tomb worthy of a royal king. There were but four small rooms and the officials were having to stack things in other things and on top of things in a desperate attempt to get them in at all. The four golden shrines that would contain the three golden coffins had had to be brought in in pieces and were now being assembled. People were pushing against each other to perform their separate duties. All dignity was lost. She leant against the wall and watched with horror as they discovered the outer golden coffin would not fit into the red sandstone sarcophagus, and workmen were called in to plane off the feet until it fitted. Then as the workmen tried to lever the huge granite lid, painted hastily to resemble the sacred red sandstone of the rest,

into place, they dropped it and it cracked with a sound
like thunder. The reverberations of the sound almost
deafened her.

'No,' she kept whispering. 'No, this must not
happen!'

More workmen forced their way into the confined
space and the two pieces of the lid were lifted and put
in place, someone plastering and painting the crack
hastily so that it did not show.

She read the words she had inscribed:

> *I am thy wife, O great one – do not leave me!*
> *Is it thy good pleasure, O my brother, that I should go*
> *far from thee?*
> *How can it be that I go away alone?*
> *I say: I accompany thee, O thou who didst like to*
> *converse with me, but thou remainest silent and*
> *speakest not!*

At the four corners of the sarcophagus four goddesses
stood with their arms outstretched to protect him.

'He will be all right,' she tried to tell herself. 'This
muddle . . . this . . .*farce* is not happening to *him*.' But
it was hard to concentrate on the deep and subtle meaning of all that was written in the tomb, all the symbolic
things that were laid out, in such an atmosphere.

'When we have all gone,' she told herself, 'then the
place of transformation will come into its own. Then the
inscriptions on the golden shrines will start to work
their magic!'

> *Thou art the Only One, who made all that is,*
> *The solitary Only One, who made what exists,*
> *from whose eyes mankind came forth,*
> *and upon whose mouth the gods came into being.*

Thou shalt be as a god, living like one of those no-ble spirits who are at the site of Horus of the Horizon in the Fields of the Blessed, Osiris, King Neb-kheper-Ra, Son of the Sun Tut-Ankh-Amun, ruler of the Two Lands, beloved of Osiris Unen-nefer.

The King, the Egg of Ra, Lord of the Two Lands Neb-kheper-Ra, image of Ra, will appear like Ra in heaven, every day, living forever and ever.

Words spoken by Isis – sister, wife, mother . . .

I have come to be thy protection, thou art my son, my beloved Horus. I have taken away the veil over thee, made by him who acted against thee. Mayest thou lift thy head to see Ra, to stand on thy feet, to walk about in the forms thou likest, to move as before. Thou hast power over the bread, thou hast power over the water, thou hast power over the wind, thou hast power over all things beautiful and clean, Osiris, Lord of the Two Lands, Neb-kheper-Ra. Thou seest with thy eyes, thou hearest with thy ears. Thy heart is thine, of thy real being, it is stable on its place forever and ever. It will not be ravished by the wicked who seize hearts, who ravish hearts in the place of burial. Thou art a justified one before Unen-nefer.

The golden shrines had been prepared without Horemheb's close attention and many things from the old days of the Aten were there, one of the shrines itself having been fashioned at the time of Akhenaten and left in a goldsmith's storehouse all this time – hastily brought out when there was not time to make another.

The Good God who came out of Ra, Noble Egg of

*Atum, who lives on Truth every day, King of Upper
and Lower Khemet, Lord of the Two Lands Neb-
kheper-Ra, chosen by Ra, bodily Son of the Sun,
beloved by him, Lord of Diadems Tut-Ankh-Amun,
ruler of the city of the sun, beloved by Osiris Unen-
nefer, this god, Lord of Ro-Setau.*

When all was finished and in place as best they could
manage under the circumstances, all things sealed with
clay and stamped with the seal of the official in charge
of the necropolis, the living left the tomb. The final wall
was completed and Ankhesenamun climbed the stairs
into the night.

A million million stars hung over the Great Place, the
Valley of the Dead.

Tents had been erected for the main protagonists in
the funeral to change into festive clothes, and long
tables laid for the funeral feast.

Ankhesenamun emerged in rich and elegant finery,
her face made up carefully so that it gave no hint of her
emotions. She took her place beside Ay because there
was no avoiding it. Horemheb was seated diagonally
opposite.

The dancers and singers, jugglers and acrobats now
came into their own. This was a feast of rejoicing. The
King was certainly regenerated and reborn in the Otherworld, the Duat. He was protected by all the spells and
prayers that had been chanted at his funeral ceremonies
and which were inscribed on his golden shrines and on
the many beautiful objects surrounding him. Bound in
the linen bandages around his body were more than a
hundred potent talismans, and jewelled necklaces,
bracelets and rings, not only priceless and unique, but
heavily charged with magic. Even the flowers that
adorned him would last in that dry tomb for a long,

long time, their sweet scent reminding him of the fields
of the earth realm until he no longer needed them
because he had the scent of the flowers of the Fields of
the Blessed. The dancers danced between the tables, the
singers sang. Jugglers and acrobats performed.
Everyone was talking, eating, laughing. The relief at the
ending of the long period of fasting and abstinence was
great and the heady wine that flowed so freely soon had
its effect. The guests who sat down so stiffly and politely
at the beginning of the feast now began to loll about and
talk too loudly, laughing overmuch at ribald jokes,
pinching the bottoms of passing serving girls.

Ankhesenamun who had drunk as much wine as the
others nevertheless stayed completely sober and looked
around her with distaste. How ugly people were when
they were drunk! She looked across at Horemheb. He,
like her, had not changed. With cold and calculating
eyes he was looking around the tables taking in
everything and everyone. In drunkenness people often
revealed aspects of themselves that were usually kept
well hidden. Ankhesenamun could see that he was
watching for these, and would use what he discovered
at a later date. She bit her lip, her heart filled with such
hatred for him it was all she could do not to pick up a
golden cup or one of the heavy stone lamps and throw
it at him there and then.

Swallowing hard and trying to bring herself under
control she looked up at the sky. A full moon was
directly above the peak of Meretseger, the pyramid
shaped peak that dominated the Valley of the Kings.
Meretseger, 'she who loves silence', must surely be
angered by the noisy celebrations in her valley. She was
a snake goddess. What if she sent an army of snakes
slithering down towards them? What if one killed
Horemheb? What if they were all killed – the whole

raucous, heedless lot were dropped into death in an instant? Present were all the powerful, influential, rich people of the Two Lands – Zais, with his smug and pudgy face, surrounded by all the most important priests of Amun – Ay, who was now nominally the King though the coronation ceremony had yet to take place – she, who was apparently the last of the royal line that stretched back to those brave and daring princes of Waset who had expelled the savage Hyksos from the country and seized the throne of Egypt back for the native Egyptians . . . What would happen if they were all killed? Would a new era dawn clean and free of all the old mistakes, the old intrigues, the old enmity? What minor official would take the opportunity to establish a new dynasty? Would her sisters come forward when they knew they had nothing to fear? What god would be the symbol of the new age? She was so caught up in her fantasy that she found herself jubilantly smiling to think that Horemheb's years and years of manipulation would come to nothing. He would *never* have the throne of Egypt. He would *never* have the privileges of a king in the Otherworld . . .

She looked up to the heavens in her excitement and was shocked to see a dark shadow crossing the face of the moon. At first she thought it must be a cloud but then realized the stars were shining undimmed. It was only the moon that was affected. And then the same cold hand that was gripping the moon seemed to grip her own heart. The thoughts she had been thinking had been dark. She had rejoiced at the destruction of everyone she knew. She had visualized a horrible death for them. What if it was the shadow of her own thoughts that was staining the purity and splendour of the moon?

No one else seemed to see the shadow and she

watched as it grew larger and larger, inexorably creeping
across the whole face of the moon. Her throat was con-
stricted – dry. She tried to take a sip of wine – but
almost choked on it. What if everything she had ever
known could be snuffed out? What if it were possible
for one's own thoughts to do this? What if one was
capable of destroying the universe with nothing more
than the intensity of one's thoughts? She knew that one
could make oneself ill and heal oneself by thought. She
knew also that by projecting malevolent thoughts on to
someone else one could make them ill, just as one could
lift their spirits and make them well by the intensity of
one's benevolent thoughts. Mind could affect mind –
there was no doubt about that, and magicians had
shown that in certain circumstances material objects
could be moved and altered by the mind. But –
something as huge and remote as the moon . . .? The
weight of such a responsibility almost crushed her.

At that moment she felt a touch on her arm, and
looked round, startled, into the face of Ra-hotep. He
was standing behind her trying to whisper something
into her ear. She could not hear what he was saying and
leaned towards him. And then her eyes were drawn to
Horemheb. He was watching her closely and there was
an expression of such malevolence and triumph on his
face she had the distinct impression that he knew what
Ra-hotep was trying to whisper and was waiting for her
anguish when she heard what it was.

She turned to the young priest of Ra and took him by
the shoulders and shook him. But he was trying to draw
back. He knew his message could not be shouted out
against the noise around. He indicated that she should
leave the table and follow him. This would draw attention. She hesitated. She looked across at Horemheb
again. With the eyes of a snake intent on its victim he

lifted his hand, pointing upwards. She looked at the moon. It was no longer a glowing silver disc – but a heavy bronze ball. Of course! These things happened and were predictable. He must have arranged the whole timing of the funeral so that this eerie and threatening event would take place just at this moment.

People were beginning to look up, following his pointing finger. The whole valley became silent – frightened – awed.

He was smiling significantly while indicating the moon. Her husband was not being gathered up into the stars – not joining the moon in its silver journey or the sun in its golden boat – he seemed to be saying. The crimes of Akhenaten's family were being acknowledged and condemned by the gods – and this was the sign to prove it.

12
THE ASSASSINATION

When Suppiluliuma received Ankhesenamun's second
letter insisting that she indeed wanted one of his sons
to be King of Egypt and giving her reasons for this
extraordinary and unprecedented step more convinc-
ingly, he called a meeting of the full council. Lupakkis
was present and was largely responsible for swaying
their initially hostile reaction towards acceptance.

He spoke enthusiastically of Ankhesenamun's personal charisma and strength, and described the state of
Egypt as bordering on chaos because there was no legiti-
mate and unchallengeable heir to the throne. Although
the venture had its risks, he suggested, for there would
inevitably be many against Ankhesenamun's solution –
General Horemheb for one – the stakes were high and
winning would give the Hittite nation immense
power.

'It is probable you will never find the Two Lands in
such a vulnerable position again. I urge your Majesty, do
not hesitate too long.'

Lupakkis had been highly impressed with the Egyptian court. It was luxurious and sophisticated in a way
he had never experienced before. The Hittites were a
strong nation and the palace in the citadel of Hattusas
was impressive, but the carvings and paintings and
furniture were crude compared to the Egyptian. He had
brought back presents for Suppiluliuma from
Ankhesenamun and presented them with pride. A bed
carved elaborately of cedar wood, inlaid with ivory and
ebony, with a comfortable base of tightly bound gazelle

thongs making it springy. All the raw materials for it had
been imported into Egypt but Egyptian craftsmen were
so admired, many countries imported back their goods
after they had been turned into beautiful objects by the
Egyptians. Lupakkis brought also jewellery and gold of
exquisite workmanship.

It was however the description of the vulnerability of
the Egyptian throne at this moment, rather than the
value of the bribe, that finally persuaded Suppiluliuma
to take a chance. Ankhesenamun had sent messages
through her contact in Kepel that convinced him she
knew what she was doing. She claimed to have the
whole priesthood of Ra working for her on this issue,
and explained that it would be they who would greet his
son on Egyptian soil – presenting his own messengers
with a charter, laying down the terms of the deal and the
safeguards for both sides. Once again she stressed the
urgency of the whole transaction.

The decision had to be made quickly and Suppiluliuma made it quickly – but not without a great deal
of argument from some members of his council. The
other great power in the Middle Eastern world at that
time was Mitanni. Tutankhamun had descended from a
Mitannian princess, Mutemwaya, who was the mother
of his grandfather, Amenhotep III. Why did Ankhesenamun not choose to write to the Mitannians for a
prince? It would seem more logical.

Suppiluliuma argued that Ankhesenamun wanted
peace with the Hittites who were harrying her vassal
states. Egypt had no fight with Mitanni at the moment.
'This is a shrewd diplomatic move on the woman's part,'
he said. 'I admire her for it.'

Lupakkis added his voice to his King's. It would be
to their advantage as well as to the advantage of Egypt
to be united in this way. He had seen Egyptian troops

and warned that they would not be easy to defeat in battle. 'It were better we had them on our side,' he said. Together – they could conquer the world!

The next question to be settled was which son was to go. The eldest, Amuwandas, was heir to the throne of Hatti and could not be spared. The second son, Mursilis, had to be held in reserve in case something happened to the first – a precaution that proved wise, for Amuwandas was killed soon after succeeding his father, and Mursilis became King after him and ruled for a long time. Hattusilis who had been to Egypt when Tutankhamun was new on the throne wanted to go, but he was a valuable general and Suppiluliuma was loath to part with him. Also he suspected that once Hattusilis got power he might well abuse it and Suppiluliuma would end up having to take second place to his own son.

Suppiluliuma looked round his sons and coldly calculated which one would be capable enough to hold a crown, and yet be pliable enough to do his father's bidding in all things. He also tried to estimate which one would be expendable if the gamble did not pay off – yet make a good enough King of Egypt if it did.

Zannanza stepped forward.

'My father,' he said. 'Let me go. I have been to Khemet and I know the Queen.'

There was an outcry from his brothers, most of whom wanted to be King of Egypt knowing that their position in the family made it impossible for them ever to be King of Hatti. Some would be positioned as kings of vassal states conquered by the Hittites – Telepinus, for instance, later became King of Aleppo – but none would have the status of an Egyptian king.

Suppiluliuma let them shout and argue for a while, sitting on the throne he himself had seized by force as

a young and ambitious prince and kept against all the
odds. He had many sons, some of whom he hardly
knew. Zannanza he had affection for though he knew
he would never make an efficient and ruthless warrior.
He was intelligent, quiet, but inwardly strong. He
would make a good king – tactful and honourable
enough to win the affection as well as the respect of
a people initially hostile to him – and not devious
enough to double-cross his father. Suppiluliuma made
his decision and silenced the hubbub in the room with
dire threats and curses against any one who questioned
his decision.

'There is no time for us to delay longer,' he added.
'Zannanza will start the journey tomorrow.'

Zannanza gasped. So soon? So suddenly the course of
one's life could change?

'Lupakkis will be in charge of the arrangements. The
party will travel incognito. Only the priests of Ra sent
by the Queen must know who he is until he is safely at
her side.'

So quickly did events move from that moment on that
there was no opportunity for any more jockeying for
position among the princes. Some were secretly relieved
the challenge had not been laid on them. There were
uncertainties and dangers ahead they would rather not
have to contend with. Some remembered the curse that
had once been laid on the capital city of Hattusas and
quoted it to each other as prophecy of dire consequences
attendant on this rash and foolhardy move. In the
ancient days before their own dynasty a conqueror had
destroyed the city of Hattusas and left an inscription for
future generations to read:

> *I took it by storm during the night, and where it had
> been, I sowed weeds. Whosoever becomes king after*

*me and again settles Hattusas, may the storm god of
Heaven strike him!*

Others were angry that they had not been chosen and
envious of their brother's good fortune.

Zannanza himself decided to spend his last night
before plunging into the unknown at the sanctuary of
the gods in the rocky hills north-east of Hattusas. His
father gave him permission and he set off with an
entourage of priests and guards to walk the stony road.
All arrangements for his journey to Egypt were to be
handled by others.

Looking back at the fortified hill that had been his
home for so many years, Zannanza suffered a pang of
regret that he had spoken out so boldly. On the other
hand the image of Ankhesenamun, the beautiful Queen
of Tutankhamun, who had struck him as being so wise
and mature, though not much older than himself, came
before him vividly. He had never fallen in love with any
woman. He had so far avoided choosing wives. He
wondered now if it was not because none of them
measured up to what he remembered of Ankhesenamun.
At the time he had not noticed it – but now he was not
sure he had not always been in love with her. When he
had heard of Tutankhamun's death he had had a strong
impression that somehow he was inexorably linked to
Tutankhamun's destiny. Now it had become clear in
what way this destiny was to be fulfilled. There was a
beautiful inevitability about his taking Tutankhamun's
place beside Ankhesenamun. He felt it had been
ordained in heaven and the pact sealed by his giving
Tutankhamun that iron dagger with the rock crystal
pommel – his own most cherished possession.

As they approached the deep double cleft in the
mountains that had become in ancient times the most

sacred place in all the Hittite kingdom, the sun was reddening on the western horizon, its rays casting long shadows. A temple had been built at the entrance and its priests opened the gates for the young prince. The lamps and torches were already being lit for it was only when the sun was high in the sky that its rays penetrated fully into the long galleries of rock.

Zannanza was polite to the priests and his attendants, but made it quite clear that he intended no formal ceremony, but a private audience with the gods. Surprised, but obedient, they drew back and Zannanza passed alone into the short gallery on the right, the gallery devoted to the sun goddess Hebut of Arinna, her son and her handmaidens. At one point, at the meeting of the galleries, she joined her husband, Teshub, the storm god of Hattusas, and his entourage of minor gods – but here in this gallery he felt he could be alone with her, the goddess, the one who had always been closer to his heart than any other.

Tall and beautiful, she stood in her flowing robes on the muscular back of a panther, her hair in long braids.

'Ah, Lady of Heaven, Giver of Life and Light,' he whispered. 'I need your strength and help. Shine on me like the sun in the sky; walk at my right hand; join with me like a yoked pair of oxen; walk by my side like a true deity should.'

She was carved on a wall of stone at the head of a procession, but he saw her as a living being, standing free, looking at him with warm and loving eyes. Was there sorrow there? Did she look at him with sadness and concern? Was the gesture she was making with her hand greeting or farewell?

'I am afraid,' he whispered. 'Strengthen my resolve. Sharpen my wits that I may not be tricked. Harden my sword arm that I may fight to win if I am attacked. Ah, Lady of Heaven, do not bid me goodbye. Come with me. Come with me to Khemet. I will build you a temple there where you will be comfortable and content. The gods and goddesses of the Two Lands will bow to you. Even Hathor and Isis will call you mother. You will be supreme. You will be happy. You will be much loved.'

He had bowed to the ground with his face in the dust at her feet, and he remained there a long time. When he rose tears were streaming down his cheeks. He had received no word, no comfort.

Zannanza's small party left at dawn. Another difficult problem had been how to protect him. If he marched south with a troop of soldiers everyone would interpret this as another instance of Hittite aggression and he would be embroiled in fighting immediately. The decision was to travel as a party carrying gifts to Egypt, not an infrequent or an unusual sight. There would be a small group of well armed guards necessary to fend off would-be robbers, and the prince and Lupakkis would dress as unostentatiously as possible. They left by the tunnel gate with no fuss, waving goodbye to the small group of high officials as though this was no more than a very ordinary expedition.

Zannanza had said goodbye to his father in his father's bedchamber, kissing his feet and thanking him for the privilege of going to Egypt.

Suppiluliuma was not a worrying kind of man but he had been lying awake most of the night partly thinking about the immense power this liaison would give his family, and partly rehearsing speeches he would make to his son in the morning – speeches that would advise him on what to do and what not to do based on his own long experience as a king. But when the time came

and Zannanza was before him he could think of
nothing to say. He bade him farewell gruffly and
indicated that he should not delay his departure a
moment longer. The prince, who had also been rehearsing a speech, found himself being bustled out of the
room without having said more than a few clumsy
words. At the door he turned and looked back, his eyes
full of emotions he could not express. The King was
seated on the edge of the bed Ankhesenamun had sent
as a gift, his grey hair long and dishevelled. Zannanza
had never seen him like this. He looked old and tired.
But even with nothing to indicate that he was a king
the old man had a kind of innate power that Zannanza
could almost feel as a physical ray emanating from
him.

'If my father were in a room,' he thought, 'and I
didn't know he was there – I would still *feel* his
presence! How do I dare to set myself up as a king,' he
sighed, 'when I don't have that . . . that . . .' He could
not name the quality his father had other than to call it
'majesty'. Perhaps it would come to him during all the
magical ceremonies that accompanied coronation. As he
walked away from his father's chamber he would have
given anything to have been able to back out of the
assignment he had volunteered so eagerly for the day
before.

But there was no going back. Lupakkis was waiting
for him. He called out something to the guards and they
passed down the long tunnel beneath the city and out
into the half-light of the early morning. To Zannanza
his country had never looked so beautiful – the harsh
and rocky hills softened by a blueish mist – the forest
in the valley alive with bird-song. Against this was set
a woman in a strange and alien land. It was true she was
beautiful and he longed to see her again – but he knew

so little about her. What if he had made a terrible mistake?

The journey south was accomplished at a gruelling pace, but without incident.

The last night before they reached Egyptian territory they made camp as usual. They were all exhausted and decided to bed down earlier than they normally would in order to be fresh when they met Ankhesenamun's envoys.

Zannanza lay for a long time looking up at the stars before he went to sleep. The Egyptians believed some part of the Pharaoh became a star when he died. What were they really? A million eyes of dead kings and queens; of gods and goddesses; of spirits of all kinds who had passed the stern trials and tests of the Otherworld – a million eyes gazing down on the earth – watching every movement – seeing into every mind? He felt uneasy. He felt the watchers watching. He felt the probers, the examiners, the assessors and the judges moving in close around him. He believed he was on trial but he did not know what crime he had committed. He had lived a fairly quiet and blameless life. He studied a great deal and enjoyed the adventure of gaining knowledge more than anything else. He looked forward to exploring all the rich and varied ancient texts of Egypt. He looked forward to talking long hours with Ankhesenamun. He felt sure she was as eager for knowledge as he was. He would tell her about the myths of the Hatti and they would compare them with the myths of Egypt, seeking the common ground that would give them the seed of truth buried in the story-shell. The stars might not be literally the eyes of spirit beings – but there was a truth in there somewhere – a hint – a clue that everything we see – everything we can explain by

physical law – is more than it appears. Physical law is by
no means the only law that governs reality – though
some believe it to be so.

He shut his eyes and took a deep breath. He must
sleep. He could hear his companions snoring already –
all but the four look-outs posted around the camp. The
light of the stars seemed to be imprinted on the inside
of his lids. It was as though he had carried the whole
spread of the sky into his own head.

He longed to know more about the stars. There was
a Babylonian astronomer at his father's court who had
taught him a lot and who could predict the movements
of the heavenly bodies. It would not be long before
there was an eclipse of the moon. He would see that
in Egypt. He would watch that with Ankhesenamun.
It seemed to him that she and he were already together
sailing in a golden boat among the stars. They were
laughing, happy, making up for all the years they had
been apart. He wondered why she had not named him
personally in her request for a Hittite prince. Surely she
remembered him? Surely she felt about him as he did
about her? Then he remembered that until a few days
ago he had not himself realized what she meant to him.
It was clearly possible for a memory to be hidden in
some secret region of the heart – and there –
somehow – without one being aware of it – for it to
continue growing until it is something very different
from what one originally thought. Perhaps she had
cried out for a Hittite prince not knowing that she was
crying out to him.

He wondered about Tutankhamun. Had she loved
him as lover? It had seemed to him at the time that she
loved him as a mother loves a child.

A boat loomed out of the darkness of the sky and
drifted past them. In it was Tutankhamun standing in

the bows with seven of the gods of Egypt. He raised his hand to greet them and there was no surprise or annoyance in his eyes seeing them together. It was almost as though he were giving them his blessing. Zannanza noticed the young King had his iron dagger with the crystal pommel in his belt. He drew it out and held it up. Starlight focused in the crystal blazed out like an exploding sun.

The Egyptians moved like shadows within shadows, making no sound.

The camp was surrounded and the guards suspected nothing. Simultaneously they were seized from behind and killed before they could cry out. Then one by one the men on the ground were murdered. Some woke in time to struggle – some never knew what had happened. The only one who survived was Lupakkis who had chosen to sleep some distance away from the others, disturbed by his companions' snoring.

He woke in time to hear the assassins depart, now no longer concerned to keep quiet – boasting about the success of the operation. They were speaking in the language of Khemet.

Horrified, Lupakkis rushed to the side of Zannanza. He was lying on his back in a pool of his own blood, his throat slit – his head stove in.

Lupakkis beat his head on the ground. How could this have happened? How could he have let this happen? The bastards! The sons of hyenas! 'Oh Teshub how could you let this happen to a son of Suppiluliuma!'

Lupakkis rushed from body to body hoping to find some others still alive. But all were dead. All, all were dead!

He stood irresolute for a while and then looked at the baggage where it had been left piled up beside the horses. The horses were all gone – no doubt secretly led off before the massacre so that they would not give the alarm. But the baggage was untouched. This had not been a raid by robbers after precious jewels and unguents. It had been a deliberate assassination, well and skilfully planned.

Ra-hotep told Ankhesenamun about the murder of the Hittite prince in a hesitant and trembling voice as soon as they were out of earshot of the other guests at the funeral feast.

She went deathly white and staggered as though she would fall – but caught at a jagged outcrop of rock and leant heavily against it for support.

'Could it have been the work of robbers?' she asked, hoping against hope that there was still some chance the killing had been for some other reason than that Horemheb and the priests of Amun had discovered her plot.

He shook his head dumbly. He was afraid. He knew as well as she the implications of this being a political assassination. When he had delivered her first letter he had not known what a part he was playing in the history of his country. Now that he knew he wished that it had been anyone but he who had become caught up in this dangerous net of royal intrigue.

'Ra-hotep,' she found herself saying, though her thoughts were racing on other matters. 'You must get as far away from Khemet as you can. Go quickly – and don't look back.' She slipped a costly ring from her finger into his hand and then gave him a slight push.

'Majesty . . .'

'Go!' she snapped. 'Get away while you can.'

'But . . .'

She could see by his face even in this dim light so far

from the lamps and torches that he was concerned for her.

'I will be all right,' she said, knowing that she would not. How would Horemheb and Zais punish her for what she had done?

Reluctantly he turned to go. He had not gone more than a few steps when she called him back.

'Ra-hotep!'

He paused at once.

'Do you know the name of the prince?'

'I think it was Zan . . . Zan . . .' His voice trailed away as his tongue stumbled over the unfamiliar name.

'Zannanza,' she whispered. 'I thought it might be he.'

Ra-hotep could not see her face as her back was to the light, but he could hear the pain in her voice.

At that moment they heard a step and Ra-hotep melted into the shadows.

Horemheb stood in front of her.

'Majesty?' he said quietly. His voice was polite, enquiring, cool – but reverberated in her heart like the knell of doom.

'General?' she answered, making a great effort to stand upright and keep her face and voice expressionless.

'Why have you left the feast?'

'Is a royal Queen, daughter of a mighty dynasty, answerable for all that she does to you – a commoner?'

'Her absence makes the guests restless,' he answered smoothly, ignoring the insult in her words and the bitterness with which she said them.

'Ah, yes, the guests,' she said sarcastically. 'We must keep up appearances at all costs!'

'Appearances are very important Majesty,' he said icily.

'More important than reality?'

He bowed slightly and for a moment she detected something other than menace in his voice, something that suggested that he had a heart somewhere in that iron frame. 'When reality has become too painful to bear,' he said, 'attending to appearances sometimes helps us to bear it.'

'So we will play this game,' she thought. 'We will go back to the feast and pretend that nothing has happened – that nothing is wrong. Will the pretending change what has happened? Will the pretending prevent what will happen? Maybe.' Maybe. If she screamed and howled now there would only be one set of events and actions that would follow. If she kept her wits about her and calmly walked back to the feast, playing for time, there might be another outcome. Her way had never been to scream and rail against the cruel blows of the world. Her way had always been to wait and watch.

When dawn came, dishevelled and drunken guests were lying about the sacred valley, exhausted. Servants were quietly going about their business clearing up the mess, helping their masters and mistresses to return home. Workmen were covering up the entrance to the tomb with piles of loose clippings and sand. Ankhesenamun, still stone-cold sober, climbed into the chair her servants brought for her and was carried shoulder high all the way back to the palace.

Horemheb had announced the date of her wedding. It would follow hard upon the funeral for the sake of peace and order. Horemheb needed all the soldiers he could muster to strengthen the Egyptian border lands against Suppiluliuma who, justifiably, would be incensed at what had happened to his son. He could not afford to have too many tied up keeping the peace in the Two Lands.

The peasants were already working in the fields, shadowy figures apparently floating in the early morning haze. The river was mirror still. Birds were winging silently towards the grain fields. Suddenly a flock of geese, honking, beating their wings noisily, lumbered across the sky. Ankhesenamun tightened her lips. The goose was one of the important symbols of Amun. It seemed to her they took a deliberately long time to fly over her little procession.

For the first time since she had heard about Zannanza tears came to her eyes. She desperately tried to hold them back. Let those mocking geese not see them! Let those screeching demons not carry the message back to Zais and Horemheb that they had finally broken her spirit, destroyed her hope and buried her future.

How she hated geese! No hunter was allowed to shoot this particular breed, but if she had had a bow and a quiver full of arrows with her at that moment, there would not be one left to land on the sacred lake of the Temple of Amun!

Her-ya Nefernefruaten, Egyptian priestess of Hathor in an alien land, rejoiced when a trusted servant brought her a message from her Hittite lover. It seemed a very long time since she had seen him and she had almost given up hope that he would ever return. Her duties at the Temple had lost their savour and she was wondering if the time had come for her to leave, calling on her sister, Queen Ankhesenamun, for reinstatement at the Egyptian court, when she heard that General Lupakkis would be waiting for her at the usual place, at the usual hour of the night. She was so excited she could hardly wait out the completion of the ceremonies – but at last

she was free. She hurried through the streets, her steps
light, her heart singing. All must be well. All must surely
be well.

But when she came into his presence in the simple but
pleasant room they had always used for their meetings,
she was shocked to see how pale and distraught he
looked. He had not slept for several nights and had been
travelling hard – one thought driving him on – one
thought festering in his heart.

She started to rush across the room to fling herself
into his arms, her face alight with the pleasure of seeing
him, but so fierce and bitter was his expression, so
dishevelled and savage he looked with his half-grown
beard and wild eyes – that she drew back.

'Lupakkis! What is the matter? What has happened?'
she gasped.

His eyes blazed at her.

'You ask *me* what has happened?' he snarled.

'Yes, I do. Why . . . why are you looking at me like
that?'

'Oh you play the innocent so well, priestess! How
many men have you deceived? How many princes have
you sent to their death?'

'What are you talking about?' She too was pale now,
genuinely bewildered. The innocence of her looks, her
beguiling beauty – seemed to enrage him even more.

'You and your treacherous Queen planned this whole
thing well! Did you think my King would send his eldest
son? Did you think you would destroy the royal house
of Hatti?'

He was advancing menacingly on her now, and she
was trying to back away.

'Lupakkis . . .'

But he would not listen. He suddenly seized her by
the throat and started to shake her. Struggling for

breath she tried to speak but he only increased his grip.

'You have killed a good man, a royal prince. You have betrayed a trust. You have ruined my life. Traitor! Liar! Murderer! Why should I listen to you. Why? Why?'

Tears were streaming down his dusty cheeks as he squeezed the life out of her. He had loved her and now his hatred and hurt knew no bounds. As she went limp he let her fall and stood over her – gazing down at her – muttering imprecations and curses.

He had come to wreak vengeance on her before he returned to his King. Now he would go and when he had delivered his message, he would kill himself. How could he live with his part in this?

He left her lying in a crumpled heap on the floor and strode out of the room and out of the house.

In the street two small misshapen shadows detached themselves from a wall and slipped into the house he had just left. They belonged to Heh and Ipi, Nezem-mut's two dwarfs, who had spent a long time tracking down Akhenaten's other daughters, believing they would be back in favour if they could but find them. They had located only one so far – Nefernefruaten – priestess of Hathor in Kepel. It was they who had intercepted Ankhesenamun's second letter from the Hittites and it was they who had delivered it to Horemheb. They were already in line for reinstatement and a reward. If they could deliver the princess to Horemheb as well, there would be no limit to the status they would have and the riches he would shower upon them.

They had not expected the Hittite general to be alive, and in following Nefernefruaten to her secret assignation they had been surprised to see him leave the house. They did not like the way he looked. He was staggering and muttering to himself like a mad man.

Inside the chamber the lamp was still burning. The bed
that should have held the lovers at their reunion was
untouched. On the floor lay the pale body of Akhenaten's
daughter. They were horrified. All that effort to locate
her – and now – this! Horemheb would not be pleased.

They bent over her. They ascertained that she was
dead, and then, without a word, they fled.

Lupakkis started off for Hattusas immediately without
rest or food, but he had not gone far when the reaction
to the rage that had driven him for so many days over-
took him. He dismounted and, aching in every limb, fell
down on the hard ground and entered a state of such
deep sleep it was almost like death. A huge moon was
rising, the stars paling beside it.

In the early hours before dawn he woke with a start.
He could not remember where he was. He sat up, wide
awake, his heart pounding – gazing around him. His
horse was a bulky shadow beside him and rocks and
bushes darker than darkness ringed him round. But
there was something else. A strangeness – a silence.
There was no insect sound, no rustling of leaves as little
nocturnal animals moved about, no breath of wind
stirring the leaves. He looked up and met the eye of the
moon. He gasped. It was no longer a shining silver disc,
but a gigantic blood-stained ball hanging in the sky – the
stars – myriads of them – burning with an unnaturally
livid light.

The deeds that had been done – the betrayal – the
murder – had not gone unseen by the gods. Retribution
would follow and retribution would be mightier than
any human could devise.

Lupakkis mounted his horse and rode on,
northwards.

* * *

When Suppiluliuma heard the news of his son's death he was like an enraged bull – his shame at being so gullible as to allow such a situation to arise, causing him to lash out at everything and everyone around him. He smashed the goblet in his hand – he overthrew the table – he even railed against the gods. Lupakkis was summarily taken out, executed and hung upside down from the battlements of the town.

Then he called a war council. The Egyptians would pay for what they had done. They would be sorry they had ever set out to trick him. The blood of Zannanza would flow in a thousand, thousand Hittite veins, would strengthen the bow fingers, the sword hands, the eyes of the spear-throwers. More soldiers than Egypt had ever imagined could come against her would pour into the Two Lands. It was true the land of Hatti was a long way from Egypt, but Suppiluliuma could envisage its vulnerability as soon as all its protective vassal states were stripped away. He was already at war with Syria and Syria showed signs of crumbling. He would clear the allies of Egypt away like a storm wind clears the sand, and then – and then he would march and fight until Egypt herself was in his hand. When a Hittite prince sat on the throne of Egypt as king, the treacherous bastards would know that a Hittite king was on the throne. He would enslave that arrogant nation. He would humiliate it, and break its spirit. His yoke would be heavy – his whip long.

Nothing was said about the murder of the Hittite prince in the Egyptian court. It was as though nothing had happened. Only the look of smug confidence on Horemheb's face as he organized the wedding and the coronation of Ankhesenamun and Ay, confirmed the suspicions of the Queen. She was powerless to resist the inexorable march of events. Ra-hotep and Ra-mes had disappeared and she feared they too had met the fate of the others who had shared her desperate bid for power. Not one of them appeared at her wedding. Not one of them could be traced. Even their names had disappeared from the Temple records. It was as though they had never been, and priests of the combined god, Amun-Ra, had always been in those positions.

Ankhesenamun and Ay were led in two separate and magnificent processions to the Temple of Amun-Ra at Ipet-Esut. The people crowded the walkways and roads, ever anxious for a glimpse of riches and power – never tired of the splendour of their rulers.

This was Ankhesenamun's third marriage. The first had been when she was very young. She had stared at the throngs of excited and admiring people, startled and afraid of their overwhelming, obsessive love. Their faces as they pushed and struggled and strained to get a glimpse of her had struck her as almost insane. What were they hoping to achieve by seeing her? Did they think they could drink her in with their eyes and absorb her into their bodies? The night of that first wedding had passed in restless nightmare. She felt herself backed against the huge wall of the Temple with the crowds pressing and pressing towards her – their mouths open – their eyes staring – their hands reaching out to tear pieces off her . . . Her father-husband had been kind and comforting when she had woken screaming – and had quietly talked her into the dawn so that she would not have to dream about them again.

Over the years she had learned to resist her fear of the populace – though she never enjoyed their intrusive attention. Her second marriage and coronation had been happier. She was fond of her half-brother Tutankhamun and felt, in contrast to his naivety, that she was very much in control of the situation. She was used to it – he was not.

But this was different. She was no longer in control.

She looked at the faces of her people and longed to cry out to them that she was a prisoner – that the lowliest of them was more fortunate than she. She saw a young woman in the crowd, about her age, and stared at her trying somehow to exchange souls with her – to exchange destinies. If she were that young woman – and if that young woman were her . . . She had heard of spirits from the dead taking over the bodies of the living . . . She had even heard of a living magician taking over the body of another living man. At this moment she wanted more than anything in the world not to be Ankhesenamun, Queen of Egypt. But no exchange happened. The young woman looked pleased and surprised to have caught the eye of the great Queen and, for a moment, wished that she could leave the drudgery of her life and ride in majesty in that golden chair . . .

But the procession passed and they both remained where they were. The young woman lifted a child to her hip to give him a better view of the magnificent scene. He was too young to appreciate it – but one day he might remember he had seen the King and Queen of the Two Lands passing by on their way to their wedding and coronation.

Just before the gates of the great Temple Ankhesenamun spotted the two dwarfs, Heh and Ipi, close beside Nezem-mut and Horemheb. She was astonished. Surely – after all that they had done they had not been accepted back into favour? What had they done now that was of such great value that. . . ?

Suddenly a thought struck her and her heart went black with rage. She was sure that no one she had trusted had betrayed her. Someone had intercepted that

letter. Who else but those two cunning and heartless
dwarfs? They were dressed as richly as princes, and as
princes, they walked boldly forward in the procession.

She scarcely heard the words that were said over
her – scarcely felt the water and the oil. The rituals that
were performed this day were empty – dead. Like a grin-
ning mask on a cadaver that had died in pain – the
ancient ceremony hid an ugly and a loathsome truth.
She looked into the eyes of Zais as he placed Mut's
sacred vulture crown upon her head, hung the jewelled
collars around her neck and placed the golden seal rings
on her fingers. How tired she was of ceremony and
ritual. How tired she was of pretence and deceit. Would
all the riches and jewels placed in Tutankhamun's tomb
make up for one night of love-making with her? Would
all this weight of treasure on her head and shoulders
bring one smile, one light moment, to her heart?

No. She was for the dark, and, looking into the icy
eyes of Zais, she knew it would not be long in coming.
He knew what she had tried to do. He knew – and he
would never forgive her for it.

She shut her eyes and remembered the Hittite boy
who had come to visit them all those years ago. She had
not meant to hurt him. She had thought to make him
great – to have him at her side when she took full power
in the Two Lands. She had thought that they together
would have started a fresh and better way of ruling.

Now all was lost. Her father was not the only one
whose great dream had come to nothing.

13
THE GLASS OF WINE

Nezem-mut made it clear to Heh and Ipi that she did not want any other of Akhenaten's daughters found – or if they were found *she* was to be told and not Horemheb. It had become clear to her that she owed her marriage to the General to the fact that she was the nearest to a princess of the royal line available. She had been fond of her nieces at one time and did not wish them harm – but neither did she wish for their return.

She was horrified to hear what had happened to Nefernefruaten and blamed Ankhesenamun for having put her in that dangerous situation. She could not understand what the Queen could have been thinking about to play such a treacherous game, and would have nothing to do with her. She could not understand why Horemheb and Ay and Zais let her continue as though nothing had happened.

'Trust me,' Horemheb said. 'It is better for the country that at this stage no one knows anything about it. But do not fear – the time will come when she will pay for what she tried to do.'

Ankhesenamun lived a more and more isolated life. Meryt-mut, her faithful woman servant, knew very little of the events that had occurred and puzzled why the Queen was being so obviously ignored. Even Ay, nominally her husband, saw very little of her. The country seemed to be running without her – Horemheb, Ay and Zais making all the decisions.

When Meryt-mut ventured to voice her concern one

day to her mistress, Ankhesenamun laughed outright –
a short and bitter laugh.

'Do not concern yourself Meryt-mut,' she said. 'I
prefer to be alone. If the whole lot of them were buried
in a sandstorm I would not shed a tear.'

But the days were long and lonely. Ankhesenamun
was bored and began to live a great deal with her
memories of the past.

One day she called Meryt-mut to her and told her that
her two youngest sisters were still alive and she longed
to see them. She told Meryt-mut that she would tell her
where they were and send her to fetch them.

'If they don't want to come to me – don't force them.
But tell them that I love them and want to see them
before I die.'

'Why do you talk of death?' Meryt-mut cried.
'Majesty, you are a young woman!'

Ankhesenamun shook her head. 'I have never been a
young woman, Meryt-mut,' she said. 'I was born old.'
She looked so tired and sad, so pale and ill, Meryt-mut
did not know what to say. Her eyes looked like the eyes
of a person who had seen all there was to see in the world
and had no desire to go on living.

'I will bring them to you, Majesty,' Meryt-mut
vowed.

'No one must know.'

'No one *will* know, Majesty.'

Ankhesenamun took her in her arms and kissed her.

'You are a true friend, Meryt-mut. I trust you.'

'I will be worthy of your trust, Majesty,' she said
quietly.

'I know.'

But Ankhesenamun never saw her sisters.

When Meryt-mut came to the delta lands where the

two young princesses had been hidden away all these years, she found neither were still there. The eldest, Neferneferure, had died earlier that year of a wasting disease, and the younger, Setepenre, had left the family who had brought her up a few days before Meryt-mut's arrival.

'Two dwarfs carrying the King's seal told us they had been sent to take her back to court,' she was told.

Knowing something of the deviousness of those two dwarfs and angry that the family should have let their precious charge go with so little evidence that it was a genuine message from the King or Queen, Meryt-mut hurried back to Waset as quickly as a boat would take her.

But at court there was no sign of the princess – nor of the dwarfs. No one had seen them. No one knew anything about them.

She tried to see Ankhesenamun – but no one seemed to know where the Queen had gone.

'She left at noon,' one of the Queen's close circle of servants reported. 'The King came for her and they walked off alone. She did not ask for any of us to go with her. Why? Is something wrong?'

Meryt-mut shook her head. She felt in her bones that something was very wrong – but she could not say what it was.

Ay had come to Ankhesenamun's quarters that day to take her to a meeting with Horemheb and Zais. Up to that time he had not known the full story of her attempt to hand over the control of Egypt to an enemy. He had thought she was somewhat in disgrace because she was trying to encourage the cult of Ra to continue separately from the cult of Amun, lending it strength by her support and even attempting to reintroduce something of

her father's outlawed Atenist rituals. Because he had
been so busy attending to all the many difficulties of
state importance that had arisen as a result of the long
period of mourning without a settled succession, he had
not made time to talk anything through with her. He
had noticed how withdrawn she was and had assumed
that, quite understandably, she had not wanted to
marry him, but had set her heart on some young man.
Horemheb's coldness towards her he understood as due
to the Ra/Amun feud.

The days had gone by, crowded and busy. He knew
he was supposed to beget an heir on the Queen – but
each night he was so tired, and each night she was so
unwelcoming that he let the time slip by. 'One day,' he
told himself. 'Not now. It is too soon. She has not
recovered from Tutankhamun's death yet.'

He walked beside her not knowing what to say. He
had been shocked and amazed at what Horemheb had
told him about her bid to put a Hittite on the throne.
He was personally hurt that she would go to such lengths
to escape marriage with him, and angry that she had
risked the future of the Two Lands in that way. Angry
that she would betray her ancestors who had worked so
hard and shed so much blood to preserve Egypt for the
Egyptians.

She could see that there was a change in him. Since
their marriage she had either seen him in the formal circumstances of a state ceremony, or at night, when occasionally he came to her chamber, said a few words and
then wearily withdrew. He had always treated her
courteously.

This time he was peremptory in his demand that she
accompany him, and his expression was severe.

'Is it now?' she asked herself. 'Is it now I am to pay?'

She kept him waiting while she dressed, changing her

mind several times, instinctively choosing garments that
would enhance her beauty. On her arm she placed her
favourite bracelet, given to her by Tutankhamun. On
her fingers she forced the rings that were now almost too
small for her, but had been her favourites through the
years – each one marking a special occasion. She spent
some time looking in the mirror, making sure that her
face was a perfect and exquisite mask. Whatever was to
happen she did not want Horemheb to have the satisfaction of seeing what she was feeling.

Ay paced up and down the antechamber restlessly.
He had no idea what Horemheb intended to do – but
now that he had learned what she had done he understood something had to be done. He thought the most
likely sentence would be exile. He would say: 'You love
foreigners so much. Go and live among them!'
Horemheb had explained why he had not acted sooner.
'It was for the country,' he said. 'The country must not
suffer from any more instability. The country must not
know that its divine Queen is a traitor who would have
destroyed it without a qualm. We have had too many
criminals and heretics on the throne lately. No one must
know what she has done. On the other hand – you must
see that she can no longer be trusted as Queen.'

Ay thought back to the child she had been. His other
grandchildren often sat upon his knee and listened to
the tales he told them. Ankhesenamun always sat alone,
listening intently, but never chattering and interrupting
and questioning as the others did. He could see her eyes
now – brooding over something someone had said.
Drawing it into herself. Giving nothing out. He had
never been able to read what she was thinking.

Why had she done what she had done? He tried to
give her the benefit of the doubt by using the excuse
that she probably thought she would bring about peace

between the two great empires. After all – princesses were brought to Egypt to be married to the king to insure the relationship between their two countries. Why not princes? But Ay knew she was not as naive as that. Her reasons, whatever they were, would not be simple.

At last she was ready.

She was dressed as Queen. Fine, almost transparent white cloth, flowed to her feet, emphasizing where it touched breast and belly, seductive curves. Jewels shone at her throat and on her wrists. Golden snakes coiled around her upper arms and a diadem of jewelled flowers encircled her head.

'She is beautiful,' he thought. 'If only . . . if only . . .'

He walked beside her down the corridors and across the courtyards. Horemheb and Zais were waiting for her in the garden pavilion where the flowers for Tutankhamun's funeral had been prepared.

'Why there?' she thought when she realized where they were going. Her favourite, precious place, where she spent so much happy time. How dare they even set foot in it – let alone choose it for this confrontation.

When she had left her chamber she was resigned to accept almost anything. She was tired of fighting. Tired of living the half-life of a royal queen. But when she saw those two she hated so much standing in her special, private place she was incensed. She tightened her lips and straightened her shoulders. She was not finished yet! Let them not believe it.

The pavilion was covered with vines and creepers through which the sunlight flickered. One could be there in the heat of the day – cool in the shade. There was a small table at the centre and a few chairs scattered about. Ankhesenamun had been known to entertain guests there informally from time to time, usually people with whom she felt she could relax. She had spoken to

Ra-hotep there when she did not want to be overheard, for it was in a remote part of the garden and no one could approach without being seen. Was it for this reason Horemheb and Zais had chosen to meet her there?

How beautiful the flowers looked this day, glowing richly from among green leaves. The ponds were full of lotus lilies, rooted in the dark, cold mud, lifting exquisite petalled faces to the hot, bright sun. Ankhesenamun mused on the strangeness of life that appeared to bloom and blossom yet everywhere hid death. Ants went about their business, bees gathered pollen, a bird sang and trilled on the top branch of a sycamore fig tree – all had such short lives yet never thought of death. Humankind paid dearly for the elaborate consciousness it enjoyed. Every step she took was more difficult than the last – not because of anything that was happening – but because she was capable of imagining what had not yet happened.

She wondered if any gods were present. She wondered if every shrub and bush hid a sacred being, a mighty spirit. She narrowed her eyes and stared into the glare of the sun reflected off the shining water of the ornamental pond, trying to see through the haze of material reality to the numinous world – the world invisible to those who were still embedded in flesh – the world that continued to exist when all around her that looked so fine was dust.

'What is the truth of it?' she whispered. She suspected that the ancient texts that spoke of other realms gave as much and as little of the truth as she saw now of the sun reflected on the water, its image distorted as a dragonfly skimmed the surface.

Horemheb and Zais were standing on the steps of the pavilion watching her walk towards them. She did not seem afraid. Horemheb, who had known her all her life, felt a pang of regret for what was about to happen. Zais felt none. She was the enemy. He did not know her in any other capacity.

She stopped when she saw them, and looked for a moment as though she would turn back and leave the place.

Ay took her arm and led her forward.

Horemheb greeted her coldly, his face stern. Zais smiled – gloating.

She noticed that there was a flask of wine on the table, with one blue faience goblet in the shape of a lotus flower. For the first time she was afraid. Up to now – the summons – the walk – the flowers – the bird – had all been part of an elaborate drama – a formalized pattern that seemed more to overlay her life than be part of it. Now she looked at the single goblet and knew what it meant. The essence of her life lay in that golden liquid – the years in the City of the Sun – the years with Tutankhamun – the long wait for the Hittite prince. When she had drained that liquid there would be no yesterday, today or tomorrow.

What was Horemheb saying? He was talking about traitors and treachery; about betraying ancestors; about irresponsibility; about shame. Who was he talking about? She listened with only half her mind. With the other she was watching the sunlight on the garden, the short shadows of noon, the sweet and potent images of life.

Zais poured the wine into the goblet, careful not to spill a drop. She saw him lift it and hold it towards her. She met his eyes.

'No!' Ay suddenly cried. 'This is not the way.' He had been standing in the background through all that was being said, looking more and more upset and agitated.

'It is the only way,' Horemheb said heavily. There was no pleasure in this for him.

'We talked about exile!'

'With exile we could not be sure a diseased age would end. This is the only way to ensure a fresh and clean beginning.'

'Nothing fresh and clean begins with a murder!'

'This is not murder.'

Zais moved closer to her. His eyes were staring into hers, powerful, hypnotic.

She could feel Ay behind her full of pain and regret, pleading silently for her forgiveness. She knew now in his old age he was not strong enough to withstand the will of Horemheb.

Zais raised the goblet and presented it to her. She wanted to knock it out of his hand. She wanted to rant and rail – to fling furniture at them – to see them cringe away from her fury. But, as though she were moving slowly under water, she saw herself raise her own hand and take the cup from Zais.

She held it silently for a while and the whole world seemed to cease what it was about. There was absolute stillness. She at the centre of a triangle formed by the three men. She holding a cup that contained her death.

She saw herself raise the cup to her lips. She saw herself drink.

And then suddenly there was noise and movement again. Having drunk she flung the cup with extraordinary force against the floor. She saw the men rushing towards her. She saw the whole pavilion whirling round. She saw the flowers of the garden ripped up as though by a gigantic wind and flung, swirling around them.

And then she saw nothing more.

* * *

When Meryt-mut heard of Ankhesenamun's death she
was shocked and frightened. She did not believe her
beloved mistress's death had been caused by illness.
Others might speak of how Ankhesenamun had withdrawn from court life and lived almost like a recluse
because she did not want the people to know she was
ill – but Meryt-mut knew that this was not so. A young
woman, in full health, had suddenly died. Her other
servants confirmed her suspicions. Ankhesenamun
when last seen leaving her quarters with Ay had been in
reasonably good health. She was pale and drawn as she
had been since Tutankhamun's death – but she did not
appear at that time more so than before.

Meryt-mut, as chief among the Queen's women,
prepared Ankhesenamun's personal belongings to lie
with her in her tomb – and she wept as she handled each
one – the silver mirror with the handle depicting a
slender swimming girl; the beautiful carved box of
sandalwood in the shape of a duck containing her rouge;
the exquisite stoppered jars of scent and oil; the fine,
fine cloth of her clothes and her glowing jewels . . .
Meryt-mut had been a child of twelve when
Ankhesenamun was born and she had been closely
associated with her all her life. She had seen her through
good and bad times. She had adorned her for her wed-
dings, her coronations and the funerals of her loved
ones. She screamed and fought when her body was
taken away by the priests of Anubis for the last preparations and she was no longer permitted to serve her.

For a while after the funeral arrangements were
complete and the Queen's beautiful coffin was laid to
rest, Meryt-mut was in a quandary as to what to do. She
knew that one of Akhenaten's daughters was still alive
and Ankhesenamun's last wish had been for her sisters'
return to court. She wanted to tell Horemheb – for if

anyone could find her and bring her back, he could –
but – if she were returned – would she suffer the same
fate as Ankhesenamun? Or would she become Queen,
ousting Nezem-mut as Great Royal Wife, and live a long
and happy life among the luxuries she had been denied
all these years? Meryt-mut blamed Horemheb and Zais
for Ankhesenamun's death, but mostly Zais, believing
that it was his dread of losing power and privilege to the
priests of Ra that had motivated him to persuade
Horemheb that she was dangerous. She had never liked
Horemheb – but she admired him and she believed he
was an honourable, if harsh, man. He was to be next
Pharaoh. There was no doubt.

It was when she saw the two dwarfs, Heh and Ipi,
leaving the quarters of Nezem-mut, laughing uproari-
ously, that she decided that something had to be done
about Setepenre. She knew Ankhesenamun had hated
them and that they had crossed her in some way and
brought about the miscarriage of her child. Meryt-mut
had been kept out of many of her mistress's secrets – but
had gathered enough by her own wits to have built up
something of a picture. She certainly knew who was
likely to help her and who was likely to harm her. Heh
and Ipi were up to some evil trick connected with the
young princess. Of that she was sure. She knew
Setepenre had left the safety of her foster home in the
company of Heh and Ipi, and yet here they were at
court – and there was no sign of the princess and no
mention of her being found.

Meryt-mut decided that of the choices available to
her Horemheb was the best. She told him how she had
been sent to find the princesses and what she had found.
She did not hesitate to say angry things about Nezem-
mut's two dwarfs.

Horemheb thanked and rewarded her at once for the

information, and suggested that when Setepenre was
Queen she, Meryt-mut, might like to serve her as she
had served Ankhesenamun. He charged her not to tell
anyone what she had told him lest harm should come to
the princess before he could offer her his protection.

'I am sure you have not lived so long close to the royal
family without understanding something of the
dangerous intrigues that go on,' he said. She knew
Ankhesenamun had not liked him as a man – but had
respected him as an administrator and general. He spoke
to her now with such calm confidence – with a face so
clear and open and concerned – she felt that she could
trust him to do what was best for Setepenre. She even
began to believe that he had had nothing to do with
Ankhesenamun's death.

14
THE PRINCESS

It had been given out of course that the Queen had died of 'natural causes' and the country mourned her – but not for as long as they had mourned Tutankhamun. There had been enough interruption to the normal routines of daily life.

There was some speculation as to who would be the next Queen, Ay's Great Royal Wife. His own wife, Tey, who had been with him since before Akhenaten came to the throne, was certainly not suitable.

It became clear to those near the centre of power in Khemet that Horemheb was preparing to make his move at last.

Since Queen Ankhesenamun's death Ay had aged alarmingly. His mind began to wander and he could no longer be trusted with any decision. Throughout three reigns he had been a rock on which many had leaned for support. Now he himself had to be supported.

The ruling of the Two Lands was more than ever in the hands of Horemheb. He had manoeuvred everything so carefully over the years that there was now a growing and vociferous demand from every side that he should be the next Pharaoh. He pretended reluctance, but was persuaded. 'For the good of the country' – one of his own favourite phrases – was used frequently at this time.

Soon Ay turned his face to the wall and died, in his last hours knowing for sure for the first time the part Horemheb had played in the lives and deaths of Akhenaten, Tutankhamun and Ankhesenamun. There had been times when he had suspected the General, but on the whole, the great skill with which Horemheb had covered his tracks, and the admirable way he had seen the country through each crisis, strengthening and controlling it and returning it to order – had prevented Ay from questioning him. It was easier to let things be than disturb things yet again. Ay had no doubt Horemheb would make a good ruler and he, on his deathbed, added his voice to the others. There was no one else no matter what he had done. It was a natural choice.

A third royal funeral followed – but this time it was only a formality. It hardly disturbed the country. Ay was old and his death was expected. Though he had achieved much in his long life it had been for the most part unnoticed and unsung. He had always been a shadowy background figure to the general population – and had never caught their imagination.

The country was buzzing with the news that Horemheb was to be Pharaoh. The fact that he was married to Nezem-mut Mutnodjemne, the daughter of Ay and sister of Nefertiti, strengthened his position.

Nezem-mut composed herself very carefully for sleep this most important night – the night before her husband's coronation as Pharaoh of the Two Lands and her own elevation to the position of Great Royal Wife and Queen. Her women worked long hours rubbing sweet oils into her body, massaging her tired muscles, preparing her for total relaxation. It would be a long hard day and she wanted to be at her best.

The marriage with Horemheb had not worked out as she would have wished. He was kind and considerate and polite – but never passionate. She could not ignore the probability that he had married her solely for her family connections and had no feeling for her at all. She

became obsessed by trying to make herself better looking than she was, dieting and exercising to make herself
slimmer, covering her skin with creams and sometimes
clay to make it softer – consulting soothsayers and magicians to find out if he would grow to love her and if she
would bear children in spite of her age.

When Heh and Ipi brought her the news that they
had found Setepenre and that she was the last of the
princesses alive, she wept at first in genuine sorrow,
remembering the pleasure she had had in her nieces when
they were young, and then shuddered to think what
Horemheb would do if he knew that there was a princess
with pure royal blood in her veins still alive. She lay awake
one whole night, tossing and turning, and wondering what
she should do to protect her own precarious position.

In the morning she called the two dwarfs to her
chamber and instructed them not to bring Setepenre to
court, nor to tell anyone that she had been found. She
told them where to take the girl, sending letters with
them to be delivered to the trusted friend who would
receive her, and to the princess herself. In each she told
a different story.

At this moment she thought only of giving herself time
to establish herself as Queen. She made no decisions about
the future.

But the night she had so specifically wanted to be
relaxed and peaceful turned out to be the opposite. She
was just dropping off to sleep when the door swung open
with a crash and Horemheb strode in, still fully clothed,
and looking angry.

She sat up rubbing her eyes sleepily, smudging all the
oils and ointments her maids had so carefully spread
over her skin just before she settled for the night. She
had not expected him, knowing that he would be busy
until late with last moment details and would probably

sleep, if he slept at all, in his old quarters to be ready for
the servants who would prepare him for the big day.

'So, Lady,' he said sternly. 'You have secrets from me.'

She looked dazed. She had many secrets from him.
Which ones did he mean?

'I am told the Princess Setepenre is still alive, and
that you have found her and are keeping her from me.'

'What nonsense is this, my Lord?' she said indignantly.

'Do you deny it?'

'Of course.'

'I will call your dwarfs to this chamber and we will
hear what they have to say.'

She was wide awake now and thinking fast.

'Heh and Ipi?' she asked. 'What have they done now?
I know, my Lord, they are capable of mischief – but
surely not . . .?'

'I have information that the princess left the home
where she has been hiding all these years in the company
of those two meddlesome dwarfs. Those same two
dwarfs were seen with you here a few days ago. They are
your close companions. It is not conceivable that they
are alone responsible for abducting and hiding her.'

'But I thought Setepenre was long since dead,' she
said with an elaborate show of innocent surprise. Too
late. He had read the guilt in her face.

He demanded that she tell him where Setepenre was
and when she would not he shouted at her, his face
distorted with hate.

'My Lord,' she said at last, haughtily, as angry now
as he. 'Ankhesenamun had good reasons for hiding her
sisters, and I have too.'

'I will not harm the girl. Do you think I am such a
monster?'

'I do not, my Lord.'

'Why then?'

'I fear that . . . I fear that you will take her as your Great Royal Wife and cast me aside.'

Horemheb was silent but the expression on his face showed her that she was not wrong.

'I used to believe,' she said bitterly, 'that you married me because you wanted me as much as I wanted you. Now I have no illusions – but I will not give you up. I alone know where Setepenre is – but I shall not tell you. And if you try to force me,' she added hastily, seeing his expression, 'or if you try to destroy me – she will die. You will never have her unless I decide of my own free will that you shall!'

He took her by the shoulders and shook her.

'You will tell me where she is.'

Her eyes told him that she would not. She was afraid but she would cling stubbornly onto this one weapon she had to keep him at her side. He could see that she no longer desired him. She desired only the throne and nothing would make her give it up.

He tried to control himself. He released her and composed himself.

'Can you not see that a princess of the ancient line should be queen for the country's sake? I will not cast you aside. You will still be my wife, my companion. You will have great riches, great privileges. You will bear my children.'

'If you can beget them!' she said venomously. None of his other wives had borne him children. No doubt he thought that with a younger wife . . .

His face darkened ominously, and a vein throbbed in his neck. He clenched and unclenched his fists, but did not raise them against her. He longed to strike her but knew that this would do no good. Horemheb rarely lost control of himself.

So she would not tell him? Heh and Ipi were heavily implicated. He would question them.

He turned on his heel and strode out of the room without another word – not even a backward glance.

She stared after him, shaking with her own anger, formulating a plan to make her niece's hiding place even more secure.

When Heh and Ipi had done what Nezem-mut had instructed them to do, they turned for home, cheerfully contemplating their reward.

'Besides,' Heh said, 'we will have something to hold over the Queen, and therefore over the King, for as long as we choose.'

They had never felt in a stronger position.

Setepenre had been placed in the care of an elderly couple, long loyal to the Atenist family, living on an estate in a remote part of the Nubian mountains. After Akhenaten's death, Khay – once called Khay-aten but now plain Khay – had been one of the nobles who had fled the golden city when it was clear the era of the Aten was over and Pharaoh's dream had turned very sour. Since then he had farmed ostriches in the dusty valley below his comfortable retreat to supply the royal family with fans. Lately, feeling his age, he had left the working of the estate to his sons and lived a quiet life in the mountains away from the aggravation and uncertainty of farming life. He had a wife, Bet, who had given him nothing but sons and who pined for a daughter who would understand all those little subtle things that the men in her life never did. She was delighted to take the orphaned girl to her heart, believing, as the letter she received said, that she was the daughter of one of Nezem-mut's close entourage, who was to be kept away from court because the death of her parents had exposed her to the undesirable attentions of a rich but brutal man.

Setepenre was tired and bewildered. She had been told by Ankhesenamun all those years ago when she had been so suddenly sent away to live with strangers in the delta region, that her life was in danger. At first she had been a sickly child, finding it difficult to adjust to her new surroundings, weeping at night for her mother. Her sister Neferneferure had tried to mother her, and eventually she settled. Then Neferneferure died and she thought she would never cease to mourn. Now suddenly she was taken away from the people who cared for her and for whom she cared, and once more told that her life was in danger and she must flee. She went south with the two strange dwarfs who bore the royal seal, expecting to be returned to what was left of her family, her mother's sister. But the boat they were on stood by in the middle of nowhere and she was left there, virtually a prisoner, with only rough men for company, while the dwarfs disappeared for several days.

Now she was brought to this rocky wilderness and left again with strangers.

'Here you will be safe,' she was told, 'but no one must ever know who you are.' The letter from her aunt reiterated this – telling her that Ankhesenamun and Nefernefruaten had both been murdered, and this would be her fate too if she ever told anyone, however trustworthy they might seem, who she really was.

She wept a lot at first, missing her friends and the lush green lands of the delta. But Bet enticed her out of her room at last and with patient and loving care persuaded her to accept her fate.

One by one the sons working the valley farm paid a visit to their parents' home. They had been starved of interesting company, particularly female, for years, and it became an amusement to Setepenre to watch them trying to outdo each other for her attention.

Most of the journey back for Heh and Ipi was overland – but when they reached the border of Nubia and Khemet, the angry white waters of the first cataract and the strange elephant-shaped rocks of the garrison town of Suan, they embarked on a ship going north. They had not gone far when they fell into conversation with two men who seemed more cultivated than the stone workers and merchants who occupied the rest of the deck. The two men invited Heh and Ipi to share a bottle of wine and a game of dice, and the cliffs of Upper Egypt were soon sliding by unnoticed as the four gambled away their possessions.

Ipi was quiet as usual, but Heh was expansive and talk-ative. He boasted of his close association with the new Queen. The men appeared to be impressed and laughingly told him that he should not mind putting his rings up as stakes in the game for he would surely be able to obtain others from his wealthy benefactress. Heh, somewhat the worse for wine – for other bottles had appeared as soon as they were down to the dregs of the first – put all his rings, his bracelets and even the royal seal ring on the boards. He lost them all. Ipi had stopped playing early in the game and was trying to prevent his companion from being so reckless. There was almost a fight between them when the seal ring went – but Heh had always been the stronger of the two and Ipi soon gave in, sitting back on his haunches, watching and worrying in silence. He began to dislike the men intensely though he could not put his finger exactly on what bothered him. He was sure they were cheating but no matter how hard he watched he could not see how it was done.

At last Ipi shrugged and decided if Heh wanted to

give up everything he had – he would not interfere. They were rich after the spying they had done on Ankhesenamun, and were likely to be even richer once they reported back to Nezem-mut. As Heh said – they would be able to demand anything they wanted for as long as they lived. He relaxed and held out his cup for a taste of the new wine that had just been opened. Heh took a deep draught of it and smacked his lips noisily. Ipi sipped it delicately – pretending a sophisticated expertise he did not actually possess. The wine was unlike any he had tasted before – but it was good. Why were the two men looking at him so peculiarly? Had he said the wrong thing about the wine? It must be very potent for he was beginning to feel extraordinarily dizzy. He wondered how Heh was handling it seeing that he was already drunk. He looked across at him in time to see him keel over on his face scattering the stakes and the dice all over the deck.

'How embarrassing,' Ipi thought. 'What a fool . . .'

But that was his last thought, for he too found himself falling into darkness. If he had had time to look at the two men he would have seen them smile grimly, their eyes cold, their demeanour completely sober. Quietly and quickly they gathered up the jewels Heh had parted with so easily, and slipped away into the crowd. They had chosen to administer the poisoned wine just before the boat drew up to the quayside. Within seconds they had leapt ashore and, before anyone realized the two dwarfs were dead, they had disappeared.

Nezem-mut later took the seal ring back, but she allowed her assassins to keep the rest of the booty, adding some further rich rewards of her own.

Now no one knew where Setepenre was except herself.

15
THE NEW PHARAOH

Horemheb sat on the throne he had worked so long and so hard to obtain and looked down on the throng of people gathered below him. Some had been with him since the first, their fortunes rising and falling and rising again with the tide of power that flowed through the Two Lands. Others were new men scarcely weathered into office.

When had he first realized it was the throne that he was after? Had he ever? Or had it just come his way as the inevitable result of the actions he had taken? He had taken those actions often because no one else would take them – though it was clear that they were necessary. He wondered at the turbulence of the Two Lands during his lifetime. Was there ever a time when so many internal conflicts had racked his poor country? He remembered an incident when he was a young captain in the army of Neb-maat-Ra, Amenhotep III, the last king of any substance this stricken country had known. At that moment he could have changed the course of history. At that moment he could have prevented so much that was later to destroy the order and tranquillity of Egypt with one decisive movement. But, at that precise moment, he was not yet ready to make such a decision and take such a step.

He was training a troop of recruits, one of them being the Prince Amenhotep, later to become the lunatic King Akhenaten. He should never have been allowed to rule Egypt! His elder brother had died and he was suddenly thrust into the position of heir.

'Take him and train him to be a man,' Neb-maat-Ra had commanded. Even he could see the boy was too feeble to make a good king. He was thin and weedy, he was a dreamer, a poet. He was the last person to take his father's place. Neb-maat-Ra was a strong king. He had ruled a long time and during his reign Egypt and its empire had never been richer, more powerful, more confident. Horemheb had boundless admiration for him. He kept order without tyranny. He manipulated people without their knowing that they were being manipulated. He was shrewd, diplomatic, unsentimental. He had only one weakness and that was his excessive love for Queen Tiye. Prince Amenhotep was her son and she was determined he would be king after his father – suitable or not.

Horemheb looked at Nezem-mut sitting on her throne with the winged crown of Mut pinching her cheeks. There were times when he had longed to have a woman to love as deeply as Neb-maat-Ra loved Tiye. The nearest he had ever come to it was the beautiful Nefertiti. He had desired her so much that sometimes he had felt he could not endure it. She flirted with him with her eyes – sometimes flagrantly in front of her husband. Once she had even offered herself to him – but there was something in him – some hard, cold band of metal in his heart that held him back. Was it a sense of honour? Or was it a fear that if he gave himself completely to a woman he would no longer be in control of his own destiny? He had not lain with Nefertiti. He had watched her grow from teasing, kittenish girl to powerful woman more worthy to be king than her peevish husband. How could she have loved Akhenaten? But she did. Of that there was no doubt. This woman – more beautiful, more intelligent, more vibrant than any other in the world, had supported that

dangerous fool through every crazy decision he
made.

What if he had let the prince die that day in the
marshes? He had come upon him separated from the
other recruits, floundering in the muddy water, his
stick-like arms stretching out to grasp the reeds just out
of reach. He had stood on the path and watched him
gasping for breath, his eyes wild with fear, water-weed
and mud clinging to his pallid face. Everything was
poised on that moment. Horemheb could have stooped
down and hauled him out with ease. He did not. Was
it because he had been instructed by his king to make
a man of him and he knew that the only way for the
prince to become a man fit to rule a kingdom would be
for him to overcome difficulties and make decisions by
himself, without aid from anyone? Was it because he
sensed even then how the country would suffer when he
held the crook and flail and wore the double crown?
Horemheb remembered how he was tempted to push
him under. Would that he had! Instead – he watched
him clamber out at last and walk away filled with anger
and hate. If he had killed him then before the country
suffered such torment he would have saved a lot of grief.
As it was he had to kill him in the end. He was not proud
of that – for a pharaoh is divine authority and should
not be touched or challenged in any way. Horemheb
sighed as his hands tightened on the symbolic crook and
flail Zais had just placed in his hands. He was not proud
or pleased with many things he had done – but he did
not regret doing them. They had to be done.

How strange to be here in this position so high above
the rest of the human race. He had always had influence
and power – but never like this. The rituals based on
ancient texts transformed him from man to god. On his
brow a golden cobra gazed fiercely out on the world

ready to protect him against any danger with its magic.
The two crowns, of north and south, weighed heavy on
his head. He smiled inwardly, remembering the boy
Tutankhamun, dwarfed by the mighty symbols of
royalty, looking out with frightened eyes. *He* was not
afraid. He had earned the right to be here more than any
who had gone before. His only regret was that he had
waited so long before he took this step. His role up to
now had been to make or break kings. He had tried to
prevent Akhenaten keeping the throne once he had
shown what he intended to do with it, and replace him
with his half-brother, Prince Djehuti-kheper-Ra, secret
son of Neb-maat-Ra and his daughter Sitamun. But the
prince had proved not to be open to influence, and in
the end had had to be pushed aside to make way for the
child, Tutankhamun, young enough to shape and mould
to Horemheb's will. Everything had looked so good
when Tutankhamun had come to the throne. He had
felt confident that he would be able to recover the vassal
states Akhenaten had lost by his weak foreign policy,
and reinstate the ancient religious structure that had
worked so well for so many millenia. But to undo the
damage Akhenaten had done took time and his programme was not complete before Tutankhamun was of
an age to want power for himself, and, under the
influence of Akhenaten's daughter, undermine his
work.

He thought about Ankhesenamun – child of troubled
times – woman of erratic convictions and moods. She
had left him facing a major war with a strong and
dangerous enemy. He did not once consider that it was
his own murder of the Hittite prince that had caused the
war, and not her letters of invitation. He did not once
consider that it might have been acceptable to introduce
new blood into the effete royal line; that the Hittites

would have been a valuable ally to have; that many kings of Egypt had foreign blood flowing in their veins and had been no less loyal to the Two Lands for all that.

He looked thoughtfully at Maya, Tutankhamun's treasurer and close friend. Could he be trusted to serve the new king? Did he, like many others, suspect him of causing Tutankhamun's accident? He hoped he could trust Maya. He was a young, vigorous and able man – well qualified for any high office he was asked to fill. Beside him stood his wife Meryt. Horemheb could see that they were close. He must make an effort to win her to his side. Horemheb had come as far as he had not least because he was a good judge of character. Maya would not follow him if he knew how much blood was on his hands – but he did not know and he did not want to know. He was honourable, but he was also ambitious and practical. The old regime was finished. No purpose would be served by dwelling on it with regret and recrimination. He would throw himself wholeheartedly and with loyalty into making the new regime work. Like Horemheb himself he enjoyed the interest and excitement of making decisions that affected many people, and would be sad to be shunted off into a backwater to lead a simple and dull life.

Carefully Horemheb looked around as the priests mouthed the sacred words and performed the holy rituals over him. He weighed up this man and that, selecting those whom he would keep in positions of power and those he would send into retirement; those whose official duties he would increase. There were some present whom he almost feared – some of the old nobility who resented the fact that a commoner had taken the throne. Some of those he would try to teach to respect him; others would meet with unfortunate accidents or be bribed into exile. He wished he had

Setepenre at his side – beautiful, young and incontro-
vertibly royal. She would lend the scene an elegance and
style that eluded Nezem-mut. Her dramatic return from
oblivion would have caused such a stir that no one
would be looking to criticize him, and Nezem-mut
would not be sitting there this moment with that expression of bitter satisfaction.

Ah, there was the incense! Zais held it out to him as
though he were a god. A god? So he was. He had the
right of life and death over every man, woman and child
in the Two Lands and over many beyond. At last this
formidable power was in the hands of someone he
trusted – not some dreamer who happened to have the
right blood in his veins – not some woman or some
child – not even some disembodied spirit named Amun
or Ra – but in the hands of himself – experienced, competent, trained. Let others believe in magic and the
supernatural. He did not. He believed in himself.

EPILOGUE

General Horemheb – Chief Commander of the armies of several kings, Attender of the King's Footsteps, Companion of the King, The King's Eyes, Scribe and Diplomat, Vice-regent and Deputy of the King – reigned for many years when finally he became King himself, counting his rule from the death of Amenhotep III, ignoring the reigning monarchs in between – Akhenaten, Smenhkhare, Tutankhamun and Ay – as though they had never existed. In the King Lists inscribed during the reign of Sety I at Abydos no mention is made of the Atenist kings and Horemheb comes between Amenhotep III and Rameses I. They were written out of history – yet – ironically – they are the ones who most fascinate us. More archaeologists and Egyptologists spend their time trying to piece together the fragments of knowledge we have about them, than they spend on all the others. Novelists write more books about them. Their tombs were smashed, their monuments desecrated, their names chipped and chiselled away – but we seek them out and we believe we know them . . .

Horemheb was a stern, strong king and restored order to the Two Lands with a heavy hand. At Karnak, the remains of a stela inscribed by him gives us some idea of the penalties evil-doers could expect – from having their noses cut off, being banished to the horrific and notorious fortress at Tjel on the Asiatic borders or sent to work the most difficult mines in the hottest and most uncompromising places – to a hundred lashes or five wounds. Law courts were set up to administer these laws.

Men-nefer (Memphis) was his capital and he spent most of his time in the north. He chose his successor from his own army, a man from the delta who had come from humble beginnings like himself and worked his way up to general and vice-regent by sheer determination and character. He, Rameses I, reigned only briefly, for, like Ay, he was already an old man when he was given the double crown. Horemheb must have seen that he had a young and able son, who showed great potential, for Sety I (as he became) was a remarkable man, strong and cultured. He was responsible for building the magnificent Temple at Abydos that we view today with such pleasure and such awe. His tomb in the Valley of the Kings is the most beautiful of all, and his fine, almost transparent alabaster sarcophagus is a joy to see at the Sir John Soane Museum in London.

Akhenaten's three youngest daughters faded from history very early on. It is not known what became of them. I have a theory that the youngest, Setepenre, married Rameses I and gave his line legitimacy, for the wife of Rameses I was Set-Ra.

Nezem-mut (whose name was also Mutnodjemne) appears on the statue made to commemorate Horemheb's coronation at Denderah. Among her titles were 'Heiress' and 'Mistress of the Two Lands', also 'Sovereign Lady exalted with the Double Plumes'. It is thought she bore Horemheb a son – but he did not live long enough to inherit the throne. Nezem-mut seems to have died in the thirteenth year of Horemheb's reign. Did she on her deathbed reveal where Akhenaten's last surviving daughter was?

Horemheb was responsible for an excellent building programme though sometimes it is difficult to tell what

is really his work and what is not, for he had no
compunction about scratching out the name of
Tutankhamun on buildings, monuments and statues and
replacing it with his own. It is fairly certain however
that he started the huge hypostyle hall at Karnak, later
finished by Sety I.

The war with the Hittites continued for several
generations. Suppiluliuma and his eldest son died of
plague brought back by his troops not long after
Ankhesenamun's death. Mursilis came to the throne
and ruled long and ably, attacking Egypt and its dependencies persistently and vigorously. The enmity
between these two great nations only ceased, interest-
ingly enough, when a descendant of the great Suppiluliuma, the daughter of the Hittite King Khattusilis,
was sent to Egypt to become the Great Royal Wife of
the Pharaoh, to seal a long overdue peace treaty.

Ankhesenamun may not have been so wrong after all
to try to make peace by love – and not war.

CHRONOLOGIES

A brief chronological summary of reigns and events in ancient Egyptian history relevant to the reader of this novel. The dates are drawn in main from John Baines and Jaromir Málek, *Atlas of Ancient Egypt* (Phaidon, Oxford, 1980).

Outside Egypt between 3000 and 2000 BC the ancient Maltese temples were built, as were Stonehenge, West Kennet Long Barrow, Silbury Hill and Avebury in Britain. The Cycladic and Minoan civilizations flourished in Crete and the Eastern Mediterranean islands. Mohenjo-Daro in India and Sumer in the Middle East reached their peak.

In Egypt before 3000 BC historians speak of the 'Predynastic Period'.

EGYPT: EARLY DYNASTIC PERIOD
2920–2770 BC
DYNASTIES 1, 2, 3

Dynasty 3: *King Djoser* 2630–2611 BC
King Djoser's great architect and sage, Imhotep, designed and built the first major stone building in the world – the first pyramid – the Step Pyramid of Sakkara. Imhotep later became deified and associated with the Greek god of healing, Asclepius.

EGYPT: OLD KINGDOM

2575–2134 BC

DYNASTIES 4, 5, 6, 7, 8

Dynasty 4: *Khufu (Cheops)* 2551–2528 BC
Khephren 2520–2494 BC
Menkaure (Mycerinus) 2490–2472 BC
These were the builders of the Great Pyramids at Giza.
Many others were built during the period of the Old
Kingdom.

Dynasty 5: *Unas (Wenis)* 2356–2323 BC
'The Pyramid Texts' were inscribed on the inner walls
of his pyramid at Sakkara for the first time. They were
wonderful poems and spells designed to help and guide
the deceased through the Otherworld.

Dynasty 6:
This ended with the long reign of Pepi II after which
Egypt seemed to sink into a decline.

EGYPT: FIRST INTERMEDIATE PERIOD

2150–2040 BC

DYNASTIES 9, 10

Central power broken. Warring local rulers. A period of
uncertainty and violence.

EGYPT: MIDDLE KINGDOM

2040–1640 BC

DYNASTIES 11, 12, 13, 14

Dynasty 11:
The unification of the Two Lands, North and South,

under several kings called Mentuhotep 2061–2010 BC.

One built his mortuary temple and tomb at Deir el Bahri next to which, much later, in the eighteenth dynasty, Hatshepsut built hers. The seat of power was established at Waset (Greek name: Thebes. Modern: Luxor/Karnak). The later eighteenth dynasty kings looked back to this period as a great one and emulated it whenever they could. At this time an expedition was sent to Punt on the Horn of Africa. Later Hatshepsut sent her own expedition there.

EGYPT: SECOND INTERMEDIATE PERIOD
1640–1532 BC
DYNASTIES 15, 16, 17

The Hyksos invaded from the Middle East, bringing with them the horse and the chariot. Their capital was at Avaris in the delta. For the Egyptians it was a dark age.

By the end of the period Theban princes led a revolt against them and drove them out of the country establishing their own right to rule the Two Lands.

Ta'o I and Ta'o II (Sequenenre) and Kamose 1555–1550 BC led the rebellion and established the next dynasty. Ta'o II had a very strong and long-lived wife, Aah-hetep I.

EGYPT: THE NEW KINGDOM
1550–1070 BC
DYNASTIES 18, 19, 20

The eighteenth dynasty and the early part of the

nineteenth is often thought to be the high point of
Egyptian civilization. Egypt was strong internally and
by conquering neighbouring states established an
empire whose tribute made Egypt rich. Pyramids were
no longer in fashion and the kings dug deep into rocky
cliffs to hide their tombs. Magnificent temples were
built.

Dynasty 18: *Ahmose* 1550–1525 BC
Warrior king. Strong wife: Nefertari.
Amenhotep I 1525–1504 BC
He had a daughter, Aah-mes, by his sister, and a son by
a lesser wife, Senseneb.
Thutmosis I (Aa-kheper-ka-Ra) 1504–1492 BC (Son of
Amenhotep and Senseneb)
Warrior king who extended the frontiers of the empire
and consolidated power with diplomatic marriages. Was
married to his sister who bore him a daughter,
Hatshepsut. His son by a lesser wife, Mutnofre, became
next pharaoh with Hatshepsut as his wife.
Thutmosis II (Aa-kheper-en-Ra) 1492–1479 BC
When he died after a short reign his son by a non-royal
wife, Ast, was still a young child. His sister-widow,
Hatshepsut, was made regent for him. She decided to
take the throne for herself and became pharaoh, taking
male titles and wearing male attire.
Hatshepsut I (Maat-ka-Ra) 1473–1458 BC
Female Pharaoh.
Famous for her magnificent temple at Deir el Bahri and
her successful expedition to Punt. (As in my novel,
Daughter of Amun, Arrow, 1989.)
Thutmosis III (Men-kheper-Ra) 1479–1425 BC
No one knows how he took over power from his
stepmother-aunt, Hatshepsut, but when he did he
reigned a long time and was a very strong warrior king.

He obliterated her name and her image wherever he could.

Amenhotep II 1427–1401 BC

Thutmosis IV 1401–1391 BC

Amenhotep III (Neb-maat-Ra) 1391–1353 BC

Long-lived, rich and powerful. Chose as his Great Royal Wife and mother of his heir a non-royal lady – Tiye, daughter of Yuya, his Master of Chariots, and his wife, Thuya (all of whose mummies have been found in a state of very good preservation). Is responsible for the Colossi of Memnon at Luxor which were actually giant statues of himself on either side of the entrance to his luxurious mortuary temple.

Amenhotep IV/Akhenaten 1353–1335 BC (Wa-en-Ra)

(As in my novel, *The Son of the Sun*, Arrow 1990.)

Moved his capital from Thebes and Memphis to a completely new site called Akhetaten (now Tel el Amarna). Overthrew the traditional religion of Egypt and concentrated all religious aspiration on the one god symbolized by the disc of the sun emitting rays which held out the sign for eternal life: The Aten. His wife, the famous and beautiful Nefertiti, given equal status. They had six daughters: Merytaten, Maketaten, Ankhesenpaaten, Nefernefruaten, Neferneferure, Setepenre.

Smenkhkare 1335–1333 BC (Possibly Nefertiti herself)

Tutankhamun 1333–1323 BC (As in this novel *Daughter of Ra*)

Ay 1323–1319 BC

Horemheb 1319–1307 BC

Horemheb reinstated the priests of Amun as a great power and turned the country against the memory of Akhenaten and his religion. In the King Lists the 'Aten kings' are left out and Horemheb is listed straight after Amenhotep III as though the others had never been. He died childless and appointed his general, Rameses, as the next pharaoh on his death.

The nineteenth dynasty with the Rameside kings now begins. By the end of this dynasty Egypt is invaded again and again and its greatest period is past.

All dates approximate.

Hittite chronology relevant to this book.

Suppiluliuma I c.1375–1320 BC
He smashes the power of the kingdom of Mitanni and extends his borders as far as Lebanon. Attacks Syria. Ankhesenamun writes to him for a husband.
Amuwandas III c.1320–1319 BC
Mursilis II c.1319–1306 BC
Consolidates his father's conquests. War with Egyptian dependencies. Wrote *Prayers in Time of Plague* and *Annals* of his and his father's reigns.
Muwatallis c.1306–1282 BC
Battle of Kadesh against Rameses II of Egypt.
Hattusilis III c.1275–1250 BC
Brother of Muwatallis usurps the throne. He concludes an 'everlasting peace' with Egypt, sealing the peace treaty by the marriage of one of his daughters to Rameses.

Some of this information is taken from *Narrow Pass Black Mountain* by C. W. Ceram (Readers Union, 1957).

PLACE NAMES

Ancient Egyptian version	Variation (often Greek)	Modern
Akhetaten	The Horizon of the Aten	Tel el Amarna
Djeser Djeseru	Djeser-menu	Hatshepsut's temple at Deir el Bahri
Ipet-Esut Ipet-Resyt	Ipet-Sut Ipet-Resut } Thebes	Karnak Luxor
Keftiu	The Island of the Bulls	Crete
Kepel	Byblos	Jbail
Khemet	Kemet, the Black Land, the Two Lands	Egypt
Khemnu	Khmun, Hermopolis	Ashmunein
Men-nefer	Menufer, White Walls	Memphis
Nekheb	The Red Mound,	Kom el Ahmar
Nekhen	Hierakonopolis	Kom el Ahmar
Per-Hay	Great House	Malkata
Punt		probably northern Somaliland, near Djibouti
Serui	Bay of Cliffs	Deir el Bahri
Suan	Elephantine, Syene, Sunu	Assuan, Aswan
Waset	Thebes	Luxor
Yunu	Iunu, Lunu, On (Bible) Heliopolis (Greek)	now buried under a north-east suburb of Cairo

PROPER NAMES

As the ancient Egyptians did not have vowels as we know them in the written word there is great variation in the translation of the different names. For instance, some authorities give 'Amun' as 'Amon' or 'Amen'. Thus we have 'Tutankhamun', 'Tutankhamon' or 'Tutankhamen'.

Some spell the sun god 'Ra' – others 'Re'. Thus we have 'Setepenre' or 'Setepenra'.

In other instances we find a varying number of vowels inserted. For instance: 'Nefernefruaten' or 'Neferneferuaten'.

To add to the confusion the authorities sometimes use the Greek version of a name instead of the ancient Egyptian. For instance: the god of wisdom is named 'Thoth' by the Greeks, and 'Djehuti' (sometimes spelled 'Tahuti') by the Egyptians. Thus we have 'Thutmosis', 'Thutmose' or 'Thutmes' based on the Greek 'Thoth', where perhaps we should have 'Djehuti-mes'. I would like to have kept to the names closest to the ancient Egyptian, but in some instances I have thought it simpler all round to use the version more familiar to the modern reader.

GODS AND GODDESSES

The ancient Egyptians had a complicated pantheon of gods and goddesses.

Brief notes on some of the main deified forces follow below.

Much fuller accounts may be found in the following books:

Hart, George, *A Dictionary of Egyptian Gods and Goddesses*, Routledge & Kegan Paul, 1986;

Hornung, Erik, *Conceptions of God in Ancient Egypt: The One and the Many* (translated by John Bains) RKP 1983;

Lurker, Manfred, *The Gods and Symbols of Ancient Egypt*, Thames & Hudson, 1980;

Rundle Clark, R.T., *Myth and Symbol in Ancient Egypt*, Thames & Hudson, 1978.

AMMIT
Hybrid monster waiting beside the scales of Maat in the Hall of Osiris to gobble up 'unjustified' souls.

AMUN (Amen, Amon)
Primeval god mentioned in the pyramid texts. Later became a powerful local god in the Theban area and a major god in the Egyptian pantheon. Usually depicted as a man holding divine sceptre and *ankh* with a crown supporting two tall plumes. The name is connected with being hidden, concealed, invisible. 'Hidden of Aspect, Mysterious of Form'; 'He Who abides in all things'. His symbolic animals are the ram and the goose. His great temple at present-day Karnak is still impressive.

APEP (Apophis, Apopis)
Appears in the form of a giant snake. Represents 'non-existence', the 'Void', which to the ancient Egyptians was a state as real as existence. The daily and nightly battle between Ra and Apep represents the constant and eternal struggle between existence and non-existence. So far Apep has always been defeated, never destroyed. The possibility that Ra might one day lose is always there. The implication is that we are only held in existence by positive action on the part of our guardian gods against Apep.

DJEHUTI (Djeheuty, Tehuti, Thoth)
'The Silver Aten'. The moon springing out of darkness to bring illuminating knowledge and wisdom. Lord of Time. Reckoner of Years. Inventor of writing and protector of scribes. Guardian of the 'House of Life', where all the wisdom texts are kept. He wears a crown of the crescent moon supporting the full moon disc. He is represented in two forms: as man-bodied with the head of the sacred ibis, and as baboon. The ibis bird is white and black with a crescent-shaped beak. The baboon was adopted from an already existing god at his cult centre Khemnu (Hermopolis). The Greeks identified him with their god Hermes, their name 'Hermes Trismegistos' coming from an inscription at Esna: 'Djehuti the great, the great, the great'.

HATHOR
Her name means 'mansion of Horus'. Her main aspect is life-giving and nurturing motherhood. She and Isis are sometimes interchangeable as mother of Horus, though she is also seen as wife of Horus. Her cult animal is the cow. Pharaoh is often seen in reliefs and paintings as sucking physical nourishment and mystical

wisdom from the udders of a celestial cow representing
Hathor. Her sacred instrument is the sistrum or rattle.
Music and dancing are very important in her cult. She
was equated with the beautiful goddess of love,
Aphrodite, by the Greeks. A child of Horus and
Hathor is Ihy, who personifies joy through music. A
well-preserved temple at Denderah is still to be
seen.

HORUS

Sky god seen as a falcon with all-seeing eyes, the sun and
the moon. The pharaoh is supposed to be Horus on
earth. 'The eye of Horus' is a very complex concept, one
aspect of which rests on the legend of Horus presenting
his own eye to his father to give him new life. He has
many forms: one is Ra-Harakhti, representing one
aspect of the sun. He is sometimes seen as the brother
of Set, sometimes as his nephew. In either case both are
opposing but complementary sides of a whole – good
and evil, light and dark. He is the Egyptian god most
readily compared to Christ. As son of Osiris and Isis he
completes a sacred trinity, and as husband of Hathor
and father of their son Ihy, he completes another. His
temple at his cult centre, Edfu, is one of the best-
preserved ancient Egyptian temples. It is still standing.
The present building was raised much later than the
reign of Hatshepsut.

MAAT

Goddess who wears an ostrich feather tied very simply
with a ribbon around her head. She personifies the order
of the universe working harmoniously with the will of
the divine initiator. You will often see a pharaoh
presenting an image of her to stress that he rules with
Maat – that is, in harmony with the divine and natural

laws of the universe. It is against her feather the heart
of the deceased is weighed in the Otherworld.

MUT
Chief wife of Amun at Thebes. Together with their son,
Khonsu, she and Amun make up one of the important
divine trinities of Egyptian mythology. She wears a
vulture headdress and the hieroglyph for her name is a
vulture, but she can also appear as a lioness or cat-
headed goddess like Sekhmet in the north. Her name
means 'mother'. The temple of Luxor was primarily
dedicated to her.

OSIRIS
King of the Living in the Underworld (known as the
'Duat' to the ancient Egyptians). His flesh is often
depicted as green as he is the god of regeneration and
rebirth. Images of him are often laid flat and filled with
Nile silt and planted with barley seed at burials. Such
Osiris-shaped trays of rooted and once growing barley
plants have been found in tombs. Ra and he are 'twin
souls', the one reigning 'above' the earth, the other
'below'. It is said he was once a king ruling on earth,
destroyed by his jealous brother Set, restored to life just
long enough by the magic of his sister-wife Isis for her
to conceive their child, Horus, the falcon-headed god.
Osiris, Isis, Horus form a divine trinity.

PTAH
One of the major creator-gods of the ancient Egyptians.
There is a record of Ptah, self-created, thinking about
the cosmos and then speaking it into existence. He is
often depicted as a craftsman-creator and plays an
important role at the 'opening of the mouth' ceremony
at funerals. This ritual prepares the mummy or a statue

to house the living *ka* of the deceased by touching his or her mouth with an adze made of meteoric iron. Ptah's cult centre was at Memphis (Men-nefer). His huge temple is currently being excavated, though most of the great blocks are missing, having been carried away in past centuries to build Cairo.

RA (Re)
George Hart says of him: 'Creator sun god of Heliopolis. Re is the quintessence of all manifestations of the sun god, permeating the three realms of the sky, earth and Underworld. Hence many deities enhance their own divinity by coalescing with this aspect of the sun god' – for example, Amun-Ra. In the myth, the sun god emerges out of the primeval waters on the first mound and as a trinity of force – Kheper (dawn), Ra (noon), and Atum (sunset) – bursts from the cosmic egg, which he/she has somehow laid, into multitudinous life. There are many creation myths in ancient Egypt, none of them logical – but many with a deep mystical integrity and power.

SEKHMET
Consort of Ptah. Lioness goddess of Memphis. 'Great of Magic'. Associated with destruction, but more often in the sense of making way for creation than destruction for destruction's sake. She has been known to cure pestilence as well as to cause it.

SESHAT
'Foremost in the Library'. Usually associated as the female counterpart of Djehuti as they are both concerned with measuring and recording. Seen with a seven-pointed star above her head.

SET

George Hart describes him as a 'god of chaotic forces who commands both veneration and hostility'. In mythology he is depicted as the murderer of his brother Osiris and the antagonist of Horus, and yet in the solar barque he defends Ra against the even greater menace of attack by Apep, the ultimate enemy of existence. He is the violent and destructive force on earth, but does not threaten the very existence of the universe as does Apep. Sometimes the energy of such a force as Set can be harnessed and redirected. Traditionally he has come to be identified with 'evil' and Horus with 'good' in the conflict of good and evil. But, as we all know, nothing is as simple as that. He is associated with the red desert regions and the sandstorms, as opposed to the rich black fertile lands beside the river.

GENERAL NOTES AND ACKNOWLEDGEMENTS

Page
10

These events are described in my novel *The Son of the Sun* (Arrow, 1990).

The exact relationships of all the various protagonists in this great eighteenth dynasty drama are sometimes obscure, but I have tried to make sense of them. The controversy that surrounds the Atenist (or Amarnan) pharaohs is still not resolved. For the purposes of writing a novel one has to take one path through the mass of confusing and divergent paths left by the exploring archaeologists and Egyptologists and follow it to the end. I am well aware that if two writers each living on either side of a family today were to write a book about that family, two very different pictures would emerge. There have been many novels written about Akhenaten's family, each different from the next, yet all using the same bits and pieces left to us after the passing of more then three thousand years and an extensive and deliberate vandalism on the part of the pharaohs who succeeded him.

When I first wrote *The Son of the Sun* (Allison & Busby, 1986) I believed that the mysterious and unnamed Amarnan prince buried in Tomb 55 was Smenhkhare, the pharaoh who reigned very briefly after Akhenaten. I have since read some convincing arguments for the theory that

Smenhkhare as a separate male pharaoh never existed at all, and that Nefertiti herself took that name and reigned briefly as pharaoh after her husband's death. These arguments have been put forward in the following books by Julia Samson and articles by J. Harris:

Julia Samson, *Amarna City of Akhenaten and Nefertiti* (Aris & Phillips, 1978), and *Nefertiti and Cleopatra* (The Rubicon Press, 1985);

J. Harris, *Nefertiti Rediviva* and *Neferneferuaten Regnans* in *Acta Orientalia* 1973 – 4.

This leaves the prince in Tomb 55 still a mystery. In the rewrite of *The Son of the Sun* (Arrow, 1990), he is named Djehuti-kheper-Ra, but keeps his identity as the half-brother of Akhenaten and the narrator of the story.

As to the question about the identity of Ay, I have followed the orthodox, but by no means unanimous, belief that he was the son of Yuya, Master of Chariots and honoured official at the court of Amenhotep III, whose well preserved body is in the Cairo Museum. As the brother of Queen Tiye, and father of Nefertiti and Nezem-mut, he is closely linked to the royal family without actually being of the royal blood-line. Again – it is well attested, but not proven – that Nefertiti was his daughter, as it is well-attested but not proven that Tutankhamun was the son of Akhenaten and a minor wife, Kia.

One relationship we can be certain of however – is that Ankhesenamun was the daughter of Akhenaten and Nefertiti.

21   'He would be bound in all nine parts of his being . . .'

'In *The Gods of Rebirth: The Mythology of Modern Magic* by Nevill Drury (Aquarian Press, 1988), there is a description of the nine parts of the individual that the ancient Egyptians believed existed.

i)   *Khat*: the physical body, liable to decay.

ii) *Ka*: the double, an abstract personality normally dwelling in the tomb – but sometimes wandering freely, ghost-like.

iii) *Ba*: the 'heart' soul, which could take a material or non-material form, and was sometimes depicted as nourishing the mummified body.

iv) *Ab*: the heart – the source of both good and evil. Conscience. It was important that the heart should be preserved in the tomb. And it was the heart that was judged in the Duat and weighed against the feather of Truth.

v)   *Khaibit*: the shadow.

vi) *Khu*: the spiritual body (soul) dwelling in the *Sahu*. It could never die.

vii) *Sekhem*: the life-force.

viii) *Ren*: the name which had to be preserved for the man to exist.

ix) *Sahu*: the greater spiritual body forming the habitation of the soul.

'The celestial body of the follower of Ra, consists of the *Ka* and *Khu* which can become a *Tet* or "Shining One" who is set like a "Jewel in the

Diadem of the Lord of Spirit and Life made
One". The noumenal essence from which both
these derive is the *Hammemit* which was supposed to revolve around the sun for a period of
one hundred and twenty (symbolic) years prior
to incarnation.'

Mr Drury's explanation is not the only one.
These are complex and mysterious beliefs. It is
enough that we remember that the ancient
Egyptians believed in life before birth and after
death, and that they believed the individual had
many life-aspects, some eternal, some not. I
sometimes wonder if our saying that a cat has
nine lives comes from ancient Egypt where the
cat was a sacred symbol.

I understand the *khu* as the 'Spirit' – that
which is part of the original and eternal being of
a person. Through this we are in touch with the
Otherworld, because the Otherworld is where
the *khu* (spirit) actually dwells. It only tem-
porarily overlaps, as it were, with this world,
while we are 'in the body'. By becoming conscious of the *khu* we become conscious of the
Otherworld. In this state of mystical consciousness we can communicate with what is beyond
our comprehension.

One's soul, the *ka*, is more local to oneself as
a personality formed in one particular time and
place. One forms it by one's thoughts and
actions in this life and at death it is 'judged'.

If it is judged 'good' it rejoins the *khu*, or
eternal spirit. If it is judged 'bad' it has to return
to earth and try again, or be denied existence
and be flung back into the Void where there is
no differentiation.

If the *ka* is judged worthy to continue, it will work its passage through many different transformations until at last it 'melts into' its *khu* and there is no longer any distinction between them. In this state, a state of perfection, it waits for the moment when that which created all things out of itself, re-absorbs all things into itself.

It will be as it was before Creation.

And then God will feel the desire to utter again and a new creation will begin.

But meanwhile, in the body, it is difficult for us to respond favourably to this magnificent eternal drama. We are much more concerned to keep the comforts of the familiar around us. In ancient Egypt prayers were uttered fervently at funerals that the deceased might have power over the 'knot' that tied the various parts of his being together so that they might not be scattered into the Unknown. The Name was crucial to this 'knot' and therefore crucial to the survival of the familiar personality of the deceased.

22 and 62-3 These quotations are taken from *Egypt of the Pharaohs* by Sir Alan Gardiner (Oxford University Press, 1961), pp. 225, 226.

The Hymn to the Aten was inscribed on the walls of Ay's original tomb at Akhetaten though it is believed it was composed by Akhenaten himself, using and enhancing ancient references to the sun god. It bears an interesting resemblance to the magnificent Psalm 104 in the Bible:

'Bless the Lord, O my soul. O Lord my God, thou art very great; thou art clothed with honour and majesty. Who coverest thyself with light as with a garment: who stretchest out the heavens like a curtain: who layeth the beams of his chambers in the waters: who maketh the clouds his chariot: who walketh upon the wings of the wind: who maketh his angels spirits; his ministers a flaming fire: who laid the foundations of the earth, that it should not be removed for ever . . .

He sendeth the springs into the valleys, which run among the hills. They give drink to every beast of the field: the wild asses quench their thirst. By them shall the fowls of the heaven have their habitation, which sing among the branches . . .

He causeth the grass to grow for the cattle, and herb for the service of man: that he may bring forth food out of the earth, . . .

Thou makest darkness, and it is night: wherein all the beasts of the forest do creep forth. The young lions roar after their prey, and seek their meat from God. The sun ariseth, they gather themselves together, and lay them down in their dens.

Man goeth forth unto his work and to his labour until the evening.

O Lord how manifold are thy works! in wisdom hast thou made them all: the earth is full of thy riches. So is this great and wide sea, wherein are things creeping innumerable, both small and great beasts. There go the ships . . .'

23   Moyra Caldecott, *The Son of the Sun* (Arrow, 1990).

33   '. . . in 1871 historians knew hardly anything about the Hittites. Today we are aware that in the second millenium BC this nation was a Great Power whose sway extended over all of Asia Minor as far as Syria, who conquered Babylon and fought successful wars against Egypt . . .'
            C. W. Ceram, *Narrow Pass Black Mountain* (Readers Union, 1957).

48   This iron dagger with the rock crystal pommel was found at Tutankhamun's side in his tomb.

52   The dream stela of Thutmose IV inscribed in this story is still in existence.

53   'The Mansion of Millions of Years' was the mortuary temple where priests performing rituals kept the name of the deceased alive hopefully for millions of years.

53   Amenhotep-son-of-Hapu and Imhotep were both so admired and respected for their achievements during their lifetimes that they were later declared 'gods' and continued to produce miracles for people who believed in them for centuries. This is a concept not unsimilar to

the idea of the Pope declaring certain people to be saints who then continue to be active in this world after they have left it.

56   The actual events in this story connected with the green crystal Egg of Ra have not been confirmed by archaeologists or Egyptologists but the ancient Egyptian obsession with the cosmic egg symbol is certainly well documented.

In *An Illustrated Encyclopaedia of Traditional Symbols* by J. C. Cooper (Thames & Hudson, 1978) we read:

'The Cosmic Egg, also symbolized by the sphere, is the life principle; the undifferentiated totality; potentiality; the germ of all creation; the primordial matriarchal world of chaos; the Great Round containing the universe; the hidden origin and mystery of being; cosmic time and space; the beginning; the womb; all seminal existence; the primordial parents; the perfect state of unified opposites; organic matter in its inert state; resurrection; hope. In Hindu, Egyptian, Chinese and Greek symbolism the Cosmic Egg, as the origin of the universe, suddenly burst asunder. Hitherto a whole, it had yet contained everything existing and potential in the limited space of the shell.' In Egypt 'The Cosmic Egg from which the sun, Ra, was hatched was laid by the Nile Goose: "It groweth, I grow; it liveth, I live".' (Spell 59, *Book of the Dead*). Kneph, the Serpent, also produced the Cosmic Egg from his mouth, symbolizing the Logos.'

In *Tutankhamun* by C. Desroches-Noble-court (Penguin Books, 1965), p.181 we read:

'. . . the graves of the masters of Thebes repeated the dramatic story of the sun's gestation and its rebirth at the fifth hour, when the god's boat slid over a pyramidal shape which protected the divine egg from which the sun emerged.'

In *The Shrines of Tut-ankh-amon*: Texts translated with introductions by Alexandre Piankoff. Edited by N. Rambova. (Bollingen Foundation Inc., New York, 1977), p.16 we read:

'Live the beautiful god . . . born of the majesty of Ra, seed of the Brilliant One, pure egg which was brought to being by Horus in the Great Castle . . .'

This refers to Tutankhamun and is from a chair in his tomb.

'The Good God who came out of Ra, Noble Egg of Atum, who lives on Truth every day . . .' Ibid., p.127.

'The King, the Egg of Ra, Lord of the Two Lands Neb-kheper-Ra, image of Ra, will appear like Ra in heaven, every day, living forever and ever.' Ibid., p.120.

Both these are from Shrine II of the golden shrines in Tutankhamun's tomb.

Horus is referred to as 'Lord of the Green Stone' in the very ancient Pyramid Texts, Utterance 301, paragraph 457c, from *The Pyramid Texts* vol.1, translated by S.A.B. Mercer, (Longman, 1952).

The idea of the Cosmic Egg being represented in clear green crystal (probably fluorite) is also used in my novel about Hatshepsut, *Daughter of Amun* (Arrow, 1989), p.135. It is this same green crystal egg that now features in *Daughter of Ra*.

In *The Book of the Dead* by R. O. Faulkner (British Museum Publications, 1985):

'I have arisen from the Egg which is in the secret land, my mouth has been given to me that I may speak with it in the presence of the Great God, Lord of the Netherworld.' Spell 22.

'I have guarded this Egg . . . If it grows, I will grow; if it lives, I will live; if it breathes the air, I will breathe the air.' Spell 59.

'I am he in whom is the Sacred Eye, and who is in the Egg, and it is granted to me to live by them . . .
Egg, O Egg, I am Horus who presides over myriads, my fiery breath is in the faces of those whose hearts would move against me . . .' Spell 42.

'O you of Nekhen who are in your Egg, Lord of the Celestial Waters, make me hale just as you made yourself hale. Release him, loose him, put him on earth, cause him to be loved . . .' Spell 71.

'I have appeared as a great falcon, having come forth from the Egg; I have flown up and alighted as a falcon of four cubits along its back, whose wings are of green–stone of Upper Egypt; I have gone up from the coffer into the Night-bark, I have brought my heart from the eastern mountains, I have alighted in the Day-bark, there are brought to me those of ancient times bowing down, and they give me worship when I appear, having been reassembled as a fair falcon of gold upon the pointed stone . . .' Spell 77.

'O Ra who are in your Egg shining in your disc, rising in your horizon, swimming over your firmament, having no equal among the gods, sailing over the Supports of Shu, giving air with the breath of your mouth, illuminating the Two Lands with your sunshine, may you save me from that god whose shape is secret, whose eyebrows are the arms of the balance, on that night of reckoning . . .' Spell 17.

What we call *The Book of the Dead* was known to the ancient Egyptians as *The Book of Coming Forth by Day* or *The Book of the Great Awakening* because it consisted of copies of ancient prayers and spells designed to assist the deceased through a series of complicated trials so that he or she might emerge at last, 'justified' and 'true of voice', to be reborn with the sun and live eternally.

The reader has probably noticed that certain parts of this book have mythic truth and certain parts have literal truth – as near as we can get it after more than three thousand years. The green Egg of Ra belongs to the realm of myth. In ancient Egyptian myth (or religion if you prefer to call it that) one of the central ideas is a Sacred Egg out of which all that exists is hatched. I have used the Sacred Egg therefore in this story as a major theme not because Ankhesenamun and the others literally struggled for possession of an actual crystal egg (though it might have happened more or less as I describe), but because, like our western European myth about Holy Grail, it serves to illustrate certain important aspects of the characters involved and, by analogy, the human race. Each pursued it for a different reason – and, like the Holy Grail, it was not only different things to different people, but sometimes different things to the same person.

Ankhesenamun's motives were initially the most noble. She basically wanted to use it to keep the balance between the different powerful factions in Egypt. She was the only one who saw its potential as a spiritual power capable of bringing about great good. Hapu wanted to destroy it because he believed Akhenaten, his great hero, wanted him to do so. He was prepared to follow a teacher blindly whether he fully understood his teaching or not.

Nezem-mut's motives were purely selfish. She wanted Horemheb and she was prepared to use the Egg as though it was no more than a magician's power-object. Horemheb saw it used as propaganda, to increase the power of his chosen god, having no intrinsic power of its own. The dwarfs saw it as a way of redressing the trick nature had played on them and becoming very rich.

Whether there was such an object or not over which they struggled is not the most important issue here. Actual objects and actual events always tend after all to be only the visible signs of huge processes that are going on under the surface. Each and every one is illustrative of the inner journey of the soul – either of the individual or of the race as a whole.

86   'I am Ra . . .' Alexandre Piankoff, *The Shrines of Tut-ankh-amon* (Bollingen, Princeton, 1977), p.34.

110   'His majesty passed through life in happiness . . .' Ibid., p.6.

115   Maya's tomb is currently being excavated at Sakkara.

124   The *djed* column is the symbol for stability and security, the hieroglyph for which is used decoratively in all forms of Egyptian art. It represents the steadying column on to which the various pieces of the god Osiris were bound when Isis put him together again after he had been dismembered by his brother Set.

127   'I am the god who resides in the Egg . . .' Georg Steindorff, *Religion of the Ancient Egyptians*, (Putnam, 1905).

136   'I have led them on water and on land . . .' From the Punt reliefs inscribed on the walls of Hatshepsut's temple at Deir el Bahri. Translation by J. H. Breasted, *Ancient Records of Egypt*, vol.2 (Chicago, 1906 – 07).

137   For the story of Hatshepsut and her temple to
        the god Amun see my novel *Daughter of Amun*
        (Arrow, 1989).

164   The 'feud' between Ra and Amun is more to do
        with the fine theological differences within a
        single religion than with the differences
        between two different and opposing religions.
        That is – more like the arguments between the
        early church fathers as to whether Christ was of
        one substance or of two, than between such
        major and different religions as Buddhism and
        Judaism.

165   'When His Majesty rose as King . . .' Sir Alan
        Gardiner, *Egypt of the Pharaohs* (OUP, 1961),
        pp.236, 237.

187   The two letters Ankhesenamun wrote to the
        Hittites are well attested historically:
            'An extraordinary event that dates from the
        time immediately following the death of
        Tutankhamun has now to be recorded. This is a
        cuneiform text quoting a letter addressed to the
        Hittite King Suppiluliuma by a young widow,
        who can only have been Ankhesenamun, though
        what appears to have been her name has through
        some error received a distorted form. She
        explains that she has no son, and begs the
        Hittite King to send one of his own to marry her
        and promises that he shall be acknowledged as
        the Pharaoh. Suppiluliuma is sceptical about the

genuineness of this request and dispatches an official to investigate. The widow indignantly protests her *bona fides*, and a young Hittite prince was finally granted, but was murdered on the way. This led to a war against Egypt though nothing is known about it from Egyptian sources.' From *Egypt of the Pharaohs* by Sir Alan Gardiner (OUP, 1961).

The text Gardiner mentions can be found in *Ancient Near Eastern Texts relating to the Old Testament*, edited by J. B. Pritchard, (Princeton, 1950) p.319.

The incident is also mentioned in *Suppiluliuma and the Amarna Pharaohs* by K. A. Kitchen (Liverpool University Press, 1962), p.22. Kitchen refers to *The Deeds of Suppiluliuma*, a Hittite text that mentions the widow of Tutankhamun 'asking Suppiluliuma for one of his sons in order to make him her husband and the King of Egypt. This event occurred in the first year of Suppiluliuma's six years' long "Second" Syrian War . . .'

The Deeds of Suppiluliuma were written by his son Mursilis II.

'Now when the Egyptians heard of the conquest of Amka, they were indeed afraid. And because their ruler had died, the Queen of Egypt, the widow, sent a messenger to my father, writing to him as follows:

"My husband has died, and not one son do I have. But of you it is said that you have many sons. If you will give me a son of yours, he could be my husband. For how may I take one of my slaves and make him a husband and honour him?"

'Now when my father heard this, he called upon the great men of Hatti for consultation . . . He sent a special envoy to determine the true state of affairs in Egypt.

"Go, and bring back to me reliable tidings. Perhaps they wish only to deride me; perhaps they already have a successor to the throne".'

The Queen evidently wrote back these words:

' "Why have you spoken these words: 'They wish only to deride me'? I have not written to any other country. To you alone have I written. It is said that you have many sons. Give me a son of yours; he shall be my husband and King over Egypt!" Now because my father was friendly he granted the woman's wish according to her word and took action in the matter of the son.'

Then follows the description of the murder.

This is an adapted extract from a translation in *Narrow Pass Black Mountain, the Discovery of the Hittite Nation*, by C. W. Ceram (Readers Union, 1957), pp. 157, 158.

The Encyclopaedia Britannica and other sources mention that the prince's name was Zannanza.

This incident is also recorded by C. Desroches-Noblecourt, *Tutankhamun* (Penguin, 1965), pp. 202-3.

205   All the known tombs in the Valley of the Kings west of Luxor, the burial place of all the pharaohs since the beginning of the eighteenth dynasty, had been opened and robbed in

antiquity and time and again since then. The archaeologists of the 19th and 20th centuries AD who finally came to them to learn about ancient Egypt found nothing left but broken bits and pieces. Only the walls painted with intricate and magnificent pictures of the Duat, the Otherworld, and all the rich mythology of religion that had endured for thousands of years, were left to them.

In 1922 AD Howard Carter, under the sponsorship of Lord Caernarvon, found a small tomb that had been almost untouched by robbers and vandals. I say 'almost' because it seemed there had been an attempt to rob the tomb only a few years after the deceased was buried in it – but only a few things were taken which suggests the thieves were surprised at their work. The tomb was re-sealed with the seal of the necropolis authority under Horemheb.

It was the tomb of the Pharaoh Tutankhamun. Up to that time very little was known about this young boy. It was a quirk of fate that has made him the best known pharaoh of Egypt's many millenia. His successor had done everything in his power to remove all traces of him.

His treasures have been on display all over the world and millions of curious eyes have stared into the eyes of his golden mask.

When I first saw that mask on display it was the time of the first moon walk, and I could not help sensing a curious eerie connection between the gold visor of the astronaut walking on the moon and the gold visor of the boy emerging from his tomb after more than 3000 years.

I felt moved to try to express it in some way.

'I will cover my face with gold
and touch other worlds –
other times.
And man
who has longed for other worlds –
other times –
will stare into my gold face –
my gold eyes –
and see
wonderful things.
And when I die
I will lie
like a young pharaoh
forever in my tomb –
uncorrupted
in the moon desert –
my treasure
a sapphire earth
set in an immensity of dark.'

There have been numerous books describing the treasures found in Tutankhamun's tomb. Here are a few of the titles I have found most helpful:

Tutankhamun by C. Desroches-Noblecourt (Penguin, 1965);
The Shrines of Tut-ankh-amon. Texts translated with introductions by Alexandre Piankoff, edited by N. Rambova (Bollingen Series XL.2., Princeton University Press, 1977);
Tutankamun – His Tomb and his Treasures by I. E. S. Edwards (The Metropolitan Museum of Art & Alfred A. Knopf, 1976);

The Small Golden Shrine from the Tomb of Tutankhamun by M. Eaton-Krauss & E. Graefe (Griffith Institute, Oxford, 1985);
The Tomb of Tutankhamun by Howard Carter (Sphere Books, 1954).

206   'I have come, that I may cause thee to trample . . .' From the victory stela of Thutmose III. Alexandre Piankoff, *The Shrines of Tut-ankhamon* (Bollingen, 1977), p.4.

208   I find it interesting that the mound of earth that was supposed to have arisen from the primeval ocean in Egyptian mythology echoes the current theory of geographers who claim that originally all the continents were joined together in one great landmass and then split and drifted apart.

208   . . . the bones . . . according to ritual texts consisted of silver and were created by the father, and . . . the flesh, of gold, issuing from the mother.' C. Desroches-Noblecourt, *Tutankhamun* (Penguin, 1965), p.193.

209   '. . . a silver vortex . . .'
'. . . the vortex of energy out of which a million worlds have been created . . .' Moyra Caldecott, *The Silver Vortex* (Arrow, 1987).

210   Some of Tutankhamun's flower garlands still in

a remarkable state of preservation are kept at Kew Gardens, London.

210   The two gigantic statues we call the Colossi of Memnon today are the two effigies of Amenhotep III mentioned here.

215   I find it very interesting that C. Desroches-Noblecourt mentions on p.178 of her book *Tutankhamun* that the coffins on arriving at the tomb were propped up on special fine white sand for the performance of the crucial 'opening of the mouth and eyes' ceremony, and that the Japanese archaeologists, who drove a thin tubular probe into a newly discovered chamber in the Great Pyramid at Giza a few years ago, were surprised to find it containing fine white sand of a type not local to Giza. I believe an explanation of one will open up an explanation of the other.

215   'I have arisen from the Egg . . .' R. O. Faulkner, *The Book of the Dead*, Spell 22.

215   'My mouth is opened by Ptah . . .' Ibid., Spell 23.

216   'O Lord of Flame . . .' a version of this ancient lament quoteed by Piankoff, *The Shrines of Tutankh-amon*, p.36.

218   'I am thy wife, O great one . . .' C. Desroches-Noblecourt, *Tutankhamun*, p.178.

218   'Thou art the Only One . . .' Piankoff, *The Shrines of Tut-ankh-amon*, p.7.

219   'The King, the Egg of Ra . . .' from Shrine II in Tutankhamun's tomb. Ibid., p.120.

219   'I have come to be thy protection . . .' Ibid., p.126.

219   'The Good God who came out of Ra . . .' Ibid., p.127.

228   'I took it by storm . . .' C. W. Ceram, *Narrow Pass Black Mountain*, p.118. A curse spoken by King Anittas of Kussara who defeated Hattusas c.1800 BC.

230   'Shine on me like the sun in the sky . . .' J. G. Macqueen, *The Hittites* (Thames & Hudson, 1986), p.152. Some ancient civilizations thought of the sun as a goddess, not a god. It seems this is true of the Hittites.